SHERLOCK HOLMES
AND THE
LUSITANIA

Lusitania
Launched 1906
Displacement: 31,550 tons
Dimensions: 761 ft x 88 ft
Machinery: Quadruple screws, turbines

SHERLOCK HOLMES
AND THE
LUSITANIA

LORRAINE DALY

Ian Henry Publications, Ltd.

ISBN 0 86025 291 4

Library of Congress Cataloging-in-Publication Data

Daly, Lorraine

Sherlock Holmes and the Lusitania / Lorraine Daly.

192 p. 20 cm.

ISBN 0-86025-291-4

1. World War, 1914-1918--Naval operations--Fiction. 2 Lusitania (Steamship)--Fiction. I. Title.

PS3554.A453554 1998

813'.54--dc21 98-40038

CIP

Printed by

Redwood Books

Kennet Way, Trowbridge, Wiltshire BA14 8RN

for

Ian Henry Publications, Ltd.

20 Park Drive, Romford, Essex RM1 4LH

CHAPTER I

I have often been asked to tell what became of Sherlock Holmes and myself after the events narrated in *His Last Bow*, when Holmes disguised as the fanatical Irish-American, Altamont, succeeded in trapping the German master-spy, Van Bork.

"But surely," friends protest, "it did not simply end there with you returning tamely to private practice and Mr Holmes retiring to keep bees in Sussex? No, John, you can't expect us to believe that!"

My percipient friends are quite right. Of course it did not end there, though Holmes was correct when he spoke of my arrangements to return to active medicine. I could foresee that if the coming war was to be as long and as terrible as Sherlock Holmes predicted many of the younger doctors would be needed at the Front and their places would have to be taken by older practitioners like myself. For that reason I had volunteered to act as locum for a fellow named Davis, who had a practice in the suburb of Ealing in west London. For convenience my wife, Violet, and I had also moved into Davis's house in Warwick Dene, a charming cul-de-sac on the edge of Ealing Common.

Obviously I was kept very busy familiarising myself with my new duties, but I willingly dropped everything when I received Sherlock Holmes's wire summoning me to meet him at Harwich with my car. The business was so urgent that we had no time for more than a brief word before we set off, driving furiously along the lanes to Van Bork's residence. During the drive Holmes outlined to me the German's recent history and explained exactly what it was he wanted me to do.

"There is a very slight element of risk, Watson," he said. "Van Bork may well be armed, but with any luck, I shall be able to deal with him myself before he can turn nasty. Chloroform is a powerful advocate," he added with a chuckle, tapping the bottle at his side. "But it is just as well you have come armed, Watson. Your old service revolver, I presume?"

"Of course," I gave my pocket an affectionate pat.

"It has been a good friend to us over the years, Watson; tonight you may be using it in the hunt for the biggest game in your life."

"Bigger than Moriarty?" I could not resist teasing him a little.

"Oh, certainly," he said. "I'm not denying Moriarty was a menace to decent society, but at least he had no wish to see the Imperial German Eagle flying over Buckingham Palace. That is Van Bork's ambition and, believe me, Watson, he came perilously close to achieving everything he desired."

"You alarm me, Holmes. I always assumed the spy menace to be greatly over-exaggerated." I broke off to concentrate on my driving through a convoluted lane with high banks that prevented me from seeing oncoming traffic until almost the last minute.

"For the most part you are right, Watson," Holmes resumed when he saw it was safe to speak again. "HMG is not likely to be shaken by the activities of a few German barbers, but Von Bork was a different animal altogether, highly intelligent, utterly ruthless and, above all, totally plausible. His charm, good looks and sporting prowess have won him friends everywhere, and that, as Mr Asquith rightly said, made him all the more dangerous, for a man who has ensured his welcome at the dinner tables of the great and the good is in a fair way to learning some of this country's most closely guarded secrets. However, the quest is over and between us we shall bring the rest of his organisation to book."

I have narrated what followed in *His Last Bow* There has been criticism of that admittedly sketchy account, with some saying it reads more like a rough draft than a finished product, and though the charge hurts my pride, I have to admit it contains a modicum of truth. At the time of writing it, however, I was compelled to show a certain reticence in the interests of national security, for instance the old woman Martha's real identity and the exact nature of the information Sherlock Holmes had fed to Van Bork. It may be that at some future time I shall be allowed to rectify these omissions; meanwhile my readers will have to fill in the gaps for themselves.

I do not propose either to dwell too much on the scene as we handed the furiously voluble Van Bark over to the nearest police station and told the bewildered station sergeant to lock him up and telephone London at once for further instructions.

Needless to say, Sherlock Holmes did not bother to cash Von Bork's cheque, as he jocularly claimed he would at the end of *His Last Bow* I have to confess that that little flourish was an invention of my own, intended to lighten the mood. The cheque would have been worthless in any case, and, moreover, Sherlock Holmes had far more pressing concerns an his mind.

As we hurried out of the station he asked me if I would drive him to Euston Station.

"Euston?" I repeated in some surprise. Sherlock Holmes had frequently departed from Victoria or Waterloo, but Euston was a long way outside his normal territory.

"Yes," he said calmly, "this time it is to be Euston, if you please, Watson, and you will have to hurry, if I am to catch the last train."

I knew better than to argue or question, so I merely turned the car around and drove back to London. During the journey Holmes spoke little as he sat in his corner, moodily chewing on one of the foul little cigars for which he seemed to have acquired a taste in his guise as Altamont. After a while the interior of the car began to smell like a particularly low-class tavern and I was impelled to utter a mild protest.

"But they are quite pleasant when you get used to them, Watson," said Sherlock Holmes, and he added with a dry chuckle, "Perhaps you would care to try one?"

"No, thank you, Holmes. I have too much respect for what remains of my health. If I were you I would throw the whole lot out of the window."

Holmes shook his head. "Can't be done, Watson," he declared, "Altamont would no more give up his favourite smokes than he would dream of parting with his cherished goatee beard."

It took some moments before his meaning sank in; then I cried, "But you said that by tomorrow the beard would be off and Altamont nothing more than a memory. Why must you continue the masquerade, when Van Bork's organisation has been destroyed?"

"His English organisation, yes, Watson," Sherlock Holmes said gravely. "Unfortunately, his American network is still very much intact and it is that towards which I now have to turn my attention. Listen, Watson," he held up his hand to prevent me from interrupting, "for a while Von Bork's capture will sow confusion among his American henchmen and that is the best moment to strike while they are still reeling from the shock. That is why," he continued deliberately, "Altamont must return to the United States without delay."

The car stopped with a violent jerk as I slammed on the brakes. To say I was horrified would be an understatement. After so many years I had found my friend again, only to hear him blithely announce that he intended to put his head into a noose, for I well knew that Altamont would be a marked man when the news of Van Bork's capture leaked out, as it surely must.

By returning to America Sherlock Holmes was daring not only the wrath of the German-Americans, many of them clandestine reservists for the Kaiser, but the far more terrifying threat posed by the committed Irish-American Fenians with their reputation for meting out brutal punishments to those they considered had betrayed them and according to their lights Sherlock Holmes had done just that getting himself initiated into the secret rites of the Fenian brotherhood in Buffalo before proceeding to capture their leader and paymaster, Van Bork.

"Holmes," I said, "you have already done your part. No one could ask you to venture into that viper's nest a second time. I beg you think again."

Sherlock Holmes laid his hand on my shoulder and gave it a friendly shake. "My dear Watson," he said, "your concern touches me more deeply than I can say, but you know very well I cannot tolerate unfinished business. So long as Van Bork's American network remains intact this country will be in danger."

"But from what I read the newspapers America would be likely to remain neutral in any coming European struggle," I said, adding vaguely, "The Monroe Doctrine and all that, you know."

"Quite right, Watson, but even so America's attitude could well be a vital factor in the days to come."

"How so?" I demanded and Sherlock Holmes gave a shrug. "I am no politician of course," he said, "but even so I can see we shall not be entering this coming struggle as well-equipped as we might be. Thanks to the sterling work of Winston Churchill, who has been an outstanding success as First lord of the Admiralty, our Fleet is ready, but precious little else. We are short of steel, munitions, raw materials of all kinds." His face illuminated suddenly by the lights of a car going in the opposite direction, was grim. "Not for the first time, Watson, this country is about to embark on a war for which it is ill-prepared, the fate of peace-loving nations throughout the ages. But this shortage in material is serious, Watson, and from where else can we hope to supply the deficiencies but the United States with her vast industrial potential?"

"Yes, I see that," I said, re-starting the car, "but I confess I see no particular difficulty, Holmes. With our gold reserves we can easily pay for these goods and we have the best Merchant Navy in the world to transport them."

"Agreed." Sherlock Holmes struck a match and lit another of his strong-smelling cigars, "but these ships are still vulnerable to the mine and the torpedo, remember, and if they tie up in New York harbour they will probably be loaded by Irish-American stevedores many of whom have no reason to love this country. That, my dear Watson, is why Altamont must return to complete his task."

A long silence followed during which I tried to concentrate on my driving, I could not in all honesty deny the force of Holmes's arguments, but though I hoped I was as true a patriot as the next man, I have to confess my heart sank when I thought of my friend running such a risk. True, he had got away with it once, but I recalled the old Greek saying that you cannot step twice into the same river, and while Sherlock Holmes was a wonderfully fit man for his age, there was no denying that he was now over sixty and that he lacked the elasticity of youth. Indeed, when we met at Harwich he had admitted that the odd twinge of rheumatism troubled him from occasionally, so if he were to be attacked by a younger, stronger man it was doubtful that even his knowledge of the Japanese art of baritsu would save him from a nasty mauling.

While I was still hesitating Sherlock Holmes said, "Watson, old friend, we have been through many trials together and in all that time you have never failed me, I beg you, do as I ask now."

I had rarely heard him speak with such feeling. I nodded reluctantly, "Very well, Holmes, I'll take you to Euston."

"That's my Watson," he exclaimed in relief. "I knew I could depend on you. Now after you have dropped me off at the station you must do one more thing for me."

"Yes?" I said warily and he laughed.

"It is nothing very terrible, Watson. You heard me arrange to meet old Martha at Claridges tomorrow morning to hear her report? Unfortunately I shall not be able to keep that appointment, so you will have to act as my deputy."

"Certainly, but what am I to do with the report afterwards?"

"Take it straight to my brother Mycroft. You remember the Diogenes Club, Watson?

"Could I forget? But I thought he had retired from government service?"

"Believe that, Watson, and you'll believe anything - as our American cousins would say." He peered at his watch. "But we must hurry, now, Watson, if you please. Unless I can catch that train I shall certainly lose my passage. It is a pity the *Lusitania* is not due to sail until Friday, for had I been able to take passage on her it would have saved me many tedious hours as I know from past experience aboard Cunard's 'Ocean Greyhound'."

"You mean you actually sailed on the *Lusitania*, Holmes?" I cried. "Well, upon my word, although this is a serious business, I must say, I envy you from the bottom of my heart. It has long been my ambition to make the Atlantic crossing either aboard her or her sister ship, the *Mauritania*. Never likely to be realised, of course. A humble doctor's salary doesn't run to those kind of luxuries, but still..." I sighed a little and shrugged.

It is not easy to convey to younger readers the degree of fascination evoked by the name *Lusitania* to those of my generation. From the laying down of her keel to her completion in 1907 she had attracted more attention than any other vessel in history. Not merely the British but the foreign press reported her progress in the minutest detail, for she and her sister were the largest and fastest passenger ships the naval architects had ever produced. Between them these 'Incomparables', as they were dubbed, had monopolised the Blue Riband of the Atlantic, and every schoolboy in the land could recite from memory, their fabulous dimensions - length 790 feet, breadth 88 feet, tonnage 30,704 and collected cigarette cards showing the great liners in all their glory of sleek black hull, gleaming white superstructure and four towering funnels painted in the famous Cunard orange-red.

"Well," said Sherlock Holmes, "it is only sensible to cross to New York as quickly as possible in the hope that Van Bork's net-work will fall into disarray after the loss of their leader - and," he added with a chuckle, "the Prime Minister did urge me to spare no expense, so it would be apt if I were to take him at his word."

"A pity you have to sail immediately," I said. "You would be in New York in just under five days aboard the *Lusitania*. Would it not be sensible to wait until Friday?"

Holmes shook his head decisively. "War will certainly break out any day now and we do not know how that is likely to affect the passage of merchant shipping. I sail on the first available vessel."

"Is it really true," I said rather wistfully, "that the *Lusitania* can work up to a design speed of 26 knots?"

"She can," Holmes affirmed. "As I say, I sailed in her before, both as a passenger and in the somewhat lowlier capacity of a steward in Second Class - that was when I was hot on Van Bork's trail, of course - so, you see, Watson, one way and another I know the *Lusitania* very well indeed."

CHAPTER II

"Ah, Watson, even though our poor country is now at war it is good to be home again," said Sherlock Holmes as he raised his glass to me.

Smiling, I reciprocated. It was a chilly evening in late April, 1915, and we were relaxing after dinner in the sitting room of Sherlock Holmes's villa on the Sussex downs. But for the fact that the fog swirling against the windows was pearl-white rather than oily brown, we might well have been back in Baker Street, for I was amused and not a little touched to see that Sherlock Holmes, always the first to insist that he was no sentimentalist but a cold-blooded man of reason, had brought with him many of the familiar artifacts of that establishment: at a quick glance, I noted the tantalus and the gasogene, the Persian slipper containing tobacco, the jack knife transfixing his correspondence to the mantelpiece (where I also noted with regret the lumps of dottle which it was my friend's insanitary habit to collect from his smokes of the previous day) and the stained deal table he used for his noxious chemical experiments.

I was about to tease him for his lack of consistency when I realised something was missing. For a moment I could not work out what it was, then, suddenly it dawned, on me that the bookshelf beside Holmes's chair contained nothing but printed books.

"Holmes!" I exclaimed, "Your scrapbooks - where are they?"

"Oh, those," he responded casually. "Well, as you see, this is a small cottage and one day I decided the time had come to be rid of those rather cumbersome works of reference on the criminal classes, so I made a great pile of them in the garden and struck a match - it was as simple as that, Watson."

"But that was sheer vandalism!" I protested. "Do you realise that means there is now no first-hand account of the Giant Rat of Sumatra or the repulsive affair of the Red Leech. How could you?"

"Very easily, I assure you, my dear Watson," he said, though I noticed he refused to meet my eyes, "Unlike you, I am not a sentimental man and the keeping of memorabilia has never been one of my weaknesses."

I said nothing, but raising my brows I looked pointedly round the room. Holmes flushed. "There are exceptions to every rule, Watson," he said and then grinned unexpectedly, "But come, don't let us quarrel over the fate of a few old scrapbooks. We have more important things to concern us now."

"You're right of course, Holmes," I said, aware that he was speaking of the War which was now in its ninth month, "but even so I can't help thinking of the loss to posterity. Those books were irreplaceable."

His eyes twinkled. "Ah, posterity will have to rely on the papers in that battered old tin trunk of yours at Cox and Co's. I must say, Watson, I would rather like to meet your bankers and take a look inside that trunk of yours, I'm sure the contents must be fascinating."

"You shall indeed," I was glad to enter into his lighter mood, "providing you give me a full and complete account of your escapades in the United States to add to them."

"I shall be very happy to do so," was his answer, "and that was one of the reasons I summoned you here, knowing of your interest in such matters. Besides, from the look of you, a weekend away from London can do you nothing but good, old friend. Is your return to general practice proving to be such a strain?"

"I do find it somewhat fatiguing to be dragged out of bed in the middle of the night," I confessed, "but one does what one can, of course. In any case it was kind of you to think of me, Holmes, and I'm very glad to be here, not least because it allows me to satisfy my curiosity about your new abode."

"Hardly new, Watson," Holmes murmured. "I have lived here for almost twelve years now."

"Any regrets at leaving London?"

"Not one!" he declared firmly. "And when I take you walking on the Downs tomorrow you will see why, my boy. However, you wanted to hear about my American travels. Well, Watson, I fear I can offer you nothing but an addition to my failures, for the truth is that I did not succeed in my quest to eradicate all traces of Von Bork's American network. Oh, we managed to capture some of the small fry easily enough, but the biggest fish of all, the one we were really after, evaded all the traps that had been set for him."

"One moment, Holmes," I interrupted, "you say 'we' - to whom are you referring?"

"Well, for the most part I preferred to play a lone hand, Watson, but from time to time I was compelled to liaise with a man named Gaunt who is with Naval Intelligence in New York."

"You mean we are spying on the Americans?" I was scandalised.

"Yes, Watson, of course we are just as they have people spying on us. These days even the most peace-loving governments have to be Argus-eyed. To resume, Gaunt had discovered that German undercover activities had suffered such a severe blow from the loss of Von Bork that the instances of known sabotage had dwindled to almost nothing. Berlin responded by sending out a new man - a fellow called Franz Von Rintelen, who has much of the courage and dash, not to say the ruthlessness of his illustrious predecessor. If I am not mistaken he will give our people in New York a hard time of it. Fortunately he is at odds with the German Military Attaché at the Embassy, Von Papen, and their mutual loathing of each other must work to England's advantage."

Far off in Fulworth Bay a ship's siren wailed, a plaintive and melancholy sound. Holmes threw another log on the fire.

"You see, Watson," he explained, "Von Papen is an advocate of *schrechlikeit*, or as we would call it `warfare of frightfulness' - that is, attempting to break the enemy's will by deliberate acts of terror. To a man like Von Rintelen such a doctrine is anathema. Of course, he longs to see England defeated, but there are limits to what he is prepared to do to bring about a German victory, whereas Von Papen and his protégé, the Tiger regard such scruples with contempt. To them all is literally fair in war, so you can understand, Watson, why Von Rintelen was so furious when he discovered upon his arrival in New York that Von Papen had gone behind his back and admitted the Tiger to the network's most secret councils. I am told that even thought of calling Von Papen out.but wiser counsels prevailed and the two men have continued to work together, though with an ill grace. No doubt we shall be hearing more of Franz Von Rintelen, but I have to say I fear the Tiger more than I do him."

Seizing the poker, he stirred the fire into vigorous life and sat watching the ladder of sparks climbing up the chimney, his fine aquiline face turned to umber by the leaping flames.

"But who is the Tiger? So far you have not told me his name."

Sherlock Holmes laughed, not very happily. "I wish I could, Watson, but to tell you the truth I simply do not know it, nor can I give you a description of him. Eight months I was on his trail and in all that time I never clapped eyes on the fellow. He seems to have a genius for vanishing into thin air at the crucial moment. I can only tell you that he is English by birth and that he operates under the code-name Tiger."

"An Englishman!" I exclaimed. "Surely not, Holmes."

"I fear so, Watson. My informant was quite definite on that point and I have never known O'Reilly to be mistaken. Ah, you probably have not heard me mention O'Reilly. He was the Fenian who sponsored me when I was initiated into the Brotherhood in Chicago - you remember, of course?"

"I do, But, Holmes, I don't understand - if O'Reilly is a Fenian himself he too must be a secret German sympathiser. Are you certain it is wise to trust him?"

"I would trust O'Reilly with my life," Sherlock Holmes answered coolly. "There was no braver man and, though it is true that he detested English rule in Ireland and had fought long and bitterly to bring it to an end, neither did his wish to see his country fall under German hegemony. For that reason I decided it was safe to take him into my confidence and I never had any reason to regret it. O'Reilly remained loyal to the end of his life."

"He is dead?" I cried.

Holmes nodded gravely. "He was murdered by the Tiger's henchmen just before we were due to meet. Somehow Von Papen and the Tiger had got wind of what was happening and took steps to silence O'Reilly before he could reveal the latter's identity to me, But let me tell you the full story, Watson."

"I should be obliged to you," I said, taking the cigar he offered me after noting with relief that it was not one of Altamont's horrors.

"Well, then, Von Papen demanded a meeting with the Fenians in New York and promised that, whatever Von Rintelen might say, he, Papen, was willing to support any measures they decided to take against the common foe, England, Germany would supply weapons, money and whatever else they might need. Finally he promised them that he was sending the very best agent he had none other than the Tiger, to England to reconstitute Von Bork's shattered organisation. At this O'Reilly saw his chance and exclaimed, 'That's all very fine, Mr Von Papen, but it goes against the grain for a fellow like meself to trust any damned Englishman. For a start I'd like to know who he really is and why he's turned traitor against his own country?'

"There were murmurs of displeasure at this blunt speech and someone called out, 'Why d'you want to look a gift horse in the mouth, Sean O'Reilly? Isn't it enough for you that the man hates the English?'

"'Quite so,' Captain Von Papen interposed smoothly. 'The Tiger's anonymity must be preserved so as to ensure his own safety. Remember, he risks a firing squad if the English catch him - I daresay,' he added, 'some of you recall the fate of Steiner and Hollis and Jack James?' (*En passant,* Watson, I must say that was a very creditable bit of work I did there).

"Eventually so O'Reilly told me, a vote was taken after which those Fenians who supported Von Papen's proposals said they would contact their friends in England and ask them to join forces with the Tiger. The rest, including O'Reilly, said they preferred to wait on events before committing themselves. Meanwhile O'Reilly was determined to learn the Tiger's identity if he possibly could and he trailed Von Papen after he left the meeting. Papen led him straight to Hoboken Docks, where the liners of North German Lloyd are berthed. As you may know, Watson, those ships have been interned since the outbreak of hostilities. There, O'Reilly glimpsed Von Papen talking earnestly to a tall man in a loose-fitting ulster, whose features were concealed by a broad-brimmed hat."

"Not much to go on," I commented. "Why, that description might fit thousands."

"Well, Watson, O'Reilly could hardly walk up to them and ask the man's identity," Sherlock Holmes's voice was impatient. "Considering the difficulties he did wonderfully well and he did follow the stranger afterwards to the Brevoort, where he registered under the name of Michael Forrester. O'Reilly was unable to learn his room number because the hotel porter became suspicious of his unkempt appearance and he was summarily ejected from the hotel. Even then he refused to give up but lurked around the back of the building where the poor and indigent of the city are wont to lurk in the hope of feeding on the scraps thrown out from the hotel kitchens.

From the gossip he heard among his fellow-unfortunates he learned that the security procedures were remarkably lax and decided it should be possible to break into the building at night and find Forrester's room. Of course, when he telephoned me and outlined his plan, I immediately begged him to do no such thing, but he was adamant and on fire with the thrill of the chase. I have to say that at first he enjoyed a remarkable run of beginner's luck too, in that over the next few days he smartened himself up sufficiently to find temporary work as a kitchen hand in the Brevoort. I should add, Watson, that O'Reilly was a handsome fellow and he possessed more than his fair share of the legendary Irish charm, so it was child's play to him to captivate one of the kitchen slaveys who prepared the vegetables and she told him it was common gossip that 'Mr Forrester' had all his meals sent up to him and in fact never appeared in the dining room. She had also learned from one of the chambermaids that 'Forrester' invariably retreated to the bedroom when his food was brought in and that one of the girls who worked on that floor had ever laid eyes on the man. Indeed, 'Forrester's' only visitor during his stay at the hotel was a short bald-headed fellow with bad teeth who spoke with a thick German accent."

"Von Papen?" I queried, and Holmes gave a dry chuckle.

"Von Papen would not thank you for that, Watson. He rather prides himself on his good looks. No, it was not Von Papen, but the waiter who brought in 'Forrester's meal as usual and was sharply ordered to leave the room was convinced he heard 'Forrester' address his visitor as 'Herr Doktor' at the moment he was closing the door behind him. A little while after that 'Forrester' and his guest were seen to leave the hotel. O'Reilly did not learn of this for some hours, by which it was too late to follow them. That was when O'Reilly at last deigned to telephone me, none too soon. I may add. 'I've a notion to search 'Forrester's' room while the coast is clear, Mr Holmes,' he said. Naturally, I attempted to dissuade him, for though brave O'Reilly was not trained in that kind of work, but he refused to listen to me. 'Sure, I'll be in and out before you know it, Mr Holmes!' he cried. 'And there'll never be a better chance. I can lay me hands on the key with no trouble at all. Then we'll really know what the fellow's game is.' He rang off before I could say anything more and that, Watson, was the last time we spoke together."

"He was caught?" I said in dismay and Holmes nodded gravely.

"I fear so, Watson. We have no way of knowing exactly what happened but two days later Captain Guy Gaunt drew my attention to a short paragraph in one of the inside pages of the *New York Chronicle* to the effect that a kitchen hand at the Brevoort Hotel had been found in the early hours of the previous morning lying at the foot of the main staircase with his neck broken. Gaunt knew of my association with O'Reilly, of course. 'It looks as if your man's cover was blown, Holmes,' he said with rather a grim smile. 'I've been in touch with the New York Police and they are not at all happy with this supposed accident". Apparently there were severe bruises a the face and body which could not be accounted for by the fall, but which bore all the hallmarks of a savage beating.'

"'So he was beaten up first and then put at the foot of the stairs to make it look like an accident,' I said thoughtfully, 'What about Forrester?'

"'Checked out of the hotel within the hour and promptly vanished,' Gaunt answered. 'He could be anywhere by now. An alarming prospect, Holmes if 'Forrester' really is Tiger. It's a pity there was nothing to connect him with O'Reilly, so the Police had no reason to hold him. Officially we can do nothing, of course. A suspicious death in New York is no business of ours, but there's no reason why one of O'Reilly's relatives, an elderly uncle, say," he glanced at me to see if I was following his train of thought I should not turn up at the Brevoort and demand his late nephew's effects. Probably the manager will be only too glad to hand them over and wash his hands of the tiresome business.' He dropped his voice. 'Will you do it, Holmes?'

"Needless to say, I tottered into the lobby of the Brevoort on two sticks, where I was received by an underling of the manager's, who thrust into my arms the pathetic bundle of O'Reilly's few possessions, some clothing, a few coins - and this."

Reaching into his waistcoat pocket, Holmes drew forth a tattered scrap of paper. "What do you make of that, Watson?"

Rather dubiously, I examined the paper, which was scribbled all over, thus:

32 33 32 23 24 23 14 42 45 13 33 33 42 42 53 24 21 25 22 32
42 21 25 11 32 41 43 32 41 24 53 12 14 34 52 21 21 11 21 44
53 24 32 25 25 21 32 43 11 21 25 000

"Why," I said at length, "I can make nothing of it. To me it looks like a collection of numbers selected at random."

"A little more than that, Watson, I fancy." Sherlock Holmes took the paper from me. "This apparently random selection cost a man's life, remember."

I cudgelled my brains. "You mean it is some kind of code?" I said finally.

Holmes smiled, "Excellent, Watson. Yes, it is of course a message written in code, as I realised the moment I saw its You may remember I am myself the author of a small monograph - now, alas, long out of print - on the subject of codes and ciphers. The problem I faced after O'Reilly's murder was to crack the code as quickly as possible and discover the message it contained for the death of O'Reilly proved that Forrester, or the Tiger, as we must now call him, knew we were on his track and would at once go to ground if he had any sense."

"Rather a tall order," I commented, "seeing he had a head start of you."

"True, but the code used was a very simple one, merely a form of the ancient Greek substitution cipher employed by Von Bork, which I knew very well, having used it so often to communicate with my supposed German paymaster last year. All that had to be done was to set down the letters of the alphabet in the form of a square and substitute letters for figures. Our German foes are a long way behind us when it comes to devising a truly impenetrable code. Let me show you."

Drawing a sheet of paper towards him, he scribbled rapidly on it.

"There you are, Watson," he laid the pencil aside. "Come and take a look."

I leaned over his shoulder and studied the curious little graph he had drawn.

	1	2	3	4	5
1	L	B	O	S	F
2	E	V	U	G	R
3	X	A	M	C	Y
4	N	T	D	Z	K
5	W	H	I/J	Q	P

"I hope that makes everything clear, Watson?" said Sherlock Holmes.

"Well, not very," I was forced to say. "For one thing I fail to understand the reason for the three noughts at the end of the message. Do they have some special significance, or have they been put there to confuse an enemy?"

"Well done, Watson!" Holmes cried heartily. "Upon my word, you are coming along by leaps and bounds! But then I always said you were inclined to belittle yourself when you wrote of my trifling affairs.

You are quite right. Those noughts are not part of the message. In the trade they are called nulls and are put there to complete the five-figure groups into which the message has to be broken down, hoping to confuse the would-be de-coder who will thus be unable to tell where the message really ends."

"Let me get this clear," I said, still glowing from the rare word of praise, "in this system all the messages are written in five-figure groups?"

"The code-groups, yes, and, bearing that in mind, our scrap of paper now begins to look like this." Seizing the pencil, he scribbled rapidly and passed the paper to me,

33334/22324/23144/21513/33334/24253/24212/52232/42212/5II 32/42212/51132/41433/24124/53121/43452/21211/12144/5324 3/22525/21324/31121/25000

"I see," I said, speaking with rather less than my usual veracity. "And the next stage?"

"Would be to substitute the figures we have here for the appropriate letters, like so. The completed message would then read thus:

AMAUGUSTKOMMTTIGERVATERLANDANGIBSCHEELEZIGARREADLER When I read it, Watson, I knew that the communication could only come from Von Bork himself, employing the same code with which we had corresponded in days gone by. I assume he had sent it to Von Papen, recommending the Tiger as a formidable recruit to their infernal cause. Towards the end you know, Watson, Von Bork had become so sure of himself and so convinced of the stupidity of the English that he neglected to take even the most elementary precautions to cover his tracks. Normally, in a message of this kind, the words would have been scrambled so as to further confuse the would-be code-breaker, but here we have Von Bork sending to the military attaché in the German Embassy in New York, himself a marked man, Watson, virtually *en clair.*"

"It may seem like that to you, Holmes," I began, but at once he interrupted me, "To save time, Watson, we will now punctuate this message and you can see what you make of it then."

AM AUGUST KOMMT TIGER VATERLAND AN GIB SCHEELE ZIGARRE ADLER, I read and looked to Sherlock Holmes for the explanation he was quick to supply.

"TIGER ARRIVING VATERLAND AUGUST GIVE SCHEELE CIGARS EAGLE - and there you have it, Watson, Adler-Eagle is Von Bork himself, of course. Remember I described him to you as a great eagle perched on the cliffs of England. I wish we could be as certain of Tiger's identity. He must be formidable indeed to have inspired the trust of a man like Von Bork."

"But the rest of the message?" I cried. "What exactly does it mean? Why would Von Bork want to tell the German Embassy in New York that Tiger was due to visit Germany in August? I must confess that makes very little sense to me. And what is all this about Scheele and cigars?"

"Ah, for the true intent behind the message, Watson, we have to dig a little deeper. Vaterland, now - what does that suggest to you?"

"Why, Germany, the Fatherland, of course," I was becoming rather irritated. "What else could it be?"

Sherlock Holmes's eyes were veiled, his voice almost abstracted as he said, "Among the German liners interned by the American authorities at Hoboken in New York Harbour, there is one named the *Vaterland*. All the interned ships are hotbeds of intrigue and the authorities keep a very wary eye on them, but of course they cannot prevent Captain Von Papen from visiting his embittered fellow-countrymen on board, since those ships constitute German territory, so, Watson, I am inclined to think that the *Vaterland* referred to by Von Bork in his message was the vessel which carried the Tiger to the United States."

"You may well be right," I conceded and he smiled.

"Let us assume that I am and proceed on that hypothesis. Now, Scheele and these mysterious cigars. You would not, I take it, want to argue that Von Bork is simply referring to a present he wished the Tiger to present to Scheele, whoever he is?"

"It seems unlikely," said I.

"Quite so. Then presumably the cigars are a code word for some-thing of a more sinister nature, maybe a kind of weapon or weapons."

"Perhaps," I said, struck by a sudden thought, "the cigars refer to arms being brought by the Tiger to the Fenians. You said Von Bork had done his best to stir up all manner of troubles for us in Ireland."

"He certainly did!" Sherlock Holmes agreed with feeling. "And your thesis, Watson, would be likely enough if the Tiger had been on his way to England, but - America?" he pursed his lips.

"It is simply not in Germany's best interests to inflame American opinion at this time - and yet the message plainly returns to material of a destructive nature. Ah!" his brow cleared as though by magic. "I have it, Watson. The Tiger is to collect the cigars for use against this country. Yes, that must be it!"

I raised my brows. "I thought you were adamant that you never guessed, Holmes. From where I'm sitting that sounds very much like a guess to me."

"My dear Watson!" he appeared almost hurt by my sally. "It is nothing of the kind - simply a logical deduction from the data. I already possess."

"Of course, Holmes," I said smoothly. He caught my eye and we both burst out laughing.

"Touché, Watson!" he chuckled. "A palpable hit! But this is not the first time you have caught me with my guard down. And you are quite right - I was allowing my imagination too much rein.

"Of course there is no proof that the cigars are anything but cigars, yet for my own part I would be prepared to wager they are something very much more." He fell silent, staring into the fire with such concentration that he might have been reading the answer to the riddle there. Finally he roused himself and said. "A small anecdote for you to add to your storehouse of odd memorabilia, Watson. Soon after O'Reilly's death some of his erstwhile colleagues were shadowed to a small wood close to town. Then something went wrong and the men successfully gave their pursuers the slip. All our people found were some circular patches which had been burned into the grass."

"Is that all?" I was disappointed, having expected the story to have a more dramatic ending.

"For the moment, Watson, yes, but since then I have found myself wondering if the Fenians went to the rendezvous to witness some sort of demonstration, perhaps the destructive powers of the notorious cigars, for I must tell you, Watson, the heat had been so fierce that the soil had fused, together and there was no trace of any mechanism arguing that it had been consumed in the flames. Possibly Captain Gaunt and I were wrong in thinking that the Tiger was to give the cigars to Scheele, perhaps it was the other way around. And, of course, if Scheele was the man with bad teeth see by O'Reilly he must have come to the Brevoort to hand over his infamous secret to the Tiger. No wonder poor O'Reilly was murdered."

"All this is very plausible, Holmes," I said, "but aren't you forgetting something? With so many German merchant ships interned by the Americans, how is the material to be got out of the country?"

"Good point, Watson, but don't forget our own ships coming and going to load up with fresh stores - very tempting targets to any would-be saboteur."

"I only hope you are wrong, Holmes," I said, and stifled a yawn. "But if you will forgive me I think I must go to bed now. Your good Sussex air is strong stuff."

"By all means, Watson," he said. "I shall sit here for a while with my violin. I trust you will not object to the noise?"

"Not at all. It will remind me of old times."

Tired after a long day, I fell asleep almost as soon as my head touched the pillow and only woke towards dawn with the sound of scales being softly played. They were melancholy and sonorous, reflecting, I assumed, the gloomy thoughts possessing Holmes for it had been clear to me as he spoke that he regarded the threat represented by the Tiger as being very serious for this country as she strained every nerve and sinew in her life and death struggle with Germany.

Opressed by my own doubts I got out of bed and went to the window. The sky was lightening perceptibly, but the mist had not yet lifted completely and the trees in Holmes's garden were all blackened and ghostly. Moisture dripped from them incessantly, while far off in the invisible bay the ship's siren still wailed on, like an omen, a portent.

CHAPTER III

Once the early mist had dispersed the day turned fine and sunny, and I readily agreed when Sherlock Holmes suggested a stroll on the Downs before I left to catch my train.

His villa stood on the southern slope and commanded a magnificent view of the Channel. Far below us the sea shifted and glittered like the scales of a python sunning itself. Apart from ourselves the cliffs appeared to be deserted, while the little village of Fulworth above its cove was caught up in a drowsy Sabbath-day enchantment. The sea also was quiet but for a dredger close inshore and the ship whose siren had made such an eerie accompaniment to the night now no more than a dot on the horizon. Yet, I thought to myself, the appearance of calm might be deceptive and these tranquil waters hide the dark grey shark-like form of a German submarines.

"These coasts are pretty well defended, you know, Watson," said Sherlock Holmes when I mentioned my fears to him. "What with our nets and barrages it would be no easy matter for a submarine to get through. Still, I agree with you that the German U-boat is the worst menace our ships have to face today, particularly the heavily-laded merchantman. But let us talk of something more cheerful on a day like this, Watson. Look, we are standing above the cove where I encountered the fearsome Lion's Mane - and learned a most valuable lesson even as I solved the mystery."

"What lesson was that, Holmes?" I asked, as ready to be diverted as he was anxious to divert me. He gave me a humorous look. "It was that never again under any circumstances would I act as my own chronicler, Watson," he said solemnly. "Having so often belittled your literary skills. I was hoist with my own petard when I foolishly allowed that smooth-talking charmer, Doyle, to persuade me into attempting a first-hand account of the Lion's Mane business - and a remarkably poor job I made of it. Looking over the work I cannot see any literary error I did not commit - it is poor stuff, Watson, dull and pedestrian to a degree. Doyle tells me it has sold well, but on my name rather than its merits - what is that worth? Ah, Watson, I have learned my lesson - talent for writing can no more be taught than a bent for observation and deduction. Henceforth, old friend," he drew himself up, "I shall not attempt to usurp my Boswell's crown and I apologise, somewhat belatedly, for the sharp remarks I have made to you aver the years as I watched you scribbling away."

"Consider it forgotten, Holmes," I said, rather embarrassed by his eagerness to humble himself, which struck me as being very much out of character. "Now," I said briskly, "show me the scene of the adventure. I must say the Lion's Mane sounds a most sinister creature. I trust there are none down there today."

Holmes willingly led the way down the cliff path to the small lagoon which had been left by the treating tide. The water was a deep pellucid green. It seemed impossible that it had once housed the monstrous cyanea which had caused one young man to die in agony and brought a second face to face with death. To my mind as I stood gazing at those innocent-seeming waters, cyanea appeared to have much in common with that sinister man-made artefact, the submarine, another silent, invisible killer against which there was no entirely foolproof defence.

"And the *Lusitanid*s former Master would agree with you, Watson," Sherlock Holmes remarked as we turned to essay the cliff-path once again. "Captain Dow, much as he tried to hide it, was in a bad state of nerves all the way across from New York and I was not entirely surprised to hear quite by chance the other day that he had been compelled to give up his command due to war strains Heaven help the man who has to take over from him; he will have to out-labour Hercules if he is to satisfy all the demands made on him, from the Admiralty and the Cunard Company, not to mention his passengers."

"Just a moment, Holmes" I said, before he could start to mount the path which tacked back and forth across the cliff-face, "I don't quite understand you. What has the Admiralty got to do with it?"

"A good deal, Watson," he turned to look at me and his face was unexpectedly grim. You see, in a sense the Admiralty own the *Lusitania* and her sister, the *Mauretania*."

"Own her?" I repeated, staring at him. "Surely, Holmes, you are not serious. The *Lusitania* is a merchant ship."

"Quite so, Watson, but when she was built in 1906 the Admiralty put up most of the money to pay for her, on the express condition that if ever this country was involved in a war with hostile powers, the *Lusitania* should immediately be handed over to them, for conversion into an Armed Merchant Cruiser."

"I think I do remember reading something about that, Holmes," I said rather breathlessly as I climbed the path behind him, "but at the time it struck me as very great nonsense. How can you hope to turn a massive vessel like the *Lusitania* into a warship? She would present far too big a target, and you could hardly hurl her about the sea as though she were a destroyer. And what about armour? A passenger liner has none; she would be desperately vulnerable to a mine or a torpedo."

"Nevertheless," Sherlock Holmes paused in his upward climb, "when hostilities commenced last year the Admiralty immediately invoked the agreement they had made with Cunard and both the *Lusitania* and her sister were taken into dry dock to have their guns mounted, and their decks strengthened with steel." He added gravely, "I have myself seen the concealed rings in the plating of the shelter-deck."

"And the guns?" I breathed, both fascinated and appalled. "Did you see them?"

"No, I did not, Watson." Sherlock Holmes's gaze sought the distant horizon, "but the Admiralty had also closed off a large section of the shelter deck and only their personnel are allowed access there, so what may be concealed inside is anyone's guess."

"But the *Lusitania* was never used as a warship," I pointed out.

"No, as I understand someone in higher authority changed their mind and the *Mauretania* became a troopship, while her sister was handed back to Cunard on the condition that her cargo holds and passenger space would now be under Admiralty control and that her contain would take his orders direct from the Admiralty rather than Cunard."

"I see," I pulled thoughtfully at my moustache, "but do these Admiralty people have any experience in manœuvring something as large as the *Lusitania*? I mean, it's somewhat different from steering a frigate."

Sherlock Holmes uttered one of his dry chuckles. "Not for the first time, Watson, you have hit the nail on the head. It is indeed very different, but the Admiralty refused to listen to advice and as a result they have turned the *Lusitania* into a most unhappy hybrid, neither warship nor passenger liner, but a combination of the worst features of the two." He gave an exaggerated shudder. "I promise you it will be a long time before I forget my last voyage on her. Normally, I like to think of myself as a good sailor, but for most of those five days I joined the ranks of those passengers who kept to their cabins while devoutly wishing they were dead. Admittedly we were unlucky. Soon after we left New York a great gale came shrieking down from the north, and big though the *Lusitania* is, she was tossed about like a cork in the rapids for twenty-four hours. There were times, Watson, when she rolled so sickeningly that I thought it impossible she could ever right herself again and I wondered if I would live to see her safely berthed at Liverpool."

"That doesn't sound like the *Lusitania*," I frowned. "Cunard have long boasted she offers the smoothest crossing of any ship afloat."

"And they spoke truly of the *Lusitania*, as she was pre-War," said Sherlock Holmes as we gained the top of the path, "but consider, Watson. The ship was very carefully designed by a leading marine architect who tried to ensure that her great height was properly balanced by the breadth of her beam. Now along come the Admiralty: they gut many of the cabins down as far as F Deck and sheathe her shelter deck in steel. Is it any wonder that she is now top-heavy and rolls villainously in all but the calmest seas?"

"No," I agreed, turning away from the broad panorama of sea and sky. "But even so, Holmes, I find it difficult to believe that these alterations to the *Lusitania*, ill-advised though they undoubtedly were, alone caused her captain to have a nervous breakdown. A man with his experience must be well-used to handling difficult vessels in foul weather."

"Quite so, Watson." Sherlock Holmes was now striding across the sheep-nibbled turf to his cottage at a great rate, his old briar pipe clenched firmly between his teeth. "In fact, Captain Dow's anxiety sprang from a quite different source, as he confided to me."

"To you, Holmes?"

"Yes," he answered, pushing open the garden gate. "Let me explain: after my recovery from my indisposition I was asked by both the Captain and Mr George Booth, cousin to the present Chairman of Cunard, if I would mind undertaking a small investigation for them - a trifling matter, Watson, definitely not one for your records - concerning such all-too-familiar minutiæ as a very valuable pearl necklace, a lady of exalted rank who was neither in the cabin nor the company she was supposed to be and a jealous maid out to blackmail her employer, but though it was a commonplace affair

Booth feared a scandal and called on me rather than their own detective, Mr Pierrepoint, and when I solved it, as anyone who was not a fool must have done, they were effusive in their gratitude. Captain Dow even asked me if I would care to join him on the bridge after dinner that evening, a rare honour indeed, for normally these Cunard Masters are too much aware of their great responsibilities to want visitors distracting them. However, while I was there Captain Dow motioned me to join him on the starboard wing of the bridge where we would not be overheard by any of his junior officers. 'Mr Holmes,' he said in a low voice, 'I can trust you, can I not?' 'I hope so,' I answered. 'I'm taking a great risk in speaking to you,' he said with a nervous glance over his shoulder. 'If any of those damned brass hats got a hint I'd lose my job and likely enough my liberty as well, for talking out of turn.'

"'What brass hats?" I demanded.

"'Why, the Admiralty, man, they who've ruined my ship and turned every voyage into a nightmare of dreading what may come if the *Lucy* was attacked by one of those filthy German U-boats. Come with me, Mr Holmes, and see what they've done to my poor *Lusitania*."

"It was then that he took me on a conducted tour, Watson, and I saw for myself the concealed gun-mountings and the steel gates locking off whole sections of the ship, Back on the bridge he faced me squarely, his hands clenched at his sides. 'Now you've seen everything, Mr Holmes. Now you can tell your friends at the Admiralty to stop loading up the *Lusitania* with these dreadful cargoes before it's too late. Mixing passengers with munitions, it's all wrong." Raising his clenched fists he shook them at the sky, exclaiming passionately, "Must we all go to the bottom of the sea before the Admiralty come to their senses?"

"'So the *Lusitania* really is carrying contraband," I said half to myself, "Even though the British Government has repeatedly denied it."

"Aye, well, they would, wouldn't they?" Captain Dow said bitterly. 'It wouldn't suit their book for the world to learn the *Lusitania*'s passengers and crew are little more than camouflage for shells and bullets, aye," he added with a sardonic smile, 'and the hundred thousand gallons of fuel oil sloshing about under our feet at this very moment. I hear you're a pipe-man like myself, Mr Holmes - well, I've been assured by the people who are supposed to know that there's absolutely no danger, so I suppose that ought to be good enough.' Suddenly he shook all over and began to weep, covering his face with his hands. "I can't go on with it, Mr Holmes," he moaned, 'it's too much for me, worrying over what may happen trying to work out a plan of action for if we get hit by a torpedo, remembering how many poor souls were lost when the *Titanic* went down. Mr Holmes, they say you're well in with these Admiralty people. If that's true for God's sake explain to them what they're doing. Make them see!

"As you can imagine, Watson, I was not particularly surprised after that to learn that Captain Dow had been given indefinite leave to recover from what has been euphemistically described as nervous strain. Poor fellow, I wish I could have helped him, but I fear he greatly over-estimated my influence with the present Board of Admiralty. They certainly would not change their policy of shipping munitions in passenger ships merely because Mr Sherlock Holmes told them it was wrong."

I left Holmes and Fulworth considerably disquieted in my mind. I knew from my newspaper that there was a shortage of ammunition on the Western Front and that many British lives had been lost because of it, but it had never occurred to me that our own Government would wilfully put civilian passengers at risk in this way and when I arrived home I discussed with my wife the possibility of writing a letter to the Prime Minister.

Incidentally, I think it is time to clear up some of the many misconceptions which have gathered round the subject of my second wife since Holmes in *The Blanched Soldier*, rather mischievously in my opinion, described my marriage to her as 'the only selfish action which I can recall in our association'. That unconsidered remark has led to endless confusion and even to a degree of ill-feeling, with some of my readers accusing me of failing to keep faith with Mary's memory - as if anything could be more ridiculous! - and others crediting me with as many wives as Bluebeard. I am not sure that Violet has ever quite forgiven Sherlock Holmes, but her anger is always tempered by the memory of how he saved her from the clutches of Jephro Rucastle, for she is, of course, that Violet Hunter of *The Copper Beeches*. The circumstances in which we met and subsequently married would take too long to tell here, but I am glad to have had the chance to set the record straight.

Violet shook her head to my suggestion of writing a letter. "I don't think that would do much good, John, dear," she said. "The authorities could only ask themselves how you managed to come by such secret, information and then follow the trail from you through Sherlock Holmes to poor Captain Dow."

"Dow, yes, I'd forgotten him, poor devil!" I exclaimed. "Certainly he already suffered enough, but it still goes against the grain to do nothing, Violet, and I tell you quite frankly, knowing what I do now, my heart will be in my mouth every time the *Lusitania* sails."

All too soon my forebodings proved to have been well justified.

As the world knows, the Lusitania was torpedoed on the 7th May this year and sank off the Old Head of Kinsale in just eighteen minutes, taking with her 1,198 men, women and children. Well do I remember the sorrow and outrage that gripped the entire country, and the anger too, furious, irrational, which made it unsafe for anyone who happened to bear a German-sounding name, to walk abroad though I am happy to say this proved to be a temporary phenomenon.

Of course, at that time I had no inkling that I was about to become more personally involved in the tragic fate of the giant Cunarder, for I had yet to become acquainted with Miss Mabel Every.

CHAPTER IV

Our first meeting was unpropitious. It was a baking hot June day and I was feeling tired and out of temper after a strenuous morning. According to most popular romantic fiction, we doctors are supposed to rise above such petty considerations as indigestion and aching feet, but if that is so I fear there were times when I failed to teach the ideal.

In my own defence I have to say that after many years in semi-retirement I had found it a considerable strain to be in general practice again and that moreover, the patients who shuffled in and out of my consulting room that morning seemed to be a singularly uninspiring lot, mainly suffering from boils and bad backs, if I remember rightly.

"Thank heavens for that!" I exclaimed, tearing off my stethoscope - as the last patient shuffled out. "Let's go and eat, Violet, before I perish from starvation!" (I should explain that Violet sometimes acted as my receptionist.)

"I'm afraid," she smiled rather wanly, "that there is someone else in the waiting room, John."

"There can't be!" I groaned. "According to the list you gave me old Noakes was the very last-"

"Yes, well," Violet shuffled her feet, failing to catch my eye, "she was getting desperate so I promised to see what I could do."

"So in fact this person doesn't have an appointment?"

"Well, no, John, but-"

"Then tell her to come back tomorrow and look in the book to see when we can fit her in," I said firmly.

Violet said, "She was very insistent, John, I think you should see her."

"You do?" I looked at her sharply. "Why, particularly?"

Violet hesitated. "It's not easy to put a thing like this into words, but - well, I think she needs to see you, John. Oh, I did try to put her off - I suggested she should go and see Armstrong, but, no, it had to be Dr Watson, she was quite clear about that."

"Curious," I said slowly. Although I try to keep up with changing medical techniques and eagerly purchase the latest medical treatise as it comes from the publisher, I have no illusions about myself; I am, as Sherlock Holmes once said I am 'only a general practitioner with very limited experience and mediocre qualifications'. True, he was acting the part of a dying man when he made the remark, but I suppose there was a grain of truth in it. The unknown lady's insistence that I must be the one to treat her was therefore somewhat puzzling. On the other hand I too was desperate, for the chance to sit down and have a cup of tea.

"Please see her, John - just for five minutes," Violet urged.

"Upon my word," I said, "you seem to be taking this very much to heart, my dear."

She nodded. "I know what it's like to be at the end of one's tether," her face was solemn, "John, I don't think you ever realised how frightened I was at the Copper Beeches."

"And you feel this lady may be in a similar case, eh? - even though her problem is of a medical, rather than a criminal, nature. Well, I daresay I can spare five minutes, Ask her to come in, but you will have to come and rescue me in," I glanced at my watch, "three minutes time. Even a doctor has to eat occasionally, you know."

Although I had given in, I still decided to put the lady in her place by pretending to be busy writing a letter as she came into the room. Childish, I suppose, but then I have never claimed to be a saint.

"Will you take a seat, Miss - er -? I'm afraid I didn't catch your name."

"Every - Mabel Every," she supplied, sitting down.

Still pretending to write, I studied her covertly, and saw a tall slender young woman of perhaps thirty, with a plain but pleasant face and brown hair coiled up neatly under a wide-brimmed hat that laid no claim to being in the latest fashion. Her clothes, too, were neat and serviceable, the cut, like the material, sober and discreet. All in all, I thought, she would never stand out in a crowd. Then she raised her head to look directly at me and I saw that, not for the first time, I had been too hasty in my judgement, for there was both power and purpose in the level stare of her hazel eyes.

"Well," I laid my pen aside, "what can I do for you, Miss Every?"

She sat still, clutching her capacious handbag to her bosom and said hesitantly, "It - it is a delicate matter, Dr Watson. Indeed, I hardly know where to begin. Will you give me a moment to collect my thoughts?"

"Take as long as you like, Miss Every," I rose to pour her a glass of water from the carafe, wondering if my ears had deceived me in catching the faintest hint of a Devon burr in her soft voice, wondering also why she had insisted on seeing me, for, apart from a nervous habit of pulling at her gloves, she appeared to be in the best of health.

She sipped the water and made a visible effort to compose herself. Despite my growing sympathy for her, I could not forbear a surreptitious glance at my watch. When I was young it was nothing to me to miss a meal or two - usually at the behest of Sherlock Holmes when he wished for my company on one of his many forays into the world of organised crime; but increasing years had inclined me to more regular habits and now my ageing stomach required feeding at the proper times, It was now five and twenty past one.

Miss Every intercepted the glance and said in a rush, "Dr Watson, I am in desperate trouble and I believe you are the only man in England who can help me." Her mouth was tremulous, her hazel eyes wide with appeal.

So that was it, I thought and half rose from my chair, anxious to prevent the fatal words from being uttered.

"Miss Every," I said quickly. "I must implore you to think what you are doing. I can't-"

"But-" she started to interrupt and I held up my hand, determined to get the wretched business over with as quickly as possible.

"In these unhappy days yours is, alas, a not unfamiliar predicament, Miss Every," I said, "Indeed it is unfortunately all too common."

She flushed. "Really, Dr Watson, I don't know what you mean!"

"I think you do, Miss Every." I carefully did not meet her eyes, "and far be it from me to cast the first stone."

"Dr Watson, I really must insist-"

"Why, I recall when I was a young subaltern in India I met a very charming -" I caught Miss Every's outraged eye and stopped at once, "but that was a very long time ago, of course," I added hastily.

She was staring at me open-mouthed, as though stupefied. It was now or never, I thought and plunged in straightaway, "I hate to cause you pain, Miss Every, but I feel it my duty to tell you that no reputable," I laid peculiar stress on the word, "no reputable doctor would consider performing such an operation upon a young unmarried woman. Quite apart from the moral aspect, it happens to be against the law to-"

There was a crash as the glass fell to the floor and Miss Every jumped to her feet, scarlet in the face. "Dr Watson, I insist on being heard!" she cried in a panting voice. "Will you please get it into your head that I am not with child!"

There was a dreadful silence. Then I uttered a groan and sank back in my chair, mopping my damp forehead with a handkerchief. I think I have never felt so mortified in my life - and it was all my own fault too, that was the worst of it. If only I had listened to her! There was only one thing to do and I did it, Rising from my chair I came round the desk with my hand outstretched. "Miss Every," I said, "through my own stupidity, I have offended you beyond forgiveness, but even though I have done nothing to deserve it, I hope you will accept my profound apologies?"

The angry colour had faded from her cheekbones and she said slowly, "When I used to read your work in the *Strand Magazine* I was often struck by the fact that in spite of your determination to run yourself down in order to make Mr Sherlock Holmes appear the more brilliant, you yourself always emerged as a perfect gentleman. Now that I have met you, Dr Watson, I see no reason to change my opinion. Of course I forgive you."

Strangely enough it was Sherlock Holmes, the supposed woman-hater, who had spoken of the fair sex's great quality of forgiveness, but I who experienced and was grateful for it now.

Miss Every was speaking again. "I daresay the misunderstanding was partly my own fault for not making myself clear at the outset." She smiled faintly, "Put it down to nerves, Doctor, I hardly slept a wink last night, worrying over what I was to say to you when we met. You see," she clasped her hands tight together, "I do need your help so very badly."

"Anything I can do, naturally,"I said, anxious to make amends. Miss Every drew a deep breath, "Then will you please tell me how I can get in touch with Mr Sherlock Holmes?" she said.

CHAPTER V

I said, "I fear that is quite impossible, Miss Every. Sherlock Holmes and I have drifted apart somewhat in recent times and now I doubt if I could even find you an address for him."

This was the story we had agreed upon before he departed for America. "For," said he, "it would be inconvenient, to say the least, if our enemies got wind of our renewed partnership, Watson."

"Yes," I said to Miss Every, "Holmes retired from London some years ago. Found the place too damp and cold for his failing health. I believe he settled in some little place near Eastbourne."

Miss Every nodded as though this was no particular surprise to her. "Yes," she said, "I had heard of Mr Holmes's withdrawal to Sussex." She smiled artlessly. "My informant told me he had found a pretty little cottage overlooking Camber sands."

I snorted. "I fear your informant has deceived you," I said. "Sherlock Holmes is nowhere near Camber Sands, He moved to a little place called Fulworth on the Sussex Downs - or so I'm told," I added hastily.

Miss Every gave me her sweetest smile. "Oh, I am sure you have got it right, Doctor," she said, "and now perhaps you will kindly lend me your Bradshaw so that I can look up the train times to Fulworth."

My brow was damp. I mopped it with my handkerchief. "Miss Every. I must implore you to do no such thing!" I exclaimed. "Going to Fulworth would be - well, you must understand it would not be the thing at all, because," I tried to think, "because nowadays my friend Holmes has become the complete recluse. Oh, yes, he hates visitors - all visitors - says they interfere with his train of thought."

"You have seen him quite recently then?" she observed.

I stared. "What makes you say that, Miss Every?"

"Well, you obviously have a very clear and up-to-date notion of Sherlock Holmes's likes and dislikes."

"I happened to see him in London a few weeks ago," I said carelessly. "We discussed his research into the roots of the Cornish language. Fascinating stuff, but a little too deep for me, I fear. It was then that he confided to me his hatred of unexpected visitors. Then there is his rheumatism," I added.

"Oh," Miss Every said brightly, "is he researching into that too?"

"No, no, you misunderstand me, Miss Every. I mean he suffers from attacks of rheumatism. Very painful it is too - at times, so you see, for a complete stranger to go bursting in on him -"

"Ah, but I'm not a complete stranger, Dr Watson." Miss Every played her trump card with a beam of triumph. "You and Mr Holmes have both met me before - though I can see you have forgotten the occasion."

"Oh, come, Miss Every," I spoke more in sorrow than in anger, "that really won't do, you know. As Holmes's biographer I am tolerably well acquainted with all his cases and I am quite certain that the name of Mabel Every does not figure among them. You will have to do better than that."

Miss Every took a firmer grip on her bag. Whatever had she got in there, I wondered to myself. "I assure you I am not lying, Dr Watson," she insisted, "Our brief meeting took place a very long time ago, so it doesn't surprise me that you have forgotten it. However, I imagine you remember Sir Henry Baskerville and the murderer, Selden."

I started. "Selden! My dear young lady, you are surely not going to tell me that you were in any way connected to that dreadful creature?"

The mention of Selden's name still calls forth a reminiscent shudder, for his murders were of a peculiarly repulsive character; it was that indeed which had caused the Home Secretary to exercise his prerogative of mercy, on the grounds of Selden's insanity. With hindsight, it is clear that the man should have been confined in a lunatic asylum, but instead he was sentenced to life imprisonment in Dartmoor, from whence he subsequently escaped and died violently, fleeing in terror from the 'phantom' Hound.

I have, of course, written of these events elsewhere and the memory of my only glimpse of Selden is still vivid in my mind. Never shall I forget that sunken, brutish face peering at me from his rocky place of concealment. Small wonder, then, that I gazed at Mabel Every's plain, pleasant features scarcely able to credit that this gentle creature could have any blood mingled with such a monster. Somewhat to my disgust, she was smiling broadly.

"No, Doctor, Selden was no relation to me, but my father was Governor of Dartmoor Prison at the time Selden was an inmate there. After the wretched man died in that horrible fashion, my father came out to Baskerville Hall to speak with Sir Henry, not knowing that the baronet had almost died in his own encounter with the Hound, so vividly and ably described by you, Dr Watson."

I said nothing but I felt a warm glow. All writers esteem praise and I confess there were times when I had felt more than a little hurt by Sherlock Holmes's biting criticism of my work. Since then many people, including critics, have told me that in fact I am a natural writer, so the matter of Miss Every's remark was not entirely unfamiliar to me, but it was nonetheless welcome and I smiled upon her with greater warmth than before.

"Pray continue with your most interesting narrative, Miss Every," I almost purred. However, before she could comply the door opened and my wife came in, obviously with the intention of terminating the interview as we had previously agreed between us. But by then I was anxious to hear what Miss Every might have to say and I motioned Violet with my eyes that she should leave us alone a little longer. She departed with a broad smile on her face.

"Well," Mabel Every resumed as the door closed, "you must remember that Sir Henry was too ill to leave his bed after the attack by the Hound, so my father spoke instead to Mr Holmes and yourself." She wrinkled her brows. "As I recall Dr Mortimer was there too. You walked together on the big lawn outside the house and then Mr Holmes took my father to look at the famous yew alley where Sir Charles Baskerville came to his death.

"I wanted to go too," she added rather wistfully, "but you said that would be unsuitable for a little girl and took me to the kitchens where Mrs Barrymore gave me rock cakes hot from the oven."

"Well, I'll be -!" The fog seemed to clear from my brain and I had a vivid recollection of the scene she described. "The little girl in the red coat!" I exclaimed. "That was you!"

She nodded. smiling, "And I'm not sure that I've ever forgiven you, Doctor, for denying me a sight of the yew alley."

"Yes, I remember you were very angry," I said. "You stamped your foot at me and cried that it "wasn't fair'. Those were your very words, Miss Every."

"Ah, well, you can hardly blame me," she said, "All the newspapers had been full of the Baskerville Case for days - and Selden too. My brothers and sisters were green with envy when my father decided to take me with him for the drive to the Hall and I had to promise them a full and detailed account of the scene of the crime. Thanks to you, Doctor," she shook her head reprovingly, "I was unable to keep my word."

I pursed my lips. "I had forgotten what bloodthirsty imps young children can be. Still," I added, "you have to admit Mrs Barrymore made very good rock cakes."

"They were edible," she agreed, "but not enough to make up for missing the yew alley." She laughed suddenly. "Own to it, Dr Watson, you were heartily relieved when my father took me away."

"Well, you have to remember neither Holmes nor myself had ever had much to do with very young children," I said, "but, speaking for myself, I found the experience stimulating. Now, Miss Every, you have established your credentials with me, so far as that goes, but you still have not given any good reason for disturbing Sherlock Holmes in his self-imposed seclusion,"

Her head drooped and I said quickly, "If you are in difficulties why not employ a private detectives I know of an excellent -"

"No," she said firmly, "a private detective would be worse than useless in this case. Dr Watson, I am not exaggerating when I tell you the people concerned move in the very highest circles of government, I see you smile, but I swear to you I am speaking the truth. The only man who can unravel this case is Mr Sherlock Holmes, a man who, as you have so often stressed in your writings, has connections in high places."

"Past tense, Miss Every," I interrupted. "Those days are over."

She laid her maltreated gloves aside and looked at me squarely. "Really, Dr Watson, you must stop treating me like some bird-brained little woman with not a thought in her head beyond the trimming of a bonnets 1 daresay Sherlock Holmes did `appear' to retire from the scene all those years ago but, given the character of the man as outlined by you, I can hardly believe he would be content to twiddle his thumbs in idleness for the rest of his days. Did he not say, `My mind rebels at stagnation - Give me problems, give me work - and I am in my own proper atmosphere'?"

"We all grow old, young lady!" I retorted. "As yet you are too young to understand that, but the time comes when the machine runs down, the sun begins to sink towards the horizon the -" I stopped, unable to think of any more similes for the moment.

"I daresay, Dr Watson," Miss Every agreed, "but you persist in talking as though a man in his sixties must be in his dotage - and you have already proved that to be nonsense by returning to general practice. And I know someone else who -" she broke off suddenly, her face swept by a blush.

Observing her embarrassment, I said quickly, 'You are most persuasive, Miss Every, but, you know, in this time of national emergency we must all do what we can. I would never pretend to be the world's most outstanding doctor, but I feel bound to offer my skills, such as they are, in the service of my country."

"Exactly!" she pounced, "And by the same token I cannot believe a man like Sherlock Holmes would be content to stand aside when his country was plunged into the most terrible war in history. And even if he preferred a quiet life," she added thoughtfully, "I feel certain that brother of his with the funny name would never allow it."

Rather shocked, I said stiffly, "I fear I don't follow you, Miss Every."

"Oh, come, Dr Watson!" she snapped, "I am talking about Mr Mycroft Holmes, the man who, in his brother's own words, occasionally is the British Government."

I drew a deep breath. "Past tense again, I fear, Miss Every. Mycroft Holmes has long since given up his old employment and retired to the fastnesses of the Diogenes Club."

She smiled. "My father was also a government servant, Dr Watson, albeit in a very different capacity and he used to say that men like Mycroft Holmes never retire - they merely appear to do so."

I bit my lips. Miss Every's knack for grasping essentials was disconcerting to say the least. How did she manage to know or deduce so much? And what was her real purpose in coming here today. To give myself time to think I walked to the window and stood looking out. The window of my surgery commanded a view of the Common where a small group of boys ran in circles pursued by an excited Scottish terrier.

"What do you want?" I turned to ask Miss Every. "Who are you?"

"My name really is Mabel Every," she answered. "I'm a housekeeper by trade, if you can call it that. I'm employed by Captain William Thomas Turner of Liverpool. Of course, you've heard of him?"

"No, I don't think -" I began and then I realised. "You mean Turner of the *Lusitania*?"

For days after the outrage the newspapers had been plastered with photographs of Captain Turner's craggy features and accounts of his career as one of the Cunard Company's ablest Masters. He had stubbornly refused to give any interviews to the press when he arrived home in Liverpool after the *Lusitania* had sunk, insisting that the matter was *sub judice* and that what he had to say would have to wait until the official inquiry into the disaster. I seemed to recall reading somewhere that the date for that inquiry had been set for the middle of June and that it would be held under the chairmanship of Lord Mersey, His Majesty's Commissioner for Wrecks.

Mabel Every said,'The Admiralty is trying to blame Captain Turner for what happened. That is why I have to see Sherlock Holmes - only he can prevent such a terrible miscarriage of justice."

"Oh, really!" I was stung. "You're surely not expecting me to believe that, Lord Mersey is renowned world-wide as an expert on maritime affairs. Of course he will see fair play."

"An expert - Lord Mersey!" Mabel Every gave a scornful laugh. "Thomas - the Captain - says he's so ignorant he wouldn't know the difference between a binnacle and a pair of binoculars!"

"Indeed?" I said coldly. I was beginning to take a dislike to this opinionated young woman. "Well, whatever Mersey's supposed short-comings, I imagine he will certainly want to get at the truth, whatever that may be."

"But that's just it, Dr Watson!" Mabel Every cried, "Lord Mersey won't be told the truth - or only that part of it which happens to suit the Admiralty. You wouldn't know, of course, but soon after the War started the *Lusitania* was taken into dry dock to have -"

"I do know something of the structural alterations to the *Lusitania*," I interrupted her.

She stared, "How do you know? That was supposed to be top secret."

"As a matter of fact," I said, "that came indirectly from the ship's previous Master, Captain Dow."

"I see," she said slowly, but I could tell that my explanation had failed to satisfy her completely. "Then as you already know so much about it, Dr Watson, perhaps you understand why it was that the Lusitania sank so quickly - she was top-heavy, thanks to the Admiralty and now they're trying to get out of it by heaping all the blame on Tho- ... on Captain Turner."

"That is a very grave charge, Miss Every," I pointed out. "Have you any proof to substantiate what you say?"

She opened her bulky handbag and took out a sheaf of papers. "These are statements from all the crew I managed to see after the sinking - also the journal kept by David McCormick, the Junior Wireless Operator aboard. Read them, Doctor. That is all I ask."

Rather ruefully, I stared at the bundle of papers. "A tall order, Miss Every," I said, "but I suppose I can spare five more minutes."

"And if after that you are satisfied there is a case to answer?" The young woman's abnormally bright eyes were riveted on my face with acute anxiety.

I smiled. "If - and I repeat if - I am satisfied, I guarantee to send my friend Holmes a wire."

So speaking, I took out my battered timepiece and laid it on the desk between myself and Mabel Every. I then balanced on my nose the spectacles I am now forced to employ for close work and picked up David McCormick's journal.

CHAPTER VI

Needless to say, the five minute deadline I had laid down for Miss Every was quickly forgotten as I found myself more and more deeply absorbed in the disturbing contents of David McCormick's journal.

"John, dear," I started violently as Violet's soft voice spoke in my ear, "lunch will be quite ruined if you don't come and eat soon. Perhaps this lady would care to join us?"

"An excellent idea," I said, closing the journal and rising to my feet. I saw with some astonishment that it was almost two o'clock.

While we were eating I explained to Violet the circumstances under which Miss Every and I had first met. Smiling, she agreed it was a remarkable coincidence and then she asked, "Tell me, my dear, how did you manage to track my husband down? He last practised many years ago in Paddington - some distance from Ealing, wouldn't you say?"

Now I came to think of it, it did seem a little odd, but I admit that my wife, like my best friend, is often far more perspicacious than myself. Miss Every laid down her knife and fork - she had eaten almost nothing.

"I traced Dr Watson through my friend, Susan Kemp," she said and added by way of explanation, "We nursed together at Barts."

"Ah, so you were a nurse?" I said, thinking that accounted for her businesslike manner. She nodded. "Susan remained in London after I left Barts and later she married a young doctor named John Stamford."

"Why, I once knew a Stamford!" I exclaimed. "He was my dresser at Barts - so this chap you knew must be a relation of-?"

"Henry Stamford was John's father," she smiled, "and he still remembers you very well, Dr Watson - in fact, he asked me to convey his regards - and when I came to London he told me of a rumour that you had moved to Ealing with Mrs Watson," she nodded at Violet, adding simply, "so here I am."

"Well, I call that a first-rate piece of detective work," Violet remarked. "I doubt if even Mr Holmes could do better."

Miss Every brushed that aside. As I had already discovered, she could be remarkably single-minded, "I had to do something," she said. "Poor Thomas has already suffered so much from the *Lusitania* sinking."

"In what way?" I asked and she answered in a low voice, "Even though the Inquiry is yet to take place there are already people who blame him for the disasters It is almost as if someone is deliberately trying to start a whispering campaign against him. There has even been a claim that he was paid by the Germans to sail his ship into danger."

"But that is nonsense," I said and she cried fiercely, "of course it is, but these days it seems that no accusation is too vile to hurl against him! He has been spat at in the streets and nearly every post brings its drop of anonymous letters." Her eyes filled with angry tears. "I cannot begin to tell you the effect all this is having on Thomas," she said, nervously twisting her handkerchief between her fingers. "He can't sleep, he eats almost nothing - and he has no one to turn to, no-one."

"But surely," Violet spoke in a gentle voice, "Captain Turner has the support of his family at least. He cannot be as isolated as all that, Miss Every."

Mabel Every bit her lip and stared at her plate in silence. At last she said, "Captain Turner has been separated from his wife for some years now. His two sons took their mother's part. That is why his sisters suggested I might become his housekeeper after I gave up nursing."

She gave us both a defiant look, saying, "I have never regretted my decision, not once, Captain Turner is the finest man I ever met in my life. I would do anything to save him, do you hear me, anything to give him back his peace of mind."

"And you really believe Sherlock Holmes can help?" Violet said after a while.

"I'm sure of it, Mrs Watson," Miss Every said eagerly. "It was Captain Dow's idea that I should approach Mr Holmes. It seems that they met when Sherlock Holmes was a passenger on one of the *Lusitania*'s last voyages - there was some trouble aboard, Captain Dow was not very clear about the details - but he was very impressed by the way Mr Holmes handled the matter and he suggested I should get in touch with him." Her face clouded, "Poor Captain Dow; he blames himself that Thomas rather than he was on the *Lusitania*'s bridge when she went down - but that's nonsense, of course - no blame could possibly attach to Captain Dow, he is a very sick man still."

"So I understand," I said and Miss Every gave me a sharp look. "How do you know that? Captain Dow's illness was kept out of the newspapers. Oh, of course, Mr Holmes told you. So you do still see him? - I guessed as much."

I was silent. Sherlock Holmes had told me of the desperate work he was now engaged upon in the strictest confidence, which I had no intention of breaking. Miss Every's pleading eyes were hard to resist, but knowing of Holmes's quest to track down the mysterious and dangerous individual known as the Tiger, I hesitated to lay yet another burden upon his shoulders.

Mabel Every saw the conflict in my face and said persuasively, "Dr Watson, you promised to send Sherlock Holmes a wire if you were satisfied after reading the papers I brought. So far you have barely had time to do more than skim through them. I beg you read them now - read them all. Mrs Watson too - and then if you say I have no case I promise to go away and never trouble you again - but please look at the papers first."

I glanced at Violet and there passed between us one of those wordless communications familiar to happily married couples.

"You haven't got a very long visiting list today, John," Violet remarked. "I'm sure Armstrong would take over for you."'

"Very, well," I threw my napkin aside. "I see I shall get no peace from you determined females until I look at the wretched things," I said and then I added sternly, "But I look to you to keep your side of the bargain, Miss Every, if I am not satisfied."

She lifted her chin. "I shall abide by your decision, Dr Watson," she said in a stately, voice.

Violet found Miss Every a book to while away the time while we were examining the papers, but I take leave to doubt whether she read a word of it, for when I glanced up now and then I saw her from the window of my study, strolling restlessly between the flowerbeds.

"Look at this, John." Violet held out a cutting from the *New York Times*. Starkly, edged in black, like the announcement of a funeral, it read as follows:

NOTICE

Travellers intending to embark on the Atlantic voyage are
reminded that a state of war exists between Germany and her
allies and Great Britain and her allies; that the zone of war

includes the waters adjacent to the British Isles; that in accordance with formal notice given by the Imperial German Government, vessels flying the flag of Great Britain or any of her allies are liable to destruction in these waters and that travellers sailing in the war zone on ships of Great Britain or her allies do so at their own risk.

IMPERIAL GERMAN EMBASSY WASHINGTON DC, APRIL 22, 1915.

Next to it was the Cunard advertisement giving details of the *Lusitania's* forthcoming voyage to England.

"In other words," Violet said caustically, "the Germans were blatantly threatening the ship before she even left New York."

"The trouble is," I said, "it may not be quite as simple as that. If Captain Dow was speaking the truth to Holmes when he mentioned some of the cargoes she was carrying - fuel-oil, shell-cases, and so forth, the Germans had every right to feel aggrieved."

She gave me a cold look. "John, you're surely not saying they were right to drown all those innocent people?"

"No, of course not, my dear," I patted her hand, "I hope you know me better than that, but, well, I can't help wishing our Government had found some other vessel to transport the weapons they needed and left the *Lusitania* alone."

"I suppose she paused to think it out,"they imagined her speed would make it impossible for any submarine to catch her."

"According to David McCormick," I said, opening the journal at the relevant place, "she was sailing at reduced speed to conserve fuel. McCormick says six of her boilers had been shut down, so she could only travel at twenty-one knots. He's added a little footnote - do you want to hear? A torpedo runs through the water at forty-five knots, so if the angle is right, no ship can hope to escape, not even the *Lusitania*."

Violet flicked through the pages of the journal. "He says nothing about the cargo."

"Probably because he knew nothing. After all, the Captain would hardly be likely to confide in him - but he does mention that the ship was seriously under-crewed. Here:" I read the passage aloud, "We need seventy-seven able seamen to work this ship properly, but Anderson [the Staff Captain] was only able to get forty-one, so that means if the worst does there'll only be one A.B. per lifeboat. Let's hope the Huns don't hear about it and start getting ideas.'"

"That's odd," Violet frowned.

"What is, my dear?"

"Well," she said, "you would have thought if the Admiralty attached so much importance to the *Lusitania* arriving safely they would have ensured she had a full crew."

"Perhaps - but personally I doubt if there is a sinister explanation for that - just normal muddle and incompetence. One of these days, Violet, you must read the account of the British retreat from Kabul and see for yourself how it is that more men die as a result of someone's carelessness than from bullets."

"I will, John, dear, but not now. I want to see what else Mr McCormick has to say."

The young wireless operator recounted how the great ship had left New York for the last time, watched by a silent, half-sombre, half-expectant crowd. Some of the passengers had taken fright after reading the German warning and cancelled, but the likes of the multi-millionaire, Alfred Vanderbilt, and Charles Frohman, the acclaimed theatrical impresario, loftily ignored both the infamous Notice and the hucksters on the quayside selling photographs of 'The *Lusitania*'s last voyage'. Presumably they preferred to believe Captain Turner's assurance that not only was the *Lusitania* too fast to be caught by any submarine and that in any case when they came into the danger area they would be safely in the hands of the Royal Navy. People might have felt a little less sanguine had they known that the ship was so seriously under-crewed it had not been possible to hold proper lifeboat drills prior to leaving New York harbour.

That the Germans were still taking an active interest in the *Lusitania* became apparent soon after she left Pier 54 when three foreigners were caught in a steward's pantry, armed with a camera. David McCormick believed they were hoping to photograph the guns the *Lusitania* was supposedly carrying. "If the Huns could prove to the world the *Lucy* was really a disguised Armed Merchant Cruiser it would give them an excuse for sinking her," he wrote, "but it's all a lot of nonsense of course. Even if we were carrying guns there's no one aboard trained to fire them.

I flipped over the next few pages in which McCormick had found very little to record, except to note ruefully that he and the senior operative, Robert Leith, were kept very busy in the Marconi Room as they tried to keep up with their routine work as well as the constant stream of messages to or from the passengers.

The first hint of approaching danger took the form of a laconic warning from the Admiralty on the 6th of May: "Submarines active off the Fastnet."

McCormick had added a caustic footnote to the effect that this was hardly an adequate warning, since it gave no indication of the submarines' whereabouts or numbers. Nevertheless, he wrote, the Old Man (Captain Turner) had taken what precautions he could, posting double look-outs all over the ship and ordering all watertight doors closed apart from those giving essential access-way. Moreover, the passengers themselves were asked not to show any unnecessary lights, while stewards bustled round blacking out the portholes. (At the time I was reading the journal I did not fully appreciate Turner's dilemma: he had to light up the ship sufficiently to show everyone she was a non-combatant liner, at the same time he did not want to draw undue attention to himself.)

Although better informed than most, McCormick was nevertheless chilled when he emerged from the Second Class Dining Room to see some of the crew removing the canvas covers from the lifeboats. Until then he had never truly believed that the Germans would have the nerve to attack the *Lusitania*. Now, for the first time, he realised that the unthinkable might be about to happen.

He mentioned his fears to the Junior Third Officer, Albert Bestie, who confirmed that all of the look-outs had been ordered to report "anything that moves - even if it's only a broom-handle floating in the water." Both men smiled easily, all too well aware that Captain Turn would not be worrying about broom handles but the telltale feathering of a stealthily raised periscope, or, worse still, the deadly white track of a torpedo.

Safely in his bunk for a few precious hours, McCormick was unsurprised to hear a rhythmic creaking as the *Lusitania's* forty-two lifeboats were swung out on their davits - a routine precaution but the sound was ominous and contributed to the mood of unease aboard the ship.

At seven o'clock the next morning, back on duty, McCormick received a warning from the Admiralty. "Submarines active off the south coast of Ireland." But there were no more details. Nevertheless, it was enough to persuade Turner to widen his margin of safety by keeping at least fifteen miles offshore from the Fastnet. Some of the passengers sighed, remembering happier days when they had sailed along the beautiful Irish coast, only a mile or so from land.

By now, Violet and I were no longer skimming but reading with absorbed concentration, for David McCormick, like so many of Celtic origin, had a certain facility with words and he skilfully evoked that last dreadful day aboard the *Lusitania* from early in the morning when she was nosing her way through thick tag which cut down visibility to less than thirty yards to those appalling moments after the torpedo struck"

"Cheer up, youngster," Leith greeted his junior with a broad smile. I've just beard on the grapevine that the *Juno*'s coming to escort us safely into Queenstown!"

"So that's why the horn's been blaring?" McCormick's remark was almost drowned by the deep bass note of the *Lusitania*'s siren. "Let's hope the Germans don't hear that!" he exclaimed, clapping his hands to his ears.

Leith shrugged. "If I were in the Old Man's shoes I'd take my chance on that rather than risk missing the *Juno* - and her guns."

Although he was several years younger than Leith, David McCormick was impressed. The cruiser HMS *Juno* had the fire-power all right, but she was at least twenty years old, a real rust-bucket, and, being un-armoured below the waterline, she would be as vulnerable to a torpedo as the *Lusitania* herself. You would have thought the Royal Navy could manage - something a bit better to protect the most famous liner in the world.

When he mentioned his fears to Leith, the latter said almost angrily, "Well, there's no point in looking on the black side all the time. Just remember the *Juno*'s got the guns to blow any sub out of the water."

Provided she sees it first, McCormick thought but did not say. He had no wish to quarrel with Leith. To him, though, the *Lusitania*'s siren had a plaintive, almost melancholy quality that chilled his blood. And if the *Juno* was out there, why didn't she damned well answer?

Before going off duty Leith mentioned the five warnings of submarine activity which had come in during the night.but none had given any additional information, so, as Leith agreed, the Old Man had been wakened five times for precisely nothing.

Once his colleague had gone, McCormick settled to work, cheered by the blessed silence now that the *Lusitania* had ceased sounding her foghorn. But was that such a good thing, he wondered suddenly. There had been no sign of the *Juno*, so the *Lusitania* must have missed her in the fog and that meant, his spine tingled at the thought, they were now coming into the danger area all on their own. His mouth tightened; even the *Juno* would have been better than nothing.

Towards noon another massage came in: "Submarines active in southern part of Irish Channel. Last heard of twenty miles south of Coningbeg Light vessel. Make certain *Lusitania* gets this." Taking it down, McCormick cursed softly. Why couldn't the Admiralty give any hint whether the submarines were behind the *Lusitania* or in front of her?

At the eleventh hour (very much so!) someone apparently woke up to the *Lusitania*'s terrible danger and at eleven o'clock a twelve word message in the most secret naval code came crackling into David McCormick's headphones. He took it down as it was transmitted and sent it at once to the bridge, aware that only Captain Turner had access to the naval codes, which were kept in his safe under lock and key, McCormick himself was familiar only with the usual MVI code in which messages to the ship were normally transmitted.

As the minutes ticked by and nothing happened McCormick found he was clenching his hands together so firmly the knuckles had turned white. He made himself relax. There was nothing to worry about now he insisted to the doubting inner voice which had been whispering in his ear ever since he entered the wireless room that morning. The powers-that-be were taking action to protect the ship. The only thing they had to wait for now was for the Old Man to finish decoding that message.

Captain Turner in fact took some time to do so, as it was the first message he had ever received in that code. Once the meaning was clear, however, he swung the *Lusitania* to port so violently that McCormick almost tumbled off his chair in the wireless room. He realised at once what had happened. Someone at the Admiralty had woken up to the danger at the last minute and diverted the *Lusitania* to Queenstown. "And about time too!" he muttered to himself. Until then he had not comprehended how frightened he was.

The mist had cleared up and the sun revealed in sparkling detail the coasts and headlands of Ireland. Beguiled by the warm sunshine the passengers came out on deck, arguing desultorily whether the tall black and white lighthouse on the nearest headland could really be the Old Head of Kinsale or even Mallin Head or Bull Rock. All these cliffs looked very much the same, one man remarked, adding that the uncertainty must add very greatly to a navigator's difficulties. Unknown to the passengers, Captain Turner had already ordered Third Officer Bestie to take a four point bearing on the lighthouse. It would take forty minutes, but he needed to fix his position with absolute accuracy if he was to thread his way up the narrow passage to Queenstown without a pilot, using the only channel swept daily for mines.

For there was no sign of the *Juno*, who should have been here to guide the *Lusitania* as she had guided other Cunard vessels in the past. No one knew the *Juno* was already back in port.

At 2.15 Robert Leith arrived to relieve McCormick. The two men chatted casually as they changed places and then it happened.

In McCormick's own words, "The *Lusitania* shuddered suddenly and there was a sound like a door banging on a windy day. She started to list. Bob Leith and I were both staggering around the wireless room like drunken men, unable to get to our feet. Then there was another explosion, a dreadful roar that seemed to throw her right up in the air. It was as if something had blown her apart.

McCormick had scribbled an afterthought in pencil in the margin: "2nd explosion much bigger than the first. They're saying it was another torpedo, but that's all eyewash. For my money, the second explosion came from inside the ship. Could have been all the stuff we were carrying in the holds - all the ammo - Admiralty say no, but then they would, wouldn't they? After all, it was them who loaded the *Lucy* up with a dangerous cargo and didn't do a damned thing to protect hers

"Some say the second bang was caused by boilers exploding under the terrific pressure, but that won't wash either because I spoke to survivors from all three boiler rooms myself and none of them mentioned any explosion, but they all pointed out there were no survivors from the baggage room just above the main orlop deck where all the you-know-what was stored. The Admiralty say there was no order to divert the ship to Queenstown. In that case why was the passengers' luggage being brought up on deck for an overnight landing there?"

The rest of the pages were blank. I closed the journal and looked at Violet, who returned my stare.

"What now?" she asked.

"I think," I said, "I must go and send a telegram."

CHAPTER VI

GREATLY INTRIGUED BY YOUR WIRE STOP ARRIVING LONDON BY FIRST AVAILABLE TRAIN STOP BETWEEN ARMIES THE LAW KEEPS SILENCE STOP HOLMES.

Thus ran the telegram from Fulworth.

"Handed in before seven o'clock," I told Miss Every, "so unless a troop train causes a hold-up Holmes should be with us by nine."

The skin between her brows creased. "I don't quite understand, Doctor. What does Mr Holmes mean, 'Between armies the law is silent?'"

"Ah, that is a classical tag, attributed to the wronged general, Caius Marius, when he marched on Rome. I seem to remember Holmes employing it at the time of the Dreyfus Case. I fear my friend tends to take a cynical view of politics and politicians. Speaking personally, I deplore the modern tendency to regard all men in public life as either fools or charlatans, when a moment's reflection will show that nothing could be further from the truth. Think of Gladstone, of Disraeli, of General Gordon, of William Wilberforce - can you truly believe that such men were motivated solely by self-interest? I fear such cynicism will end by harming our nation."

"Excellent, 'Watson!" A cool slightly mocking voice spoke from the doorway. "As I have said before, you are the one fixed spot in a changing universe."

"Holmes!"

Smiling affably, he handed his hat to the maid and moved forward to exchange civilities with Violet, who had hurried to welcome him.

Mabel Every was staring at him as though some fabled quadruped, a unicorn, say, had entered our prosaic drawing room, and for a moment I too found myself looking at Holmes through the eyes of a stranger seeing him for the first time, that tall spare figure in his sixties with lines in his face and receding hair, which, however, remained black and glossy. To my mind he still very much resembled the pictures Mr Paget had produced for *The Strand Magazine*, many years ago now, alas. The grey eyes were as piercing as ever, the aquiline features as sharp, and as for the brain within the bony casement of the skull. No-one who knew anything of the long pursuit of Von Bork could seriously think Sherlock Holmes had lost any of his mental acuity.

Having greeted Violet as an old friend, as indeed she was, Holmes turned to me, "Well, Watson?"

"It's good to see you again, Holmes!" I cried,

"And this," he transferred his gaze to Mabel Every, "must be the young lady in the case." Retaining her hand, he studied her with obvious interest. "And how long is it since you gave up active nursing, Miss Every?" he inquired.

"Oh, about twelve years," she said casually and then she gaped at him. "How did you know that, Mr Holmes? Or was it a lucky guess?"

"Certainly not," he sounded aggrieved. "Watson here will tell you I never guess. Your hands gave you away, of course."

"My hands?" she fluttered them self-consciously behind her back. "What about my hands?"

"They are well-kept," he answered, "but the nails are cut very short, which in my experience is a characteristic of those in the nursing profession. However, your skin is soft and well-kept, arguing that, although you have been a nurse at some time, you are no longer one."

"But I might have been a lady typewriter, Mr Holmes," she said teasingly. Holmes considered for a moment before he shook his head decisively. "No, for the sleeve of your dress shows no sign of the giveaway double line above the wrist where the typewriter presses against the table. You remember, Watson, the Mary Sutherland case?"

"I remember it vividly," I answered, guessing that Holmes had adopted this unusual approach to put Miss Every at her ease, and had succeeded wonderfully well, for she already appeared to be much less on the defensive.

I said, "As I told you in my wire, Holmes, Miss Every has a remarkable tale to unfold."

"So I perceive," said Sherlock Holmes, adding with a smile, "No great mystery there, Miss Every, but when a lady clutches her handbag with such fierce determination as you did when I first entered the room, it is plain that it must carry something of value to her."

"Yes, I- " she began, but Violet interrupted her.

"May I ring for some tea before you begin? Mr Holmes must be thirsty after the train and we shan't be eating for some time yet."

"An excellent suggestion, Mrs Watson," Holmes responded and he smiled again. "You are obviously endowed with the practical sense of the incomparable Mrs Hudson, and, believe me, I could pay you no higher compliment than that."

Thus it was that, having refreshed himself with not one but two cups of tea and received permission to light his cherrywood pipe, Holmes crossed his long thin legs and invited Mabel Every to begin.

I will not repeat her exact words, since the account she gave Sherlock Holmes tallied exactly with the version of events she had already given Violet and myself and she concluded by reading from McCormick's journal.

Holmes listened in silence, his face turned away from me, so that his formidable profile was sharply silhouetted against the dark-red wallpaper.

"Yes," he said at last, "I believe I have the picture now. By chance I happen to be fairly familiar with the *Lusitania*, although some of this material is quite new to me and requires thought. As to our previous encounter, Miss Every," his voice lightened, "I remember very well a child who pest- I mean, who asked a great many questions."

"And here I am after nearly thirty years still asking questions, Mr Holmes," she took him up, "but different ones this time. Do you think you can find me some answers?"

"I am not sure as yet," he replied. "It depends a great deal on other factors. Will you be good enough to hand me David McCormick's journal, please?"

Rather reluctantly she gave it to him. Holmes sat still for a moment with the book in his hand, making no move to open it, but staring with great interest at the cover.

"Interesting," he said at last, "but you realise, Miss Every, it would be entirely worthless if presented as evidence in a court of law?"

Mabel Every went white. "I don't understand you, Mr Holmes," she stammered. "Surely a complete and accurate record of the *Lusitania*'s last voyage- ?"

"My dear Miss Every," Sherlock Holmes interrupted with an air of weary patience, "it is quite clear that this journal was written by McCormick when he returned to England after the events he describes." He held it up. "As you see, there is no sign of prolonged immersion. It is therefore nothing more than an account of events David McCormick thinks he remembers."

"So?" While he was speaking Miss Every had managed to regain some of her poise. "David McCormick has an exceptionally good memory. That is as true and accurate an account of what happened as you are likely to get."

Sherlock Holmes said in a crushing voice, "Miss Every, I rather doubt if a busy man like Lord Mersey will be interested in the ramblings of the *Lusitania's* junior wireless operative, who has obviously been embittered by his very distressing experiences after the ship sank and is looking for someone to blame. I daresay, too, he hoped to earn himself a measure of notoriety by blurting out the so-called 'truth' at the Inquiry. As we all know the gutter press will pay almost anything for sensational stories nowadays."

Mabel Every sprang to her feet. "Mr Holmes, you are unjust. Far from making money out of his story, as you imply, David McCormick is likely to suffer in his career for revealing what the Admiralty would prefer to keep hidden. Doubtless that is why they have insisted that Robert Leith is to give evidence at the Inquiry, even though, as he admits himself, he was not on duty during the morning of the 7th."

"But McCormick?" I said. "Lord Mersey will surely want to hear what he has to say?"

She shrugged, "Maybe, but he will not get the chance, Dr Watson. David McCormick is not to be called as a witness."

I glanced at the silent figure sitting by the fire. "Rather unfair to Captain Turner, wouldn't you say, Holmes?"

"I imagine the Admiralty must have their reasons," he answered noncommittally.

"But if the *Lusitania* really was diverted into Queenstown-"

"'If' being the operative word," he said pettishly. "As a reasonable man, Watson, ask yourself why the Admiralty should wish to deny bringing the *Lusitania* into Queenstown, if indeed that was their intention?"

"Oh, I can tell you that," Mabel Every broke in, "it was because they made a mess of it. Not that that was anything new," her voice was biting. "From the beginning they did nothing to protect the ship. Captain Turner was given no proper course instructions - he even had to go to the Admiralty building in New York and ask for them. They told him none had arrived and it would be best for him to follow the same course he used before. Do you call that taking proper precautions? I don't."

Sherlock Holmes drew on his pipe. "No doubt there is a perfectly sensible explanation for the Admiralty's action," he said. "If that is the gravamen of your case against them, Miss Every, I feel bound to tell you I do not think much of it."

"Oh, but there is more, Mr Holmes, much, much more," she declared. "That was only the beginning. If the Board of Admiralty were here now I would have some things to ask:, I can tell you!"

"I'm sure of it," Holmes murmured *sotto voce*, but unheeding she swept on, "After the German threat why was there no escort for the *Lusitania* after she came into the War Zone? Why was the *Juno* recalled to Queenstown? Why were there no patrol boats searching the area for submarines, especially after three ships had been sunk there in the previous twenty-four hours?" She was shaking with anger.

"Three ships?" Sherlock Holmes made a note, "Named?"

"The *Earl of Lathom*, the *Candidate* and the *Centurion*," she reeled them off without pausing to think.

"I see." Sherlock Holmes drew on his pipe again, only to find it had gone out. Taking out his pouch he began to stuff fresh shag into the bowl. While he was thus engaged he said casually, "But it is possible these sinkings occurred too late for the Admiralty to alert the *Lusitania*."

"No, Mr Holmes, it is not possible," she contradicted. "The news was all over Liverpool in the early hours of the 7th. There was plenty of time for the Admiralty to do something about the *Lusitania*, but they did nothing. Why?"

She was so brave in her defiance.so convinced of the rightness of her cause that I was tempted to cheer and I looked hopefully towards Holmes, certain that he would at least admire her spirit, but his grey eyes remained cold and there was an undercurrent of menace in his voice as he said softly, "It may be that the Admiralty believed, wrongly as it turned out, that a Master as experienced as Captain Turner would know how to protect his own ship."

Giving her no chance to speak he continued, "Indeed, it seems to me, as a layman, that Captain Turner has a great deal to answer for in his navigation of the *Lusitania* - sailing too close to headlands, failing to steer a mid-channel course- "

"But, Holmes..." I tried to interrupt. Sherlock Holmes held up a hand to silence me and went on with the damning indictment.

"Not merely that, Miss Every, but the Captain reduced his speed to an absurdly low rate of knots, and, worst of all, he failed to zigzag." He smiled crookedly. "Short of stopping dead in the water, I cannot think of a single error the *Lusitania*'s Master failed to commit. He almost seems to have gone out of his way to make sure a U-boat got him and in my opinion, Miss Every." Holmes paused to light his pipe, "Captain Turner can think himself lucky not to be facing a charge of treason rather than simple negligence."

"Holmes!" I was determined to be heard and for the moment. Mabel Every appeared to have been stunned into silence by the ferocity of Holmes's attack. "No doubt you will think this a mere quibble, but I have never heard the southern part of the Irish Sea described as a `channel' - how then could the Admiralty expect Turner to steer a mid-channel course?"

Sherlock Holmes's granite features softened a little. "That is a fair point, Watson, and I must own it had not occurred to me."

"Perhaps," Violet said unexpectedly, "anything that helps to blacken Captain Turner's character suits the Admiralty's case - so the Irish Sea becomes a channel, for the time being, anyway," she added with a wicked smile.

Holmes's lips twitched but he said seriously, "Far graver is the charge that the Captain was not zigzagging at the time of the attack, as all merchant captains had been ordered to do if the danger to their vessels appeared to warrant it."

Mabel Every's head went up, "Mr Holmes, the Admiralty instruction to zigzag was only issued to merchant captains *after* the *Lusitania* had left New York, and that I can prove because I have here," she dived into the capacious recesses of her handbag, "signed statements from the captains of the *Candidate* and the *Centurion* confirming that neither of them was zigzagging when attacked. Perhaps you would care to read them."

"I should be happy to do so," he answered her, amusement tinged with respect in his eyes. "You have been remarkably thorough, Miss Every. It is perhaps unfortunate that Cunard did not employ you to prepare their case for them."

"I wish they had!" was her spirited rejoinder. "But as I have already explained to Dr Watson, none of this will be admissible as evidence at the Inquiry, so Lord Mersey will never hear of it."

Nodding impatiently, Sherlock Holmes read quickly through the documents she had brought with her. His face had taken on that immobile Red Indian cast that made it impossible to tell what he was thinking and we all three waited in some trepidation to hear what he would have to say.

"Well, well," he leaned back in the armchair and put his fingertips together, "as I see the problem, it will be our task to present the evidence to Lord Mersey in such a way that he cannot ignore it. How that is to be done, I cannot tell as yet, but done it must be."

For a moment I could hardly credit What I was hearing, but then I saw Miss Every's transfigured face and heard her joyful cry, "Mr Holmes, you'll take the case!"

"Naturally," he said, as though there had never been any doubt of it, "the matter clearly requires investigation and then pressure must be applied to those who, for reasons best known to themselves, are concealing the truth." His brow contracted in a frown. "We shall meet with considerable obstruction, no doubt, for the political turmoil following the *Lusitania* disaster has been unprecedented and not merely in this country. I am told that feeling in America, following the drowning of so many of her nationals, runs so high that President Wilson, against all his naturally pacific instincts, may be forced to declare war on Germany."

"But, Holmes," said I, "Why should President Wilson's attitude have any bearing on our trying to establish the truth about the *Lusitania*?"

"As yet I am not quite certain myself, " he answered, "but, well, our own Government is hard pressed just now and governments under pressure are capable of almost anything." His eyes were veiled as he said in an abstracted voice, "Indeed, history is littered with the crimes of otherwise decent and honourable men acting out of a mistaken sense of patriotism." He added in a meaningful voice, "By the way, Watson, are you still in touch with your old schoolfellow who used to work in the Foreign Office?"

"You mean Percy Phelps," I said. "He was the only friend I had who moved in such exalted circles. Funnily enough, Holmes, we were talking about you only the other day. He is still very grateful to you for saving his career by recovering the Naval Treaty."

"Ah, so you are still in touch?"

"Very much so."

"And Phelps is still at the Foreign Office?"

"Yes, indeed," I said, "though his career never quite recovered after he was branded as the man who lost the Naval Treaty. It got about in Foreign Office circles that Percy Phelps was 'not quite sound' and he was passed over time and time again when there was talk of new appointments. Not even the influence of his uncle, Lord Holdhurst, could procure him a job worthy of his talents. After Lord Holdhurst died, Tadpole, as I still call him, left the Foreign Office for a while and tried to start a new life in America, but he is back now."

"Hm," said Sherlock Holmes, "but even in a lowly capacity he must be privy to many Government secrets. How do you feel about sounding him. out, Watson?"

Miss Every and Violet both turned to look at me. I said, "Tadpole Phelps is an old and valued friend. I will do nothing to force his confidence, but I will undertake to go and see him in the morning."

"Good man, Watson!" Sherlock Holmes rubbed his hands. "While you are telephoning Phelps -" I gaped and he said impatiently, "no point in wasting time, old friend. As I say, while you are telephoning Phelps I will go through the rest of the papers brought by the indefatigable Miss Every and see if anything further may be gleaned from them. If I am any judge we have a long hard fight ahead of us. The Board of Admiralty will not yield their secrets very easily. Come, Watson, no need to look so gloomy. Remember that when the Greeks despaired after the death of Achilles, they found the wily Ulysses to devise the stratagem of the Wooden Horse."

CHAPTER VII

Just before we sat down to dinner I managed to catch Sherlock Holmes on his own for a moment.

"The Tiger?" I said in a low voice. "Have you succeeded in tracking him down?"

"No, Watson, I have not," he answered wearily. "Despite my best efforts the trail appears to have simply petered out in a myriad of false trails. There are no reports of increased espionage activity in this country or of outrages which could be traced to the machinations of the enemy - or so I am told, anyway."

"And Scheele's cigars?" I pressed him. "Do you have any idea what they might be?"

"Again, no, Watson," he shot me a humorous look, "at this rate I shall be losing the reputation you have grafted upon me for near-infallibility. Let us hope I shall be more successful with the *Lusitania* Case, but to you alone, Watson, I will confess that I have my doubts. Government bodies are usually reluctant to yield up any of their secrets, and I am sure the Admiralty will be no exception. Much will depend on you, Watson, and what you learn from your friend Phelps tomorrow."

As we were preparing ourselves for sleep that night Violet said to me, "I don't know if Mr Holmes is aware of it, John, but I suppose you realise that young woman is head over heels in love with her employer?"

"Miss Every? In love with Captain Turner? Come, Violet, you're letting your romantic imagination run away with you."

"I've never been a romantic person, as you well know, John, but I've been watching Miss Every since she came into this house and what I'm telling you is the truth. Haven't you noticed the way her face fights up when Captain Turner's name is even mentioned? Then there is her ferocious determination to defend him from every possible charge. And how many housekeepers do you know who would be willing to spend so much time tracking down witnesses and then spend their hard-earned money on a trip to London in quest of the most famous detective of them all? John, if that isn't love I don't know what is."

I looked at her. "Are you implying that the relationship between Miss Every and Captain Turner is an improper one?" I demanded.

"Of course not! What an idea!" she was indignant. "I'm just trying to warn you that Miss Every is a very partisan witness and that Captain Turner may not be the innocent victim of circumstance she makes him out to be. You and Mr Holmes would do well to weigh very carefully everything she says."

"You could well be right, my dear," I said, unclicking my back collar stud, "and I promise to be on my guard. Still, Holmes believes that one glance at the Admiralty Signals Register for 7th May will settle the matter. If it can be proved beyond doubt that the *Lusitania* was diverted into Queenstown, Turner is home and dry, if not-" I, sighed and added pensively, "Poor Miss Every - I'm glad she can count on the support of the Stamfords, at least. What an extraordinary coincidence that the son of my old dresser at Barts should be- "

"Yes, John," said Violet, and blew out the lamp.

***

Usually I am a sound sleeper, but that night, twist and turn as I would, slumber evaded me as my mind seized first upon this conceit and now upon that. For example, the real identity of the mysterious individual known as The Tiger and the exact nature of the sinister 'cigars' he was either to receive from or give to the brilliant but unsavoury Doktor Scheele.

Now, hard upon the heels of that mystery crowded another. The *Lusitania*. What could be the explanation behind the Admiralty's apparent disregard both for the safety of the vessel and of her hundreds of civilian passengers? And why - and for me this was the nub of the matter - why had my old schoolfriend's voice been charged with an unfamiliar note of wariness and caution when he spoke to me on the telephone, "The *Lusitania*, Watson." A long pause, an unsuccessful attempt at a laugh. "My dear old boy, that's an Admiralty matter - nothing to do with the Foreign Office."

"But," said I, "you must have an opinion, Tadpole?"

Another prolonged pause before he said, "Well, maybe I have, but since I am not a naval man, it would be without value."

"Nevertheless, I think I would rather like to hear it," I persisted. "We have been friends for longer than I care to remember - surely you can trust me?"

"Of course I do, Watson, how can you doubt it?" he protested at once. "But do try to understand, old man, I'm in a damned difficult position. As a public servant, I simply can't speak my mind as freely as I would like, not even to an old friend."

"I see," I said, "so it is true that the Government have something to conceal about the fate of the *Lusitania*?"

"I never said so, Watson," he interposed quickly.

You had no need to, Tadpole, your voice gave you away. I'm afraid you have never entirely mastered the civil servant's art of hiding your true feelings."

"Have you become a mind-reader in your old age, Watson?" he tried to make a joke of it.

"In a way, A general practitioner can learn a great deal by listening to the tone of a man's voice. I know anger and distrust when I hear them."

The sound of his indrawn breath rustled down the telephone. Then he said. "I suppose you'd better come and see me. Four o'clock tomorrow afternoon suit you?" He rang off before I could answer.

"We're getting on, Watson," Sherlock Holmes had said when I reported this conversation to him. "I hope your long-suffering colleague will not mind you departing to Surrey on the morrow?"

"There will be no need for that," said I. "The Phelpses live in London now and Briarbrae is now a convalescent home for wounded officers."

"It's a pity you won't be going to Briarbrae, John," Violet remarked casually, "The gardens must be at their loveliest just now." She smiled reminiscently. "Annette was saying only the other day how deeply she envied Joseph for being able to enjoy them while she and 'Percy were stifling in the London house."

"Joseph!" Sherlock Holmes's fork clattered to the plate and he turned quite white. "My dear Mrs Watson, can you possibly be referring to Joseph Harrison?"

"Why, yes, of course," Violet replied. "Did John not tell you, Mr Holmes? Joseph is running the convalescent home."

"No, Watson did not tell me that." Sherlock Holmes had become very thoughtful. "The last I heard of Joseph Harrison, he was living abroad, having made England too hot to hold him after he stole the Naval Treaty. Upon my soul!" he added, "it is surely very magnanimous of Percy Phelps to allow Harrison to live at Briarbrae, seeing that his career was blighted.and he might have been stabbed to death by that worthy."

For those among my readers who need to have their memories refreshed I would refer them to my story *The Naval Treaty*, edited by Arthur Conan Doyle. Briefly, however, my old schoolchum, Percy Phelps, had been asked to make a copy of a treaty aimed at restraining the belligerence of Kaiser Wilhelm, that Harrison had stolen it and that Tadpole had summoned Sherlock Holmes to aid him. In recovering the treaty cleverly concealed at Briarbrae, the Phelps family home, Holmes had also unmasked Joseph Harrison as the thief and would-be traitor. However, the incident had dealt a body blow to Tadpole's hopes of a distinguished career at the Foreign Office. From then on he had been repeatedly passed over whenever one or another coveted post fell vacant. Nor was his cause helped by his marriage to Annette Harrison, Joseph's sister. The fact that they loved one another and had been contracted to marry long before the disaster cut little ice with the civil service mandarins. In truth my old friend had been shabbily treated by his superiors.

"Personally," Sherlock Holmes was still pursuing his own train of thought, "I would have, felt inclined to prosecute Harrison for treason, not to mention attempted murder, for I am firmly convinced, he meant to kill Percy Phelps that night."

"Out of the question, Holmes," I said briskly. "Lord Holdhurst was a key member of that Cabinet. His enforced resignation might have brought down the Government too and let in the opposition at a very tricky time in international affairs. Rather than risk linking the Foreign Secretary's name, however tenuously, with a scandal of that kind it was easier to let Harrison quietly vanish abroad."

"Where did he go, I wonder, after the débacle?" Holmes mused, twirling the stem of his wineglass between long fingers while he studied the colour of the wine, "Berlin? Vienna? One imagines there must have been gentlemen in the Kaiserhof and the Schonbrunn who would willingly have availed themselves of his services."

Violet had been showing signs of agitation for some time and now she burst out. "Mr Holmes, I am surprised at you! Did you not once say that to put a man in prison would be to make a criminal of him for life?

"I did indeed, Mrs Watson," Holmes said gravely, "and for the most part I stand by that statement, but I am not sure I would ever be willing to view Joseph Harrison in that light."

"Nothing would serve to convince you he has genuinely and

entirely turned over a new leaf?" Violet's colour had risen and her little foot beat a rapid tattoo on the floor. I who knew her well could tell she was very angry indeed.

Sherlock Holmes looked at her flushed face and gave the faintest of shrugs, "Oh, anything is possible, I suppose," he said ungraciously.

Violet glared at him. "It may interest you to know, Mr Holmes, that Joseph has done wonderful work at Briarbrae and his patients think the world of him."

Holmes nodded. "He always was a plausible fellow," he said in an absentminded voice. "Once he almost persuaded me that he was a regular solid citizen."

Violet bristled. I sent her a warning glance and, she subsided reluctantly. When she left us to our port and cigars I tried to explain to Holmes why she felt so strongly.

"She and Annette Phelps both serve on the same committee for Belgian War Relief," I said,"so they have naturally seen a great deal of each other these past few months, Before Briarbrae was opened as a convalescent home Joseph Harrison frequently came to the London house, where Violet met him and formed her present high opinion of his character."

"But presumably she became aware at some time of what had happened in the past, the theft of the Treaty and so forth?" Holmes looked at me interrogatively.

"Harrison told her himself."

"Did he now?" Sherlock Holmes pursed his lips in a low whistle.

"He said he had no wish to sail under false colours and she had.better know the worst from his own lips rather than a stranger's."

Sherlock Holmes uttered a soft chuckle. "I seem to remember the notorious Baron Adalbert Gruner employed a similar technique to ensnare Miss Violet de Merville; now I come to think of it, those two had much in common. Harrison now - " he enunciated the name slowly and let his voice trail into silence while he gazed into space.

"Holmes," I said with dawning apprehension, "what are you thinking now?"

"It's late, Watson," he stood up abruptly, "and I have had a long day, with the journey and other matters." He smiled at me. "Let us go and seek our rest, old friend for tomorrow; we have a great deal of work to do, you and I."

CHAPTER VIII

True to his word, Sherlock Holmes came down early for breakfast the following morning, saying it would be no bad thing for him to arrive at the Admiralty before anyone was fully awake.

I looked up from my ham and eggs, "Do you anticipate so much difficulty, Holmes?"

"Well, let us say I am prepared for a certain amount of obstruction," he replied, sipping his coffee. "Whatever the rights and wrongs of the *Lusitania* Affair, it is plain that the Admiralty failed in their primary duty to protect her and I for one would rather like to know why. Was it simply negligence, as Miss Every believes, or is there some darker explanation?"

"Which do you believe, Mr Holmes?" Violet asked him and he smiled, "I am rather hoping Watson will be able to tell me that after he has seen Percy Phelps."

He pushed his cup aside and rose to his feet, one hand idly playing with the gold sovereign on his watchchain, which he always wore as a memento of the incomparable Irene Adler and also as a reminder of his own fallibility. Then, with an air of decision, he bade farewell to us and hurried from the room.

Before we could settle to our breakfast again the door was pushed open to admit Mabel Every, whose haggard face and reddened eyes spoke of a sleepless night.

"Forgive me, Dr Watson," she faltered, "I felt I had to come and see you for one last time before catching the train to Liverpool.Where is Mr Holmes? I must speak to him-tell him-"

"I'm afraid," Violet said kindly, "that Mr Holmes left the house some minutes ago. Come and sit down, my dear, and have some breakfast - then John can drive you to the station."

"I don't want anything to eat, thank you." Mabel Every subsided into the chair I drew out for her.

"Some coffee then?" Violet suggested, filling a cup for her.

Mabel Every twisted her hands together,"You must think me very rude and peculiar," she said, "but I particularly wanted to see Mr Holmes. There were things I had to tell him and somehow I never managed to get round to saying them last night. I had it all planned out, you see what I was going to say but last night the words wouldn't come. Mr Holmes has that way of looking at you as if he has a job to believe you and I - oh, I can't explain."

"You wanted to tell him something about Captain Turner?" Violet said gently and Mabel Every nodded her head with poignant force.

"The Inquiry," she said, "I'm so afraid of Thomas giving Lord Mersey the wrong impression. Sailors often make bad witnesses - no one knows why - and Thomas has a rather abrupt manner sometimes." Smiling faintly, she added, "That was why Cunard took so long in promoting him to Captain. They were afraid he would be unable to cope with the First Class Passengers. Some of them can be very autocratic, and Cunard believed Thomas might be provoked into saying something he shouldn't."

"I believe," said I, "that the captain of a liner once remarked every ship carrying passengers has three sides, the port side, the starboard side and the social side."

"That's what I mean, Dr Watson," Mabel Every said eagerly. "Thomas was more outspoken even than that, but only to me or members of his family. He is an outspoken man, but he always speaks the truth, he would never tell even a white lie to save someone's face." She stared into her cup of cold coffee. "He told me once his father wanted him to become a minister, but he hated the idea and ran away to sea." She smiled again. "He tells some wonderful stories about his days before the mast - he was in sailing ships as a boy - I could listen to him for ever."

She remained sitting in silence for a while and then she stood up. "That was all I wanted to say, " she announced simply.

Violet was just opening her mouth to reply when there came a furious pounding at the door and a moment later the maid came hurrying into the room, her eyes popping,

"There's a young chap outside wants you to come and see his missis, Doctor!" she squeaked. "He says she's been took mortal bad!"

This I found to be no exaggeration when I hurried to the blue and red waggonette in the road. The white-faced young fellow at the horse's head gestured towards the rear of the shabby vehicle into which a mattress had been crammed. Upon it lay a young woman whose golden hair was soaked with sweat and whose face was twisted with pain, the severity of which could be judged by the strength of her moans.

"She says it 'urts 'er 'ere, Doctor." The man left the horse to its own devices and came up to me, tapping his right side.

"All right, my good man, I'll take a look at her," I said, clambering not without difficulty into the cart, where I began a hasty examination. The woman's pulse was alarmingly weak and her right side was so tender that she cried out when it was touched. I straightened up.

"I fear your wife has appendicitis," I said quietly. "The appendix is just about to rupture and give her peritonitis."

"Cripes, I'd better get 'er to the 'ospital quick!" he gasped.

"No time for that, I fear. You will have to put your trust in me."

The young man gulped. "Whatever you say, doctor. What must I do?"

"First we must carry her into the house where I can make a proper examination."

I was far from feeling as calm as I sounded, for, though in order to keep myself up to date I had made a point of reading every surgical treatise I could lay my hands on, I had never in my life performed an appendectomy, On the other hand, one glance at that clay-white face was enough to convince me that the patient might die en route to the nearest hospital and it therefore seemed to me that I had very little choice but to attempt the operation myself.

Telling the young man, Dobbs was his name, a qualified plumber according to the notice painted in scarlet letters on the side of the wagon, to stay with his wife, I hurried back into the house and explained the situation to Violet.

"We will have to use the kitchen table," I said. "Can you find me a clean overall while I go and scrub my hands," I turned to Miss Every. "Will you help me?" I asked.

She hesitated. "I haven't nursed for some years-" she began and then she nodded. "Yes, of course I will."

Fortunately, Violet had faced similar emergencies in the past, though nothing so grave as this, and she calmly ordered Jane to bring down blankets to cover the table and herself boiled up some water, while young Dobbs gently lifted his moaning wife from the cart.

I do not propose to go into details about the operation. Suffice it to say that the woman lived, as she might not have done had I delayed, for the first incision confirmed my diagnosis that the appendix was about to rupture. The anaesthetic was administered by Mabel Every, who behaved throughout with the utmost coolness, causing me to say as I stripped off my makeshift mask, "It is a great pity you ever gave up nursing."

"Do you think so, Doctor?" she smiled rather crookedly. "I was surprised to find I remembered so much, but, no, I'm happier as I am, or I would be if-" she broke off and bit her lip.

Studying her downcast face, I became convinced that my wife had spoken truly when she said Miss Every's feelings for Captain Turner were warmer than is normally the case between employer and housekeeper and inwardly I sighed for her, remembering her description of the Captain as a man of strict principle. A young woman who allows herself to fall in love with her married, albeit separated, employer risks laying up a great store of grief for herself in my opinion.

The ambulance came to take Mrs Dobbs to hospital and I prepared to get on with morning surgery, first bidding farewell to Miss Every, who said she would go back to the Stamfords to collect her things before catching the train home. As I was not free to drive her I insisted on calling a cab. She lingered in the hall for a moment.

"You will remember what I said this morning, Doctor, about the Captain, I mean - and tell Mr Holmes?"

"Be assured I will," I told her.

"And if there is any news-?"

"Mr Holmes will contact you right away if there is anything to impart."

"I shall wait to hear from you then," she said and left somewhat reluctantly in the taxi.

Fortunately I did not have a long surgery that morning and my visiting round was short. I say 'fortunately' because the strain of operating had tired me a good deal and I wanted to be fresh for my visit to the Phelps, later that afternoon. I knew I would need all my energy to persuade my car to behave.

The Ford is a good little motor on the whole, but it can be recalcitrant when I have to crank the engine, and many a time have I been forced to stand in the road, swinging the starting handle until my face is red and my language reverts to a more military idiom.

The day followed a normal pattern and some time elapsed before the engine coughed into life and I was able to clamber aboard, mopping my face with the handkerchief Violet held out in silence. At the last minute she had elected to come with me.

Apart from having to jam on the brakes when a foolish errand boy wobbled out from a side turning and almost shot under the front wheels, the drive to Cheyne Walk passed uneventfully and we were soon drawing up outside the Phelps's imposing residence which boasted a wonderful view of the Thames.

The butler who opened the door to us was such a commanding figure that I immediately felt shabby even in my best suit. I offered my card. He inspected it gravely before announcing in tones worthy of Sir Henry Irving, "Her Ladyship is expecting you. Dr Watson. Will you have the goodness to follow me, please?"

In the split second that his back was turned I winked at Violet, who smiled back, though with a reproving little shake of the head. We entered the magnificent drawing room.

In the *Naval Treaty* narrative I have described Annette Phelps (Annette Harrison, as she then was) as 'a striking-looking woman, a little short and thick for symmetry, but with a beautiful olive complexion, large dark, Italian eyes, and a wealth of deep black hair.' Nearly thirty years later, she was still striking, her complexion unfaded, her eyes as beautiful as ever, though once Violet confided to me that the blackness of her hair now owed something to the hairdresser's art.

Be that as it may, I think perhaps I should add to my earlier sketch by mentioning Annette's determined little chin, which imparted so much character to the lovely face and reminded me forcibly of the determined young woman who was so unshakeably convinced of her fiance's innocence, who nursed him devotedly through an attack of brain-fever, and who afterwards did much to sustain him when his once-bright prospects faded and he was shunted into a dreary succession of mediocre appointments.

"Well," she said, after she and Violet had exchanged embraces and we were all sitting down."Percy told me this was not going to be a social call, so I think we should get down to brass tacks right away. Why do you want to see him, John?"

One should never forget, I reflected, that she was an iron-master's daughter from Yorkshire, where blunt speech is almost a way of life. Deciding to match her at her own game I said, "I need some information from him, Annette."

"Confidential information, presumably?" Her eyes never left my face.

"Some people would call it so," I agreed. "But not everyone approves of the Whitehall mania for secrecy at all costs."

"Foolish talk, John," she retorted. "Some Government business has to be carried on in secret, as you know very well."

I shrugged, "Secret manœuvring did nothing to save this country from becoming embroiled in a terrible war."

I could tell from her expression that that had struck home.

She said sharply, "I won't have you dragging Percy into your private vendettas, John. He's already suffered more than enough from wagging tongues. I'll not stand by and see him go through that again."

"Thank you, my dear," said Tadpole Phelps as he came into the room, "but I think we should have learned to trust John Watson by now. Remember that but for him I should be living in the shadow of an appalling disgrace."

I should say that Tadpole Phelps now bore very little resemblance to the nervous, emaciated man I have described in the *Naval Treaty*. Over the years he had put on weight and put off hair. His pale complexion was now ruddy and the bright blue eyes were now covered by gold-rimmed spectacles, reminding one irresistibly of Mr Pickwick.

When he removed them, however, one saw the sepia-coloured skin round his eyes and noticed the deep new lines about the mouth, betraying both the public man carrying great responsibilities and the private individual who had suffered bitter trouble himself. His smile as he greeted me seemed genuine enough, but the eyes were guarded behind the twinkling glasses. If he knew anything, I thought, It would not be very easy to extract it.

However, I decided there was no point in delay and plunged into my tale without more ado. While I was speaking Tadpole's expression changed from a polite social smile to a look of very great trouble. More than that, he looked furtive, almost guilty.

"No more, Watson, please," he interrupted. "As I explained to you last night, this is not a Foreign Office matter." His voice was cold.

"But your private opinion?" I pressed him.

"Really, Watson, I have none. The sinking of the *Lusitania* was a most unfortunate incident and, naturally, I regret the loss of innocent lives, but as an official at the Foreign Office, the torpedoing of a merchant vessel is not my concern."

I said, "But she was not just any merchant vessel, Tadpole. She was the *Lusitania*."

"Yes," Tadpole nodded impatiently, "obviously she was the most prestigious vessel afloat and, believe me, Watson, the threat posed to her by U-boat activity was constantly under review at the Foreign office. The general consensus was that her status would protect - that the Germans simply would not dare to attack such a ship." He grimaced, "Unfortunately, as you know, our bluff was called in the most tragic manner."

I studied him, wishing Holmes could be here to put the questions. I was convinced that Percy Phelps was hiding something, but I lacked my friend's genius for eliciting information.

Then a thought came into my mind and I set it down here as the only time I have experienced the phenomenon known as telepathy in my life. "Of course," I said, "since her demise the *Lusitania* has become something more than just a ship. The German torpedo has made her into an unusually potent symbol - some say she may even be the *casus belli* to bring America into the War."

Tadpole's face underwent an extraordinary change; his expression became blurred, almost as though someone had passed a wet sponge over his countenance. His jaw dropped and he said in a croaking voice, "How do you know that, Watson? Has someone been talking out of turn to you?"

I shook my head, "Nothing like that, I promise you, " I said, "but it just came into my mind to wonder whether the United States would be more or less likely to enter the War because of what happened to the *Lusitania*."

He gave a sickly grin. "That kind of intuition might have brought you to the stake at one time, Watson," he said.

"You have not answered my question, Tadpole," I pointed out.

"My dear Watson, do you seriously expect me to? These matters are confidential, you know."

"Also," I said, "the possibility of alliance with America has been discussed?"

"Discussed, yes, Watson," Tadpole was visibly exasperated. "But that means nothing at all, you know, A discussion is simply that, a discussion. Many such topics come under review from time to time."

Violet said thoughtfully, "An alliance with the Americans would be a great prize, would it not, Percy? I cannot help wondering if the

Admiralty were given a hint that they need not go to any great lengths to protect the *Lusitania*?"

"Violet!" Tadpole was on his feet now, the lines sharply etched in his white face. "That is an outrageous suggestion! I am deeply mortified that you, the wife of one of my oldest friends should even think that I would haveany part in such - such beastliness!"

Breathing hard, he stared down at her, his fists clenched at his sides, as though he feared to forget himself and strike her. Violet stared back at him with an appearance of calm, though her colour had risen and her bosom rose and fell uneasily.

"Percy," Annette Phelps' voice cut through the thick heavy anger in the room."I think you are going to have to tell them the truth.

CHAPTER IX

"It was in the early part of January this year," Tadpole began. "I was summoned into the office of Sir Edward Grey, the Foreign Secretary, who asked me to draft a paper attempting to forecast the political consequences of a British passenger liner being sunk with Americans on board."

"Good heavens!" Violet ejaculated softly.

Ignoring her, Tadpole went on, "Sir Edward stressed the need for the work to be done quickly and in great secrecy. 'You are to make two copies,' he told me, playing nervously with his watch-chain. 'One for this department and one,' he hesitated for a moment, "for the First Lord of the Admiralty.' Sir Edward smiled. 'Try not to keep him waiting, Phelps, there's a good fellow. Winston is not the most patient of men.'

"I'm aware of that, Foreign Secretary," I said, smiling in my turn. Winston Churchill was a byword throughout the Civil Service for his impetuosity. I therefore returned to my office and started work immediately."

"One question, Tadpole," I said, "why did Sir Edward ask you rather than anyone else to write such a paper?"

"As you know, I have travelled extensively in the United States and I know many of the top people there, including the President, Woodrow Wilson. I am also a close personal friend of the American Ambassador, Walter Hines Page, who has been a frequent guest at Briarbrae. I imagine those were the reasons why I was chosen." Tadpole looked questioningly at me. "Shall I continue?"

"Please do. I am sorry I interrupted."

"First then, I must explain the background to you a little. You may be aware, of course, of President Wilson's reluctance to see his country drawn into what he regards as a purely European conflict and, despite much urging from those who take a different view he has remained determinedly neutral. Against that, I have to stress his willingness to turn a blind eye to the steady stream of raw materials exported from the United Spates to this country. Obviously this traffic is known to our German enemies, who have furiously accused the Americans of a pro-British bias, a charge which the Americans angrily refute, saying they would as willingly supply the Germans, though knowing full well that nearly the whole of the German merchant fleet is either interned or lurking fearfully about in the oceans of the world, knowing that in the near future the Royal Navy must inevitably find them."

"And the *Lusitania*?" I asked. "Where does she fit in?"

Tadpole said reprovingly, "I am coming to that, Watson. When I discussed that matter among others with Ambassador Page, he was of the opinion that President Wilson might be forced to abandon his neutral position if the Germans were foolish enough to commit some spectacular outrage against American nationals.

"You can understand I chose my words with care when putting my next question. 'Would that,' I said, "include a hostile act against a particular vessel, Walter?' He smiled at me. 'I guess you mean the *Lusitania*,' he said, `and what would happen if the Heinies lobbed a torpedo into her.' (Americans are so blunt, Watson!) Walter Page said seriously, I wouldn't bank on that, Percy. The Germans would have to be completely insane even to consider such a thing. They already have as much as they can handle against the Allies - they sure wouldn't want to find themselves fighting us as well. It just wouldn't be worth upsetting Uncle Sam that much over a few items of contraband.'

"`Perhaps not,' I agreed, `but tell me, Walter, off the record and merely to satisfy my curiosity, what do you think it would take to bring your country into this conflict?'

"'A direct threat to any of our territories,' he answered promptly, `that would do it, as sure as God made little apples. But the *Lusitania*? Personally, I would like to believe we'd find ourselves standing shoulder to shoulder with the British and the French inside a week, but, knowing Woodrow Wilson as I do, I guess that isn't going to happen.'"

Phelps lapsed into silence and stared fixedly at the oil painting of his uncle, Lord Holdhurst, hanging above the carved marble mantelshelf.

"Well," he resumed, "that was the gist of my argument in the paper I prepared for Sir Edward Grey: that the possibility of the United States becoming involved in a European struggle because of an attack on the *Lusitania* was so remote that it could hardly be considered a possibility."

He was silent again, his gaze still averted from me as he industriously polished his spectacles with a silk handkerchief.

"What was the reaction to your paper, Tadpole?" I asked.

"At the Foreign office? Very little, Watson." His smile was not without bitterness. "Sir Edward thanked me for my work, but since then I have heard no more about it and I assume my report has been quietly pigeonholed somewhere."

"But you told us you had to make two copies," said Violet, "one of them for the Admiralty."

"Ah, there the reaction was very different. I understand Winston Churchill denounced it as a lot of defeatist nonsense. He had convinced himself, you see, that such an incident must be enough to bring President Wilson charging to our aid on his white horse:and everyone who opposed that view must be either mad or bad, perhaps both." He paused and added thoughtfully, "A remarkable man, Churchill, who combines in himself the qualities of romantic visionary and ruthless man of action. I remember being very much struck by something he once said to my Minister, Sir Edward Grey, 'You know, Edward, at the summit, true politics and strategy are one. 'The manœuvre which brings an ally into the field is as serviceable as that which wins a great battle.'"

Phelps finally withdrew his gaze from the portrait to look directly at me. His eyes were haunted. "Since the *Lusitania* sank, Watson, I have often found myself remembering those words and pondered what was meant by them. Is it possible that more than a thousand lives were sacrificed to gain an alliance with the United States?"

"Surely not," I exclaimed, a thrill of horror going through me at such a monstrous conception, Holmes had spoken of the policy of deliberate terror pursued by some of the German commanders; *schrechlikeit* he had called it, warfare of frightfulness, arguing that the tactic went back to Roman times. That was as maybe, I thought, but that an English statesman would involve himself with such infamy was too much for me to swallow.

"But, Tadpole," I said, "it was a *German* boat that sank the *Lusitania*."

"I know that, Watson," he said. "I merely find it rather strange that the *Lusitania* was allowed to sail unescorted into an area where a U-boat was known to be waiting and I find myself recalling Arthur Hugh Clough's couplet: "Thou shalt not kill, but need'st not strive officiously to keep alive." And I wonder why the Admiralty did so very little to protect the ship, Watson."

"The Admiralty are trying to blame the Captain," I said.

"Of course," Tadpole spoke in an acid voice, "we have to have a sacrificial victim to offer the public, as I know to my cost. I can feel for that poor devil of a Captain, Watson, I can tell you. It isn't easy to be an official scapegoat. That is why you are here now, my friend, and why I have told you the things I have. Not so that you can use them as evidence at the Mersey Inquiry - even you must see that would be out of the question - but in order to give you a clearer picture and help Mr Sherlock Holmes to build up a satisfactory case for my fellow-sufferer."

I thought it was not entirely the loss of the Naval Treaty which had blighted Tadpole Phelps's career; he had too much genuine warmth of heart to be a satisfactory official machine. But I could never tell him that.

Fortunately, perhaps, the door opened and the splendid butler came in, adopting the manner of one of the gods entering Valhalla. (How many tedious evenings did I endure in the Baker Street years when Sherlock Holmes heard of a Wagner concert somewhere or other and dragged me along with him, willy-nilly, to worship at the shrine of that thundering bore!)

"Mr Joseph on the telephone, m'lady," the butler intoned to Annette Phelps. "Shall I ask him to call you back?"

"No, no," she rose, a smile of pleasure lighting up her face, "I'll speak to him now."

She glided from the room. Tadpole consulted his watch. "I would offer you some refreshment," he said, "but I fear I really do have an appointment. I only hope Master Joseph does not keep Annette on the telephone for too long."

Although his urbane expression gave nothing away, as always I could detect a faint underlying coldness in his voice when he spoke of his brother-in-law. And small wonder, I thought, given what had happened in the past, though it was only fair to add that Joseph Harrison's efforts to make up for that had been truly Herculean.

Strangely enough, even though my wife and Annette were good friends, I had myself only once encountered Joseph Harrison since his return to England and then it had hardly been more than a bare exchange of greetings, accompanied by a vague affable smile from him. He had grown very much stouter, I noticed, Neither of us had mentioned the Naval Treaty. Since then, a natural delicacy had kept us apart. In any case Joseph Harrison was far too busy running his convalescent home at Briarbrae to come to London very often, and I too was much occupied with my practice.

"How is Briarbrae these days?" I inquired of Tadpole. "Flourishing, I suppose?"

"If you care to put it that way, Watson," said Tadpole.

"There is, unfortunately, no shortage of patients, nor will be for the foreseeable future. Joseph has done good work there," he added, "Of course.he always was a capable fellow when he set his mind to it," The coldness in his voice was now unmistakeable, and I marvelled how Violet, normally the shrewdest of women, could have missed it.

Tadpole stood up, bowing himself over Violet's hand, "Let me know how you fare in your quest, Watson," he said, turning to me, "I should be most interested. to hear."

Thanking him for his kindness promised I would and followed Violet out of the room. In the hall Annette Phelps waved to us from the small vestibule under the stairs where the telephone was kept.

"I must go, Joseph," she said into the mouthpiece. "You know what Percy can be like if I keep him waiting - What's that? - Yes, of course I'll speak to him about the pigeon-loft - Yes, I promise - But you do. understand it must not be anything too unsightly - Oh, tonight, I suppose, if he's in a good mood, but I warn you, Joe, I am not going to upset him on account of your prize fancies. Look, I must go now, our visitors are leaving."

Replacing the earpiece, she came out of the vestibule and hurried over to us.

"Really, you two, I hope you weren't thinking of leaving without saying goodbye to me!" she scolded affectionately. "I'm sorry I was away so long, but Joseph is a perfect fanatic about his wretched pigeons. He talks of nothing else these days. I tell him it must be his Northern blood coming out, "

On the way home I stopped briefly at the King Edward Hospital to inquire after Mrs Dobbs, I was assured she was doing very well and complimented upon my surgery.

"I had an able assistant, " I said, thinking of Mabel Every. By now, I imagined, she would be back in Liverpool, her hopes pinned to whatever information Sherlock Holmes might have discovered at the Admiralty today.

But when we arrived back at Warwick Dene Sherlock Holmes was just alighting from a cab and one glance at his haggard face was enough to tell me his visit to the Admiralty had not borne fruit, and so it proved when we three assembled in the drawing room before dinner.

"I fear, Watson, that I shall have to disappoint Miss Every," he said without preamble. "Despite the most exhaustive searches at the Admiralty, I found no evidence whatsoever of the *Lusitania* being diverted to Queenstown. However," he added, and his eyes sparkled. "I did find ample evidence of the wish to conceal something and I am therefore inclined to believe that every word in David McCormick's journal was the absolute truth."

CHAPTER X

"The first thing I did," Sherlock Holmes told us after receiving Violet's permission to light his pipe, "was to take a look at the Admiralty Signals Register. I will not bore you by detailing the stratagems I employed to examine such confidential records. Since I had been anticipating some-thing of the sort. I was not greatly surprised to discover the page of the Register for the 7th May this year had been ripped out, I believe it is self-evident that the reason for this crude censorship must have a great deal to do with the fate of the *Lusitania*."

He drew on his pipe. "Naturally, that whetted my appetite for fresh discoveries. I decided that my starting point would be to find out the degree of care the Admiralty had shown for the liner's safety. We all know that, despite the German threat, Captain Turner was merely told that since no sailing orders had arrived from London he should 'follow the same course as before' - a somewhat cavalier approach in the face of a known danger to my mind, but perhaps, I thought to myself, the Admiralty were as offhand when issuing instructions to their warships."

"How very clever of you to think of that, Mr Holmes!" cried Violet and my friend executed a little bow in her direction, his thin cheeks darkened with a flush of pleasure as he proceeded: "I soon found the battleship *Orion*, to give but one example, had been issued with very detailed and practical instructions, issued to her captain personally, as to the course and speed she was to adopt when returning to Scapa Flow after refitting at Chatham. Now why, I wondered, had a captain in the Merchant Navy been treated so very differently from a post captain in the Royal Navy. Why had Turner been left to rely on vaguely-worded wireless messages and a bundle of random advices many of them contradictory from which he was supposed to make his choice. Was this mere carelessness on the part of the Admiralty, or have you, Watson, some other, perhaps more sinister explanation to offer after your visit to Percy Phelps?"

Clearing my throat, I told him what had transpired at the house in Cheyne Walk. Sherlock Holmes heard me out in silence, but his face, always of an austere cast, became grimmer by the minute.

"I see," he said at last, "from what you have learned today, Watson, it would appear that the Germans were not alone in wishing the *Lusitania* at the bottom of the ocean and," he added with a sigh, "from our point of view, old friend, that is a great pity."

"Why so, Holmes?"

"Well, Watson, leaving aside the moral implications - and they are monstrous enough, Heaven knows - can you seriously imagine any government would admit in public that it had been an accessory to such a:ghastly crime? No it would be easier for us ta prove a charge of negligence, and that, I am reasonably certain I can do."

"I must say, you sound very confident, Holmes. From your demeanour as you entered the house I imagined our cause was lost."

"Not a bit of it, Watson! As a famous American commander declared in an apparently hopeless situation, 'I have not yet begun to fight'. No , Watson, I have my suspects and by the time Lord Mersey opens his Inquiry I shall be ready to indict them publicly."

"Who are these suspects?" Violet demanded and Sherlock Holmes smiled at the sceptical note in her voice, "I can best tell you that, Mrs Watson, by describing the events of my day in some details But first my pipe needs rekindling. Will you have the goodness to pass me my tobacco pouch, Watson?"

Judging by her expression, I do not think my wife wholly welcomed the reek of tobacco fumes in her pretty drawing-room, but such was the hold that Sherlock Holmes could exert over an audience that the lines of annoyance were quickly smoothed from her face and she listened with the same eager attention as myself.

"As you know," he began, "I have been privy to many Government secrets since my recovery of the Bruce-Partington plans, so I was able to draw extensively on the Admiralty's goodwill by bearding the Chief of Naval War Staff in his room on the vague prextext that I wished to offer my services 'for the duration'. Never the most patient of men, Admiral Sir Henry Oliver clearly thought I was wasting his time, but before I was bundled out, I did manage to take a god look at his room, which was what I really wanted."

"His room?" I repeated. "But whatever for, Holmes?"

"It was vital to see the conditions under which Oliver normally worked," he explained. "Obviously, something went wrong the night before the *Lusitania* was attacked - the warnings that went to her were either too late or so vaguely worded as to be worse than useless. I had to know why this was so. You, Watson, have already advanced the conspiracy theory. Against that, I put my personal conviction that the ship fell victim to incredible carelessness and cite in evidence Admiral Oliver's desk, heaped high with a mountain of papers, not to mention the constant interruptions. While I was there at least ten people entered the office with this or that query, each one of which the Admiral insisted on dealing with personally. Surely you understand my inference, Watson?"

"I feel bound to confess I do not, Holmes, " I said, frowning.

"Why, man, it is obvious!" Holmes cried. "Admiral Henry Oliver is a deeply conscientious officer who refuses to delegate, that is why, I heard later, he is always twenty-four hours behind with his paperwork and this is the man who, as Chief of the Naval War Staff had overall responsibility for the safety of the *Lusitania.* Now do you understand, Watson?"

I did, and was appalled. Although obviously equally troubled, Violet recovered more quickly and said, "But, Mr Holmes, granting what you say about Admiral Oliver is true, he must still have had people working under him. Who was the officer directly responsible for the *Lusitania*?"

Sherlock Holmes nodded, appreciating the fine distinction my wife had drawn. "As a merchant vessel," he explained, "the *Lusitania* was the charge of Captain Webb of the Trade Division. I'm afraid he does not come out of this very well. Captain Webb possessed exact knowledge of nearly all the U-boat activity in the Irish Sea, thanks to - well, I had better not name the department. In the circumstances it is bizarre indeed that Webb has been entrusted with the task of drawing up the Admiralty's case against Captain Turner, which will shortly be presented to Lord Mersey, I happen to possess a copy of this remarkable document, which would give great pain to Miss Every, were she to see it, for Webb loses no opportunity to blacken Captain Turner's character, accusing him of stupidity recklessness, obstinacy and treason. To my mind," he added, "Webb missed his vocation by not becoming a maker of fairy tales."

He drew on his pipe, found it out and laid it aside. I looked at him severely. "Holmes," said I, "how did you come by such a document?"

"I stole it," he answered disarmingly. "No, to be serious, it was given to me by a young man named Kenworthy, who happened to be on duty on the fatal night, working in the Admiralty's cryptography department and he saw at once that the *Lusitania* was in great danger. According to his own account, he implored Captain Webb to seek the authority to have the ship diverted before it was too late. When Webb refused, Kenworthy protested with some vehemence and he learned today that he is to be transferred to the Malta Station for his pains."

"What will you do now, Holmes?" I asked. "The Admiralty are not going to admit any of this at the Inquiry, nor will Tadpole. For practical purposes, you have no case."

"I don't think it is quite so bad as that, Watson," Holmes protested, "but I agree with you in saying that our side needs a little more concrete evidence, that is why I have decided a trip to Liverpool is now essential." A glint of the old fire was in his eyes as he looked at me. "What do you say, Watson? Will you come?"

"My practice!" my conscience forced me to exclaim.

"Nonsense, John," said Violet, "I'm sure Armstrong would willingly stand in for you. There are not many patients tomorrow in any case."

I turned my eyes to Sherlock Holmes, who had been listening to our little exchange with a smile upon his face. "I suppose one or two nights away would make no difference," I said.

"Good, Watson," Sherlock Holmes rubbed his hands together. "I was so certain you would not fail me I took the liberty of making our reservations at the Adelphi Hotel and also sent a wire to Mr Alfred Booth of Cunard, warning him to expect us. Now, while we eat, you can tell me all about your visit to the Phelps's as well as the latest gossip about that rascal, Joseph Harrison, who seems to be such a reformed character these days."

CHAPTER XI

Euston Station has never been a favourite venue of mine and, looking through my notes, I find I have never described any of the adventures I shared with Sherlock Holmes which involved a departure from that particular terminus. Today I found Euston more than ever depressing, with its usual noise, bustle and grime augmented by the sad sight of a fleet of ambulances bringing the wounded to the station for embarking to hospitals nearer their homes. It was a terrible thing to see so many fine young men so fearfully injured, the only softer note, being struck by the tender solicitude of the nurses, bending over each stretcher-bound form as it was carried to the train. I stared at them, shaking my head as I reflected what a judgement it is upon mankind that our noblest achievements all too often walk side by side with the greatest horrors.

"Come, Watson!" Sherlock Holmes put his hand on my arm and I could tell by his voice that he too, was deeply moved. "Our train is almost ready to go and we must not lose it."

We almost did, for halfway along the platform I collided with a porter, whose vision was obstructed by the two large wicker crates he carried, the contents of which rustled and flapped in the most disconcerting manner.

"Beg your pardon, sir," the man said, deftly clutching his swaying burden before it could fall to the platform. "Guard forgot all about these, so I had to get 'em out quick, like."

"What on earth have you got there?" I demanded.

"Pigeons, guv'nor," the porter answered promptly. "Going all the way to the Western Front, they are."

"To eat?" I stared, thinking that from all I had heard pigeon pie would be a most welcome addition to the diet of our armed forces, though I could hardly see two crates going very far.

Sherlock Holmes laughed, shaking his head at me. "Surely, Watson, you have not forgotten the racing pigeon has been used to carry messages for the military since time immemorial?"

Before I could reply a whistle shrieked and Holmes pulled me aboard the train just in time. Rather breathlessly, I subsided against the upholstery as we lurched out of the station. Sherlock Holmes tossed the bundle of newspapers it was his invariable custom to purchase when-ever he embarked upon a railway journey on the seat opposite and took out his favourite pipe. For a wonder we had the compartment to ourselves and I was disposed to make conversation.

"That's a curious coincidence, Holmes," I remarked.

"What is, Watson?" His manner was not forthcoming,

"Why, those pigeons," I said. "Seeing them reminded me of something I learned yesterday at the Phelps's."

This time Sherlock Holmes did not even trouble to open his mouth; he merely raised an eyebrow, his expression politely bored.

"Yes," I ploughed onwards, "it seems that Joseph Harrison, of all people, has taken up the art of pigeon-fancying, of course, prefers the ornamental varieties - the tumblers, pouters, cochin-chinas - that sort of thing."

"Of course," Sherlock Holmes echoed and then he appeared to lose interest in the subject, picking up one of the newspapers and immersing himself in the contents. As I recall, he was reading of a devastating fire which had swept through a munitions factory in Kettering.

Left thus to my own devices, I made myself as comfortable as possible and settled down to sleep. From time to time I swam upwards to consciousness when the train halted to take on more people, but I did not finally rouse myself until we arrived at Rugby, where Sherlock Holmes tipped a porter half a crown to fetch us two cups of tea from the station buffet. The hot beverage was most welcome, for the train was unheated and the day chill and overcast, an all-too-familiar phenomenon of the British summer.

The journey had been long and tedious, and for my own part I was very glad when the train at last ran through the red sandstone cutting into Lime Street Station, which, like Euston, was also a scene of noise and bustle. Before leaving the compartment I observed Sherlock Holmes carefully tearing out the item about the factory fire and placing it in his breast pocket and, I meant to ask him the reason, but the matter soon slipped my mind as I looked about, me and said, "I suppose we had better engage a cab and ask, the driver to take us to the Adelphi, since I do not know Liverpool at all."

"The Adelphi is quite close at hand in point of fact, Watson," Holmes said, "but a cab would be most useful in transporting our baggage."

And so we left behind us the vaulted, glass and iron roof of the station and emerged into the open air, where our ears were immediately assaulted by noise of a different kind, the judder of the trams crossing the steel network of lines outside the station and the clatter of the traders' carts. Even I, who am well used to the roar of London traffic, had to admit Liverpool possessed a clamorous vitality all of its own.

Answering Holmes's raised finger, a cab drew up beside us and started to load our bags with remarkable alacrity into his vehicle. As he worked he informed us in his distinctive Liverpudlian accent that the Adelphi was the finest hotel in north of England, far better his manner implied, than anything on offer in the south.

In a few minutes he drew up outside the Adelphi's imposing façade and we were mounting the steps into the foyer, where the desk clerk informed us that Mr Alfred Booth of Cunard wished urgently to see us.

"I fancy we have enough time for a wash and brush-up, Watson," Sherlock Holmes remarked to me in the lift, "before we go to see Mr Booth."

"Do we really have to go right away, Holmes?" I was not best pleased, to tell the truth. Although suffering, like every other institution, from wartime exigencies, the Adelphi was still a luxury hotel and I had been looking forward to sampling what it had to offer. But Holmes was inexorable.

"Right away, Watson. We really have no time to waste. I daresay," he added kindly, "it may be possible for us to have dinner here tonight..." I brightened "...providing our inquiries are complete."

"Oh, of course," I said glumly and he smiled. "Poor old Watson," he said, "I fear you have had a good deal to suffer from me one way and another."

"Perhaps," I agreed, adding, "but the rewards are such that, it is of no consequence."

After a pause Sherlock Holmes said, "Thank you, Watson," and I fancy his voice was not quite so steady as usual.

Following a hasty toilet, another cab was engaged to take us to Pierhead, where the glistening new Cunard Building looks out proudly over the river Mersey and its seven miles of dockland.

A smooth-faced young functionary conducted us to the Chairman's office and as discreetly withdrew from the room. Mr

Alfred Booth rose at once and came from behind his vast shining desk to shake hands with us.

"It is a great pleasure to meet you, Mr Holmes," he said, smiling all over his long narrow face. "I have long been an admirer of yours - and of Dr Watson's too, of course. Pray sit down gentlemen, and tell me in what way I can assist you."

"I should say the boot was rather on the other foot," Sherlock Holmes observed as he took one of the chairs indicated. "I have come about the *Lusitania*, of course."

"Yes, I know." Alfred Booth's ready smile had lost some of its warmth and his eyes were guarded. "May I ask how that unhappy vessel has become the concern of Mr Sherlock Holmes?"

"My friend chose not to answer him directly. "This morning you appeared to desire my intervention, " he observed mildly.

"That was before-" Alfred Booth began and checked himself abruptly.

"So," said Holmes, "I see that position has now changed. I don't suppose," he added casually, "that could have anything to do with the naval car speeding in the opposite direction as we were coming along Water Street?"

Alfred Booth played nervously with his gold fountain pen. "I really have nothing to say."

"Mr Booth, we are wasting time, a precious commodity with the Mersey Inquiry only days away. I know very well what has just happened here. You heard from Admiralty representatives warning you to hold your tongue - am I not right?"

"No comment," Alfred Booth said stubbornly.

Sherlock Holmes had risen to his feet. "You would do well to listen to me, Mr Booth," he said in a quiet voice, "for if ever a man needed help it is you. I am here to offer you that help."

Alfred Booth flushed, but his voice was even as he said, "We have already engaged an excellent counsel in Butler Aspinall, who will represent the owners as well as the Captain. I am sure your intervention is kindly meant, Mr Holmes, but really it is unnecessary."

Sherlock Holmes smiled. "Is that a polite way of telling me to mind my own business?"

"You can take it that way if you like. And now, if you will forgive me, gentlemen, I have a great deal of work to do," He bent over his desk, writing very busily. It was an obvious signal to us to leave. I glanced at Holmes, who shook his head slightly.

"Mr Booth?" he said.

"Yes, Mr Holmes?" Booth's tone wobbled on the edge of civility.

"One question before I go: who told you the *Lusitania* was to be diverted to Queenstown on the 7th of May?"

Alfred Booth's head jerked up. "How do you know about that," he gasped and my friend heaved a sigh. "Surely it is obvious. At the moment the torpedo struck the passengers' luggage was being fetched up from the hold twenty-four hours before the ship was due to berth in Liverpool. Had the *Lusitania* not been about to dock at Queenstown, that would have been a completely pointless exercise, particularly for a vessel lacking so many crew."

"An intelligent guess, Mr Holmes," Alfred Booth insisted, "but merely a guess on your part."

"No," Sherlock Holmes said calmly, "the evidence of my own eyes. I have been a passenger on the *Lusitania*, but more than that I have also sailed on her in the guise of a steward, for reasons we need not discuss here. I know the routine when one of your ships has to divert into Queenstown and that the first rule is that the passengers must not be incommoded in any way - hence the speedy transfer of baggage."

Alfred Booth had been listening intently, an urbane smile masking whatever emotions he may have felt, "I did not realise you had actually served with us, Mr Holmes," he said and then he shook his head. "Even so, what you have just told me is not proof."

"Possibly not, but it is a clear indication of a break in the *Lusitania's* normal routine. But perhaps you are right, Mr Booth," Sherlock Holmes added blandly, "for I see the Admiralty found you an apt pupil when they coached you as to what you could and could not say, but it grieves me beyond measure to see an eminently truthful man like yourself struggling to tell lies."

"This is intolerable!" Alfred Booth's face was a surge of colour. Raising a hand he pointed a shaking finger at the door. "I must ask you both to leave at once."

Sherlock Holmes placed both hands on the desk, bending down so that he could look the Chairman directly in the eyes. "I am going, Mr Booth," he said quickly, "but first I ask for five minutes of your time. Five minutes, no more, no less. After that, if you still wish me to leave I will certainly comply with your request."

Alfred Booth considered, his gaze roaming round the panelled walls, hung with oil paintings of previous Cunard Chairmen. His eyes finally came to rest on the portrait of Sir Samuel Cunard, the founder of the world-famous steamship company. The painted eyes of the old man gazed shrewdly back.

Finally Alfred Booth nodded and sketched vague gesture with one long white hand:

"Very well, Mr Holmes; say what you have to say, then go, please."

"I shall begin," said Sherlock Holmes, not at all put out by the Chairman's abrupt tone, "by outlining what I have managed to learn of the *Lusitania*'s recent history and the conclusions I have drawn from it."

He proceeded to give a brief account of Mabel Every's visits Captain Dow's remarks to him, and David McCormick's journal, as well as the statements Miss Every had managed to obtain from surviving members of the *Lusitania*'s crew and the Masters of the *Candidate* and the *Centurion*, the two ships which had been sunk on 6th May, presumably by the same U-boat which had accounted for the *Lusitania* herself.

Naturally, this took much longer than five minutes, but Alfred Booth had apparently forgotten the stipulation and sat listening with absorbed interest, his chin propped upon his hand.

"Yes, it is true," he said at last. "We at Cunard do feel we have been badly served by the Admiralty. They did neglect to give Turner a proper course, and some of the ship's cargo was undoubtedly contraband."

"Was that fair to the passengers?" I could not resist saying and Alfred Booth gave me an angry look.

"It's easy enough to be wise after the event, Doctor!" he snapped, "I plead guilty to believing Admiralty assurances that there was absolutely no risk to our passengers. Safety has always been our watchword at Cunard, you know. In fact our instructions to captains specifically say, 'Your ship is loaded it take her; speed is nothing, follow your own road, deliver her safe, bring her safe back - safety is all that is required.'

"Quite so," said Sherlock Holmes, with a warning glance at me not to interrupt again. "With that in mind, can you tell me when you first began to feel alarmed for the *Lusitania*'s safety?"

"As soon as I learned of the sinking of the two Harrison steamers, *Candidate* and *Centurion*," Alfred Booth answered promptly.

"And what did you do?" Sherlock Holmes inquired.

"I called immediately on Admiral Stileman, the Senior Naval Officer here."

"With what result?"

Alfred Booth hesitated. "The Admiral stressed that he was speaking to me off the record," he said. "All I can say is that I left his office convinced that measures were already being taken to protect the *Lusitania*." He bit his lip. "I was so sure that I cabled my cousin, Paul Crompton, who was a passenger on the ship not to wait about in Queenstown, but to take the night packet across to Liverpool, as I needed to see him rather urgently." His fingers drummed the table impatiently. "The Admiralty now tell me I was mistaken," he said, "and that they never had any intention of diverting the *Lusitania*. Yet at the time I was certain that was their meaning."

"Your cousin could bear you out in that at least," I said, risking Holmes's annoyance a second time. Booth slowly shook his head.

"I fear not, Dr Watson, Paul Crompton, his wife and six children were all drowned." There was grief and anger in his voice as he burst out. "But why did Stileman give me that assurance if the Admiralty were going to do anything. Why did he go out of his way to remind me of a similar scare we had last January and the steps that had been taken then?"

"What scare was that?" Sherlock Holmes's expression was very alert. For a moment a shutter seemed to come down over Alfred Booth's face and then he said, "Since you appear to know so much already I see no reason not to tell you. Last January another of our ships, the *Transylvania*, oddly enough she was commanded by Captain Turner at the time, was escorted into Queenstown by the cruiser *Juno* to berth there in safety because there was a U-boat lurking about." He looked at Sherlock Holmes with weary eyes. "Do you not find it strange, Mr Holmes, that the Admiralty were not prepared to exercise the same care for the *Lusitania* her illustrious sister? Many and many a time since the *Lusitania* sank I have found myself wondering on that and never find an answer."

It was as well, I thought, that Alfred Booth knew nothing of the secret paper written by Percy Phelps. Sherlock Holmes, however, had become preoccupied with quite another aspect of the matter.

"In view of what you have just told me," he said to Alfred Booth, "Captain Turner must have been very relieved when he finally received the signal ordering the *Lusitania* into Queenstown?"

"He was," Alfred Booth agreed absently, "he told me so himself, but you see, Mr Holmes he can prove nothing. As you know, the wireless log went down with the ship. Even so," he added with vicious satisfaction, "the Admiralty have had a hard job trying to coach him as to what he can and cannot stay. Poor Will Turner, the most honest soul alive, forced, to get up in public and make up a string of lies just to save the Admiralty's face. In some ways I find that the most sickening aspect of all in this disgusting business."

"But they have tried to coach you, have they not, Mr Booth?" Holmes probed. "Is that why you were so anxious to get rid of us?"

Alfred Booth said, "When I first got your wire, I was over-joyed for until then I had been at my wits' end. I knew Butler Aspinall has been increasingly worried at the kind of showing Will Turner is likely to make on the witness stand. Your promised intervention was like the answer to a prayer - and then, early this morning, I had a visit from two very senior naval officers warning me to have nothing to do, with you. If I dared to disobey them, I was told Cunard and Captain Turner would suffer. What could I do, Mr Holmes?"

"But you changed your mind and decided, to help us after all?" said Sherlock Holmes.

"I did; there have been enough lies." Rising, he went to a cabinet and drew out a bulging folder. "Turner's personal file," he said, adding with a grim smile, "It will show you the kind of man he is and explain why you will not be welcome if you go to see him. He is a taciturn fellow at the best of times and recent events have not made him more outgoing. If you can,persuade him that he must cooperate with Butler Aspinall, otherwise he will be without a proper defence when Edward Carson and F E Smith go to work on him."

He accompanied us to the door of his office and shook hands with us, asking politely, "Have they made you comfortable at the Adelphi? I did stress on the telephone that nothing could be too good for the great Mr Sherlock Holmes."

"Most kind." Sherlock Holmes's expression showed how little he relished these attentions, but fortunately Alfred Booth turned away without seeing his face.

CHAPTER XII

"Are you very hungry, Watson?" Sherlock Holmes asked as we emerged from the stately portals of the Cunard Building.

'Well-" I hesitated, for I had eaten nothing since the early morning and, though the sunshine was brilliant, the wind blew keenly off the Mersey and the rumbling of the Overhead Railway resembled the condition of my stomach.

Seeing my downcast expression Holmes took pity on me. "Very well, Watson, we will return to the Adelphi for luncheon before taking the electric train to Great Crosby. But first I would like you to come with me a little way. "

He took me to the landing stage where the *Lusitania* had berthed in her days of glory and stood there for a while, his scanty hair ruffled by the wind, his expression unreadable.

Finally he turned and said abruptly, "Come, Watson, it is time we were on our way."

I would have been fascinated to stay a little longer and watch the crowds disembark from the ferry which had just chugged across from Birkenhead, black smoke pouring from its stumpy funnel, but Holmes now appeared to be in a very great hurry and, seizing me by the arm, propelled me through the jostle of humanity to the corner of Chapel Street where he was able to hail a cab.

"Our plans have changed, Watson," he said over luncheon, which had been sent up to our suite at the Adelphi. "I have to go out for little while, so we will postpone our visit to Captain Turner until this evening."

I laid down my knife and fork. "May I come with you, Holmes?"

"Not this time, Watson," he smiled at my crestfallen expression, "but you can, if you will, be of the very greatest assistance to me by familiarising yourself with this." He tipped Captain Turner's personal file, which lay on the table at his elbow.

"With what object?" I asked.

Sherlock Holmes neatly cut up a piece of meat and ate it before he replied. "I need to know a little more about Turner," he said. "So far we have only heard the testimony an his side, but Miss Every and Alfred Booth are clearly prejudiced - very naturally so, but one must on that account treat their evidence with caution. The Admiralty have built up a very strong case against Turner. Perhaps his personal file will show whether or not he was a foolishly obstinate captain. There may be some incident in his past which will reveal the truth. You don't look very happy, Watson, I daresay you feel this is like going behind the man's back, but it is better for us to be forewarned if Turner's past contains anything to his discredit."

"I suppose so," I said reluctantly, "but you're quite right, it goes against the grain with me to behave like some scandal-loving journalist. After all, everyone agrees Turner was an outstanding Master."

"In peacetime,Watson," said Sherlock Holmes. "Possibly he found himself unable to cope with the realities of war and tried to sail the *Lusitania* as though this country were still at peace. Turner is about the same age as ourselves and there is a saying about an old dog and new tricks, is there not?"

He stood up, pushing his plate away, "I will be with you in a few minutes, Watson," he said and withdrew to his room. With a sigh, I picked up the file and chose the most comfortable sofa for my afternoon of unwelcome study. I had barely skimmed the first page when the door opened again and a bizarre figure shuffled into the room, leaning heavily upon a stick.

I say `bizarre' because surely nothing like this crusty old seaman with his stained pea jacket and battered cap covering a tangle of white hair was ever seen in the elegant Adelphi before.

Breathing stertorously, he limped towards me. "I take it I pass muster, Watson," said the familiar voice.

I sighed. "It all depends," I said, "whether you really want to create a scandal here. Seriously, Holmes, has this masquerade any point?"

"Indeed it has, Watson," Sherlock Holmes retorted and I could tell that my implied criticism had nettled him more than somewhat. "I have decided the time has come for me to have some serious conversation with the *Lusitania*'s surviving crew-members, so I am now on my way to the Sailors' Home, my pockets stuffed with the wherewithal to buy spirituous liquors, my ears alert for any unconsidered trifles of information which may be let fall to a fellow-seaman, albeit one fallen on evil days." He coughed ostentatiously and thumped his chest.

It was in my mind to ask how a man fallen on evil days had a pocketful of guineas, but I desisted for the sake of peace.

"I leave you to your studies, Watson," he said and limped out. I was strongly tempted to follow him, just to see how he managed to evade the hotel porter, but I too had work to do and I picked up Turner's file.

Holmes returned surprisingly quickly - in his normal persona, much to my relief, just as I was about to ring the bell for some tea.

"No time for that, Watson!" he cried, tossing me my hat and stick. "We have an appointment at Great Crosby, remember?"

"Now you mention it," I said heavily, "I do remember, although I would not have thought," I added in a rare display of sarcasm, "that five minutes would make much difference one way or the other."

I should of course have remembered that when he was working on a case, Sherlock Holmes became wholly indifferent to the pangs of hunger and thirst and that I, as his chosen companion, was expected to display a like fortitude. It was not always easy.

When we were seated in the electric train and rattling on our way to Great Crosby, however, I had recovered my good humour and asked Holmes what success he had had in talking to the *Lusitania's* crew. He looked chagrined. "None, Watson, I regret to say. I have been told over and over again, 'At the time of sailing the *Lucy* was in good order and well found,'" his voice perfectly mimicked the flat northern vowels. "She was unarmed having no weapons for defence against an enemy and she has never carried such equipment."

"I presume," I said, "you are trying to tell me they had been coached beforehand."

"Of course they had, " he said impatiently, "I guess, mind you, but as you are aware, Watson, I have my own methods and I believed that by showing a little patience I could get what I wanted, but not a bit of it! Someone had managed to put the fear of God into the *Lusitania's* crew and all they would do was repeat, parrot-fashion, the words that had been drilled into them. As with the men.so with the officers - their eyes were eloquent enough but their lips remained mute."

"Even David McCormick?" I was surprised. Reading that young man's journal had given me the impression he was something of a rebel.

"Ah, McCormick," said Sherlock Holmes as we rattled through Seaforth. "According to his landlady that young gentleman had gone to visit his relatives in Aberdeen. However, while I was talking to her I saw a curtain twitch at an upper window and I know very well he was there. I must say I would very much like to know who it was managed to cool the ardour of that young firebrand. He must be a formidable fellow indeed."

"Perhaps," said I, "it might be this Admiral Oliver you mentioned? He after all has a great deal to lose if Mersey's verdict goes against the Admiralty."

"It is certainly possible," Sherlock Holmes admitted after a moment, "but somehow I doubt it, Watson. Oliver is clever man - oh, yes, make no mistake - this *Lusitania* business has not shown his best side as a most capable and conscientious officer - but whoever is trying to make life difficult for us here is of a very different stamp, I should say, a born intriguer, Watson, whose abilities match his enjoyment of his work."

"Is there such a person?" I asked. "Recently I have gained a very different impression of the Admiralty."

"There is a man," Sherlock Holmes's face wore an abstracted expression. "I worked with him briefly last year while I was after Von Bork - but I understood he had been moved to another department, otherwise I should have no hesitation in attributing this sudden outbreak of reticence to him. But never mind that for the time being, Watson," he turned briskly to me, "I want to hear your impressions of the unfortunate Captain Turner."

"He appears to be an outstandingly able officer," I said. "A little eccentric, I suppose. Apparently, he refuses to wear his uniform cap except when he is on the bridge of his ship; otherwise he always insists on wearing a bowler hat. This has earned him the nickname 'Bowler Bill' throughout the Cunard Fleet." I grinned at Sherlock Holmes, himself not remarkable, for the conventionality of his attire. "However, Cunard seemed willing to tolerate Turner's idiosyncrasies because of his splendid seamanship. He commanded the *Mauretania* when she made her record-breaking run to New York and back in ten days and when the *Aquitania* made her maiden voyage last year, Cunard chose Turner to captain her. Reading his dossier through, Holmes, it does not seem likely to me that Turner could ever have been the foolishly obstinate man the Admiralty are trying to depict. For one thing, Cunard would not have employed such a booby."

"It would seem, Watson," said Sherlock Holmes in a faintly amused voice, "that you have become almost as firm a partisan of Turner's as Miss Every. There, there, I am only teasing, my dear fellow," as I bristled, "and indeed you may well be right, I shall be interested to see for myself."

Captain Turner lived in a large square redbrick house in its own garden to which we were admitted by an anxious Mabel Every.

"He has gone out," she said, twisting her hands in the familiar gesture. "He was very angry when Mr Booth telephoned to say you were coming. He says you have no business to come here interfering, Mr Holmes," she was blushing, "and that the best thing you can do is take yourself back to London immediately for he will not see you."

"Perhaps," Sherlock Holmes smiled, in no way put out, "the Captain's temper will be improved by a walk with his dog. I understand Blundellsands is a delightful spot at this time of year."

Mabel Every gave quite a start. "How did you know we keep a dog, Mr Holmes." Her gaze swept round the hall. "I am sure I keep everything very tidy here."

"Oh, immaculate," Holmes assured her, "but I noticed some very faint scratches on the door there. Clearly the dog has been used to beg for entry to his master's private sanctum. I take it that is the door to Captain Turner's study." When she nodded he added swiftly, "Do you mind if Watson and I take a look?"

She hesitated and then nodded.

Inside, the room was nothing more nor less than a record of Captain Turner's life at sea. Paintings and photographs of ships of every type, from the graceful sailing clippers of a bygone age to the gigantic iron-hulled *Aquitania* crowded the walls - with one significant omission. A square of faded crimson wallpaper indicated where the *Lusitania*'s likeness had been used to hang. I surmised that Turner found it too painful to have it there now.

Holmes, meanwhile, was roaming round the room, touching this, disturbing that in his slow perambulation. His eye alighted briefly on a violin case. Opening it, he plucked one of the strings which sounded somewhat out of tune to me.

Mabel Every said, "He taught himself to play years ago. He used to play a great deal, but he seems to have no heart for it since-" She bit her lip and tears came into her eyes.

"Quite so," Sherlock Holmes said soothingly and turned his attention to a framed cabinet photograph on the desk. "Come and look at this, Watson," he said.

Appreciating his tact, I hurried to his side and looked at the photograph of a short grizzled man whom I took to be Captain Turner standing beside His Majesty, King George V. "Good heavens!" I said.

"That was taken when His Majesty and Queen Mary came aboard the *Mauretania* two years ago." Mabel Every had recovered herself and come to join us. "The King made him a Commander in the Royal Naval Reserve that day," she added with a touch of pride.

"A signal honour indeed to have received his rank from the monarch's own hands," Sherlock Holmes smiled kindly at her. "Captain Turner must have been a proud and happy man that day."

"He was," a harsh voice spoke just behind us. We turned to the man of the photograph who stood glaring at us, his light blue eyes burning with fury from a face weathered to the colour of old bricks. "And now, gentlemen," he grated, "perhaps you would be good enough to leave my house." His northern accent was very noticeable.

"Captain Turner, will you allow me to introduce myself? I am-"

"I know who you are, Mr Holmes," Turner interrupted. "It makes no difference. The *Lusitania* case is closed."

"Not quite, I believe, Captain Turner." Sherlock Holmes was not dismayed by the hostile reception. "That is the reason for my presence here - to see what can be done in your defence."

Captain Turner uttered a short barking laugh and ran a hand through his grizzled hair. "I can tell you that, Mr Holmes, and save you the trouble of inquiring. According to Lord Fisher, the First Sea Lord is a scoundrel who ought to be standing trial as a German spy. Others say I was such a bad Master of the *Lusitania*. I'm not fit to be in charge of a rowing boat, so you can puzzle out the right answer for yourself on your way to the station. There's a train to Liverpool every hour, so you'll not have to wait long." And he turned his back, making it plain he had nothing more to say to us.

Sherlock Holmes glanced first at me and then at Miss Every before addressing that rigid back.

"I am not inclined to take even Admiral Fisher's opinion as the final verdict upon a man, Captain. A close study of the available evidence has convinced me you are being very harshly treated."

Captain Turner made no reply and after a moment Holmes went on: "I have sometimes been called the last court of appeal, Captain. Men turn to me when all else has failed."

"Used to, you mean," the Captain turned his head just a little. "I understood Sherlock Holmes died years ago."

There was a faint smile on his lips as Holmes said, "I have to join Mark Twain in saying, the report of my death has been greatly exaggerated. As, you see, I am very much alive - and at your service."

Turner continued to hesitate and my friend said quickly, "Mr Booth was hoping you would find yourself able to cooperate with me. No doubt I shall eventually arrive at the truth with or without your help, Captain, but only at the expense of wasting time."

"Tell me just one thing, Mr Holmes," Turner thrust his grizzled head forward and his blue eyes blazed with the light of battle. "Who put you on to this case? From what I remember it's not your line of country at all. Was it Mr Booth?"

"No, Mr Booth is not my client." Sherlock Holmes did not so much as glance at Mabel Every, who had turned so white I thought for a moment she was going to faint.

"Mr Aspinall, then?" Turner pursued. "Come, Mr Holmes, I have a right to know. Who's been meddling?"

"Let us merely say you have a well-wisher, Captain, a secret well-wisher."

"Sounds like a tuppeny romance," Turner commented, "And you won't tell me who it is?"

"No, Captain, I never breach a client's confidence."

"Fair enough," Turner shrugged, "You'd best sit down, the pair of you, and get it over with. Mabel, fetch us some tea, there's a good lass."

There was an impatient scratching at the door. When the girl opened it a curly-haired retriever ambled into the room and collapsed in a heap on the rug beside what was obviously the Captain's chair. Turner absently fondled her ears during the following interrogation.

Sherlock Holmes began by asking, "When you left New York on the first of May had you personally received. any warning that the *Lusitania* might be attacked?"

Turner shook his head. "I only knew what I read in the papers."

"The Senior Naval Officer in Now York, for example, did he say nothing to you?"

"No." The flat negative was, I thought, more damning than a flamboyant diatribe.

"But you were aware the ship had been threatened?" queried Sherlock Holmes and Turner uttered a snort of impatience.

"I read the papers like everyone else, Mr Holmes, and I saw that damned German notice, of course I did, so you could say I was aware the *Lusitania* had been threatened."

Sherlock Holmes ignored the sarcasm. "You must have been a very worried man when the ship came into the War Zone?" he observed.

"Naturally. That was why I had the boats swung out and the water-tight doors closed - as a precautionary measure, of course. You have to tread a very fine line in these cases, Mr Holmes. On the one hand you have to consider the safety of your passengers, on the other you don't want to panic them."

Holmes nodded, appreciating the point Turner was trying to make. "What time did you pass the Fastnet?" he asked.

"Eleven o'clock on Friday night," Turner replied, adding, "by dead reckoning, of course."

"Yes, I understand. Between that time and the moment of the attack, did you see any submarines?"

Turner shook his head, his face bleak. "None whatsoever. There was no sign of them."

"But it would not necessarily have been possible for you to see them, is that not so, Captain? I understand there was thick fog off the Irish coast."

Turner conceded that this was so.

"You were on the bridge, naturally. What action did you take?"

"I gave orders for our speed to be reduced to fifteen knots, Mr Holmes, what is the point of these questions?"

"Fifteen knots would be well below the *Lusitania*'s normal capabilities, of course." Sherlock Holmes ignored the Captain's growing impatience. "I believe, however, " he added, guilelessly, "that it is the cruising speed of HMS *Juno*."

"Really?" Captain Turner refused to give an inch.

"Come, Captain, you know very well it is, the *Juno* escorted you into Queenstown during the submarine emergency of last January when you were in command of the *Transylvania*."

Turner said, "I fear I am not at liberty to discuss that, Mr Holmes." But there was bitter anger in his face.

"Captain, did you receive special instructions from the Admiralty that morning before the torpedo struck?"

"I did," Turner conceded grudgingly.

"Will you tell me what those instructions were?"

"No, Mr Holmes, I will not."

"Will you at least tell me whether you carried them out."

"Yes, to the best of my ability," Turner answered and closed his lips tightly, indicating that he intended to say no more about the instructions the Admiralty had given him.

Sherlock Holmes leaned back in his chair, looking not at Turner but at the photograph we had been studying when the Captain returned. For a few moments there was silence and then Holmes smiled suddenly, as though a peculiarly knotty problem had just unravelled itself before his eyes.

"Ah, yes, I understand now!" he exclaimed. "Of course, of course, it was perfectly obvious from the start!"

Captain Turner stared at him in bewilderment, clearly wondering what he could have said to provoke such a reaction in my friend.

Mabel Every rose and went silently out of the room. I looked at Holmes.

"May I ask Captain Turner one question, Holmes?"

"By all means, Watson, providing the Captain does not object?"

"No, I've no objection, Doctor - what do you want to know?"

"Did you at any time ask the Admiralty for an escort?"

Captain Turner stood up so quickly that the dog started to her feet and darted hopefully to the door. "No, I did not!" he exclaimed. "I leave that to the Admiralty. It's their business, not mine. I simply carried out my orders."

The door opened and Mabel Every reappeared, bearing a laden tea tray.

"You'll stay and have a cup?" Captain Turner said gruffly.

The curly-haired dog sprang up wagging her tail and looked at the plate of cakes with beseeching eyes. "Sit, Nell!" the Captain said sternly and she obeyed him at once, giving her long tail an occasional thump as she regarded her beloved master.

Teacup in hand, Sherlock Holmes had wandered back to the

table displaying Turner's memorabilia. "You have an intriguing collection here, Captain," he remarked. "What is this I see here? Ah, the Humane Society's Silver Medal. The letters are so small I cannot quite make out the inscription."

"I can tell you all about that, Mr Holmes," Mabel Every said eagerly. "Thomas dived into the Alexandra Dock and rescued a boy from drowning. He-"

"That's enough, Mabel," Turner said irritably. "Mr Holmes won't want to hear about that."

"On the contrary, I am very interested to-" Sherlock Holmes was beginning to say when Mabel Every rounded on her employer.

"It is not enough! People only hear the bad things about you - someone has to show them the good side, and if you're too stiff-necked to do it for yourself then I must. And I will!" she added defiantly, though her eyes shone with tears.

Turner looked at her, half opened his mouth to speak and then closed it again. His gaze shifted to Sherlock Holmes.

"Forgive me, Mr Holmes, Dr Watson. It's been a pleasure to meet you both." He gave us a stiff bow and walked from the room, the dog following closely at is heels. A moment later we heard his footsteps going up the stairs. Mabel Every made a movement as if to follow him when Sherlock Holmes caught her by the arm.

"I should leave him be for the moment," his voice was gentle. "Captain Turner strikes me as a proud man who would not care to make a public display of his feelings, even to a valued friend like yourself."

She swallowed, then turned away and began to collect up the cups and saucers, piling them haphazardly on the tray.

"Mr Holmes," her voice was muffled, "you will be honest with me I know. Is there any chance that we shall win this case?"

Sherlock Holmes hesitated and I gained the impression he had been embarrassed by the question.

"The truth, please, Mr Holmes," Mabel Every insisted, lifting the heavy tray and turning ta look into my friend's face.

"The truth, Miss Every, is that, although I am more convinced than ever of Captain Turner's innocence, I cannot in all honesty tell you our side is likely to win since we still lack any concrete evidence to put before Mersey. Moreover, I think Butler Aspinall is likely to have a tricky time when he has to put your Captain on the witness stand.

That blunt manner of his may not go down well in some quarters."

Mabel Every set down the tray. "Would it help," she said, "if I could put into your hands the chart Thomas was keeping during the *Lusitania*'s last voyage?"

Sherlock Holmes looked startled. "The very greatest help, Miss Every provided it is genuine. I was told all the *Lusitania*'s papers had gone down with her."

"They had," Mabel Every assured him, "all except this one. Thomas says he remembers thrusting it into his breast pocket at the last minute. Then he forgot all about it."

"Very natural," Sherlock Holmes said rather grimly. "A man struggling for his life in icy water is likely to have quite different priorities. But surely the chart must have been ruined by the salt water."

"No - it is very much stained, but still perfectly clear. You will be able to follow the *Lusitania*'s course all the way from New York to the Old Head of Kinsale where she-"

"Quite so," Holmes said quickly. "And where is the chart now?"

"In Thomas's desk over there," she nodded towards it.

"Can you get it for me now?"

Mabel Every shook her head regretfully. "That desk is always kept locked and Thomas keeps the only key on his watch-chain."

With a bound Sherlock Holmes was by the desk, crouching to examine the lock, his expression that of a headmaster whose most promising pupil has unaccountably failed him.

"A pity you did not mention this when we met in London, Miss Every," he said severely. "Had you but done so I would have brought the necessary equipment with me - as it is I suppose I shall simply have to force the lock. Kindly hand me the poker."

Mabel Every laughed merrily, "There will be no need for that, Mr Holmes. I can open the desk myself. I am quite skilled at picking locks," she added modestly.

"Indeed?" Sherlock Holmes's brows lifted, "Where did you learn that particular art, may one ask?"

Her hazel eyes were limpid. "One of my father's old lags taught me," she said. "I'll bring the chart to your hotel tonight without fail."

CHAPTER XIII

Punctually at nine o'clock Mabel Every mounted the steps into the main lounge of the Adelphi, her glance flicking across the chattering groups seated here and there until her eyes alighted upon Holmes and myself, whereupon she smiled and came straight up to us, apparently oblivious of the curious stares directed towards the unfamiliar spectacle of a young woman entering the hotel unescorted.

"Ah, Miss Every," Sherlock Holmes had risen at once to his feet, "I am glad you were able to come." Smiling, he offered her his arm and we went up the short flight of steps to the panelled room used mainly for business conferences. Having seated Miss Every at the long polished table, Holmes carefully secured the doors.

"I have the manager's personal assurance we shall not be disturbed here," he said.

"Is that likely, Mr Holmes?" Mabel Every looked surprised.

"I am not sure," he answered, "but my experiences today at the Seaman's Home warned me to take no chances. Someone is anxious to prevent the truth from reaching Lord Mersey and I have no intention of playing into his hands. Did you succeed. in getting the chart?"

"Yes, I have it here," Mabel Every rummaged in her bag.

With a quiet, "May I?" Sherlock Holmes took the chart from her and spread it on the table. Looking over his shoulder I saw with a thrill of horror that at the moment the submarine fired its torpedo the *Lusitania* had been seventeen miles off-shore and twenty-five miles from safety.

"So near and yet so far, " I commented sadly. "If only -"

"Never mind that, Watson!" Sherlock Holmes interrupted. "The point is that the Admiralty are resting a great part of their case on the accusation that, Turner disobeyed their orders by sailing too close to land, yet here we have the documentary evidence that the *Lusitania* was more than fifteen miles out to sea when the torpedo get her, a fact of which the Admiralty must be perfectly well aware since the wreck has been buoyed, yet they still insist on their figure of eight miles and it is one of their strongest cards in this case."

"I see all that, Holmes," I said, staring at the pencil marks of Turner's plotted course, which ended abruptly at the Old Head of

Kinsale where the single, poignantly laconic word, "Sunk" had been scribbled, but when all's said and done, where does it get you?"

Sherlock Holmes's mouth had thinned to a hard line. "It proves that the Admiralty have been lying," he said.

"You don't change, I see, Holmes." The speaker was a short slight man in naval uniform who had just entered the room. His white hair fluffed out like a monk's tonsure round his gold-braided cap but the unwinking black eyes that looked coldly into mine for an instant did not belong to a monk.

"Well, well," Sherlock Holmes's placid smile might have been calculated to infuriate, "this is an unexpected honour, Blinker. Do you make a habit of intruding on private gatherings?"

"Only, when I think it necessary," the captain was unyielding, "and I have already heard enough to convince me that in this case it was necessary. Besides, since when did you become so scrupulous? I seem to remember you boasting of the time you and Watson listened to a very intimate conversation between Charles Augustus Milverton and - well, perhaps it is better not to mention names even now."'

Sherlock Holmes turned to us. "Miss Every, Watson, allow me to introduce Captain Reginald Hall of Naval Intelligence - sometimes known as Blinker."

Years later, I read the memoirs of the American Ambassador, Walter Hines Page, who wrote that Captain Hall could `look right through you and see the very muscular movement of your immortal soul while he is talking to you.'

My own impression at the time, for what it is worth, was that we faced a very formidable opponent and I braced myself for the coming attack.

Initially, however, Captain Hall preferred to exercise his undoubted charm and made to take Mabel Every's hand in a display of old-fashioned gallantry. But she shrank back, her violent antipathy for the uniform he wore plain to see. Captain Hall quickly, withdrew the hand and blinked several times, very rapidly. Holmes told me afterwards that this nervous tie had earned him the nickname by which he was known throughout the Service.

Throwing his cap on to the table Captain Hall went on, I am pleased to make your acquaintance at last, Miss Every. It is time we met, I think."

"You know my name?" In her surprise she ignored or did not heed the second part of his speech,

"Oh, yes," said Captain Hall, "I know all about you, Miss Mabel Every - even to the prank you played on one of the senior consultants in the days when you were a student nurse and threw an orange at him." He wagged an admonitory finger. "You were always an impulsive young lady."

Mabel Every was pale faced. Sherlock Holmes said quickly, "Suppose you tell us why you are here, Blinker, instead of playing childish games?"

Captain Hall right eye gave a violent twitch. Clearly he did not relish the adjective. He sat down, placing his hands flat against the table. "You are causing the Admiralty a great deal of trouble, Holmes," he rasped. "I am here to see that you stop it, that is all."

He was looking at the outspread chart. Intercepting his gaze, Mabel Every snatched it up and clutched it fiercely to her bosom. Captain Hall sighed. "Really, Miss Every, you must give up this absurd campaign of yours," he said.

"And if I won't?" she said defiantly.

Captain Hall's voice was soft. "You obviously have no experience of women's prisons, Miss Every. They are not pleasant places, I assure you. I do not think you would relish finding yourself in one of there."

Mabel Every smiled. "Are you threatening me, Captain Hall? How very ungentlemanly - and quite pointless."

"How so?" Captain Hall's eyes were watchful.

"Because even if you were to silence me I hardly think you could expect to get away with putting Mr Sherlock Holmes behind bars. The world's foremost detective treated like a common gaolbird - there would certainly be questions asked about that! And what of Dr Watson? Are you going to arrest him too?"

The betraying eyelid quivered again. "You have plainly forgotten we have an Official Secrets Act in this country, Miss Every -"

"Official phooey!" she retorted. "If I choose you can do nothing to stop this story becoming public property and you know it. You made a great mistake in coming here like this, Captain Hall. Now I know how frightened you, and your masters really are."

Beside me, Holmes was doubled up with silent laughter. "I think you have met your match at last, my friend," he said when he could speak. "Miss Every is not to be denied. And she is quite right, of course. The gentlemen of the Press are like bloodhounds once they get on a scent and if there is even a hint that the Mersey Inquiry is not to be entirely fair and above board you and your people are likely to be torn limb from limb. Heads will surely roll at the Admiralty, I can see it coming."

Captain Hall studied Holmes's face for a moment. He did not seem to be angry so much as thoughtful, "I have no quarrel with any of those arguments, Holmes," he said. "You make your points very succinctly, but as a man of the world, you must know quite well that a public admission of failure by the Admiralty is out of the question."

Sherlock Holmes's eyes were veiled, "You think so, Blinker?"

"I know so, Holmes," Captain Hall corrected him, "and so do you. With the stalemate in France and our military losses mounting every day, you know quite well the British people must not lose their faith in the Royal Navy's ability to protect them. Our superiority at sea is the last good card we have and, by God, I mean to see we keep it."

At that moment with his face thrust forward and his eyes blazing with the light of battle, he was a frightening figure.

Sherlock Holmes refused to be intimidated. "Yet something must be done," he declared. "An innocent man has been unjustly pilloried. We are no better than our enemies if we wilfully allow Turner to be condemned."

"And that is your last word, Holmes?"

"Yes, Hall, I am afraid it is. Do I take it that Watson and I, along with Miss Every, are now under arrest?"

"Not so fast. Are you so anxious to be martyred. Let us talk this over a little like sensible men and see if a compromise can be reached."

Holmes said warily, "What sort of compromise have you in mind?"

Captain Hall mused, "Well, for instance it might, I only say might, be possible for part of the truth to emerge at the Inquiry."

There was long silence, during which Sherlock Holmes kept his eyes fixed on Captain Hall's face, as if making a determined effort to read his mind. Finally he said in a quiet voice, "Explain yourself, Captain Hall."

The Captain's voice was low, "A certificated copy from the wireless station in Valentia, containing all the signals sent to and received by the *Lusitania* on 6th May, has been sent to Admiral Sir Frederick Inglefield as part of his brief - he is to be one of the Naval Assessors at the Inquiry. I have seen it, Holmes, and I can vouch that it is genuine."

If Sherlock Holmes was excited, he did not show it. Instead he asked, "Does it by any chance include the full wording of a signal ordering the *Lusitania* into Queenstown?"

Captain Hall shook his head, "The W/T operatives at Valentia had no access to naval codes. They merely recorded that a message had been sent to the *Lusitania* at two minutes past eleven, using that code; but if Mersey has any brain at all he will surely put two and two together and realise that the matter is a little more complex than might at first appear."

"And you would be willing to let Mersey see it?" Sherlock Holmes sounded frankly sceptical.

Captain Hall smiled. "At a price, yes. Now don't look down your nose at me, Holmes. We are living in the twentieth century now and, as old King Lear remarked, 'Nothing can come of nothing.' If you want my help," he paused deliberately, "you must first find out who was responsible for the destruction of the battleship *Bulwark* at her moorings in Sheerness last November."

CHAPTER XIV

"HMS *Bulwark* was thirteen years old battleship of the pre-*Dreadnought* class," Captain Hall began as he drew back a chair and seated himself. "On the morning of 25th November last she was anchored with other vessels of the Channel Fleet in Kethele Reach at Sheerness. Suddenly she was shaken by a terrific explosion. An enormous column of smoke mounted slowly to the sky, while pieces of flaming debris rattled down on to the deck of the *Prince of Wales*, the next ship in the line. When the smoke cleared there was nothing to be seen of a once-proud battleship but a few items of wreckage and the bobbing heads of the dozen or so survivors, all that remained of a crew of seven hundred and fifty men."

I uttered a shocked sound and Sherlock Holmes remarked, "I had, of course, heard something of the tragedy, but I was pre-occupied with other matters at the time," he exchanged a smile with me, "and, sad to say, the loss of HMS *Bulwark* tended to be crowded out of the newspapers by the appalling news from France."

Captain Hall nodded, "In any case the Press were encouraged to play the story down. It was even argued in some quarters that the loss of one elderly battleship was no great matter. What most people failed to realise is that a trained crew is not so easily replaced. To resume, however, there was an immediate investigation into the tragedy and it was concluded that somehow the temperature in the ammunition passages had become dangerously high, igniting the loose cordite stored there and thus accidentally exploding the racks of shells, all of them fully armed and operational. In other words, the ship had fallen victim to a tragic mischance."

"But you don't agree, Blinker?" Sherlock Holmes looked up from his task of filling his pipe with loose tobacco.

"No, Holmes, I don't, " said Captain Hall. "For my money the *Bulwark* was the victim of deliberate sabotage."

"Hm." Ignoring Captain Hall's expression of distaste, Holmes got his pipe going and then through the trail of drifting bluish smoke he asked, "'Your reasons?"

Captain Hall hesitated. "I have nothing more to offer than my instinct that matters are not quite what they seem - and I have a distinct impression that someone somewhere is laughing up his sleeve at us."

I expected my friend to direct the withering blasts of his scorn at the hapless man, but Holmes said merely, "Well, Blinker, when we last worked together, I remember that this so-called instinct of yours very often pointed you in the right direction, so it is not for me to say your theory that the ship was deliberately sabotaged is nothing but moonshine. Still, I think you will need something more concrete to stir your colleagues at the Admiralty into action."

"Oh, they will do nothing!" Captain Hall's voice was bitter. "According to Admiral Oliver the *Bulwark* case is now closed. He even refused my suggestion of a few preliminary inquiries among the civilians at Sheerness, who witnessed the disaster."

"What incredible folly!" Sherlock Holmes smacked his fist into the palm of his other hand. "Any trail there might have been has long since gone cold, thanks to Oliver's blinkered short-sightedness. Really, I cannot see what I can do now. Without data I am powerless."

"But there is some data, Holmes." Captain Hall leaned forward, his expression reminding me of a crafty friar; such a one as might have played adviser to Cardinal Richelieu. "In the past few months there has been a spate of mysterious fires breaking out up and down the country, always in factories and warehouses dedicated to the War effort.

"Like this?" His eyes gleaming, Sherlock Holmes drew from his pocket the newspaper cutting of the fire in Kettering which had so absorbed him aim our train journey to Liverpool.

Hall stared in astonishment. "You know of this?" he exclaimed.

Holmes shook his head. "I know very little, Blinker. I kept the cutting because it seemed to have a possible bearing on another matter I have been investigating."

"I see," Captain Hall was clearly far from satisfied by the explanation, but for the moment he asked no questions. "Well, Holmes, I have a whole file of similar cuttings and after seven attacks I believe I am right in saying there is a distinct pattern in these apparently related incidents."

"What pattern?" Sherlock Holmes puffed at his pipe, his grey eyes wonderfully alert. Mabel Every and I listened intently, both of us enthralled by the rapid-fire question and answer between these two men, who at the same time were so alike and yet so dissimilar.

Captain Hall, ostentatiously cleared his throat, looking pointedly at Holmes's pipe. "Well, as I have already said, these fires occurred without exception in plants that had contracts from the British Government, For instance, this one, Harts' & Co," he showed Holmes a tattered clipping, "a wood-turning establishment, making rifle-butts, among other things. I think you had better read it."

Holmes studied the cutting. "It says here the blaze spread so rapidly that nothing could be saved?" He looked at Captain Hall for confirmation.

"Yes," Captain Hall nodded, "that was the common factor in all the cases I studied - a fire breaking out suddenly and with such ferocity that not only the stock but the entire building was destroyed. I could quote you more than a dozen examples - a boot manufacturer's in Northampton, a concern that made tinned beef in Leicester, a precision instrument-maker's in London, all of which had recently signed Government contracts."

"You need not labour the point, Blinker," Sherlock Holmes remarked with an amused smile. "I understand very well what you are saying, but to my mind you still have to prove any link between these incidents and the destruction of the *Bulwark*, Is it not possible that, like the *Lusitania,* she fell victim to an enemy torpedo?"

"No, Holmes, I don't believe it," Captain Hall said forcefully, "for a torpedo always throws up a fountain of white spray as it strikes the ship's side. Those on adjacent vessels who witnessed the explosion were all of them adamant that they saw only a huge column of smoke and flame, followed by a tremendous detonation as the ship blew herself to pieces."

While Sherlock Holmes pondered the significance of this, I myself put a question to Captain Hall. "Did you yourself manage to speak to any of the survivors from the *Bulwark*?"

"Yes," Captain Hall replied, "but they could tell me little - suffering as they still were from the effects of shock and pain. Their only memories were of smoke and flame and the ship's masts shaking violently in the last moments before catastrophe overwhelmed them. I suppose," he added slyly, with a sidelong glance at Sherlock Holmes, "the next step logically would have been for me to question the civilians who had recently been aboard, but that was the point at which my inquiries were forcibly ended by Admiral Oliver."

Holmes brushed that aside, personalities as such being of no interest to him when he was on the scent of something. "There were civilians aboard the ship?" he said. "You did not mention that before."

"Because there is no great significance in that, Holmes. There is always a great deal of coming and going when a ship lies at anchor, you know. Stores of all kinds and fresh provisions are taken on daily - not to mention the dockyard workers engaged on essential maintenance. In fact, a working party had been aboard the *Bulwark* the whole of the previous night and, luckily for them, were taken back to Chatham shortly before the explosion."

"Presumably," said Holmes, "these men were thoroughly interrogated by the Court of Inquiry?"

Avoiding Holmes's eye, Captain Hall answered shortly, "They were not."

It was rare indeed for me to see my friend so thoroughly taken aback as he was now. I am ready to swear that his jaw dropped as he exclaimed, "But surely-!"

"The Court of Inquiry were under pressure from the First Lord of the Admiralty and the First Sea Lord to issue their findings as soon as possible," Captain Hall's voice was defensive; it was plain from his heightened colour how very much he disliked this line of questioning, and it gave me an insight into the difficulties we faced in trying to unravel the *Lusitania* case. If the Admiralty had put a stop to Captain Hall's efforts to get at the truth concerning HMS *Bulwark*, how much less were they likely to welcome the intervention of a complete outsider like Sherlock Holmes. I could not blame Captain Hall for being loyal to his Service, but in the circumstances it seemed to be a great waste of time and I knew my friend felt the same way as he said impatiently, "I would have thought a thorough interrogation of everyone surviving from the *Bulwark*, including civilian workers, purely elementary in the circumstances, Not everyone in this country is wholeheartedly in favour of the War effort. For all we know there are disgruntled individuals at Chatham working in the dockyards there, who have their grievances about their pay and conditions. Then again, there are committed pacifists who might have felt impelled to use extremist methods to get their point across, and then-"

"And then there are spies and traitors," Captain Hall's eyes gleamed. "My money is on them, Holmes. As we all know to our cost, the Germans had been planning long and carefully for war - and the weakening of the Royal Navy must be among their foremost aims. It may be that the destruction of HMS *Bulwark* was the first shot to be fired in a long, pitiless campaign."

Sherlock Holmes's face had assumed its inscrutable Red Indian cast; there was nothing in his expression to suggest the surge of excitement which gripped him, as he told me later, when Captain Hall's remarks appeared to suggest a possible link between a series of outrages across England and the faceless individual known only as the Tiger, whom the German High Command had chosen to spearhead their campaign to destabilise the English enemy. After months of waiting Sherlock Holmes's first opportunity to get to grips with the Tiger had finally come. But he gave no hint of this as he said rather pettishly to Captain Hall, "What you say is so very generalised, Blinker. You offer me nothing in the way of a distinctive trail. Even I cannot be wrestling with the purely nebulous."

Captain Hall looked at him calmly. "Then hear this. When the good people of Sheerness ran down to the sea wall after the *Bulwark* blew up they found a stranger already there, gazing up-stream towards the warship anchorage."

Sherlock Holmes nodded rather wearily. "Did any of them describe this man?" he asked.

"Yes," Captain Hall had reddened a little at my friend's obvious scepticism, "they say he was dressed like a well-to-do farmer, about sixty years old, with a clipped moustache and a military carriage."

Sherlock Holmes had a hand to his mouth to cover his smile. "Upon my word, Watson!" he cried. "You've been at it again have you? I would have thought the near-disaster that almost overtook you in Charles Augustus Milverton's grounds sufficient to put you off a criminal career for life!"

"It was." My humour was more restrained than his. It was, after all, my ankle which had been gripped by the detectives' clutching fingers as I made my escape over the wall. Even now, to think of the terrible consequences, personally and professionally, if I had been arrested were enough to bring me out in a cold sweat.

Mabel Every's strained face had relaxed into a smile. "They say everyone has a double somewhere in the world, Dr Watson!" she exclaimed mischievously. "Perhaps the man at Sheerness was your doppelgänger."

"His name was Robert Clarke Townsend," Captain Hall had no time for badinage. "He was arrested later at the scene of the fire at Harts - the timber people, you remember?"

"Yes, I do - so you managed to catch the fellow?"

"Not me, unfortunately. Townsend was arrested by an unusually vigilant young constable who had been called to the scene. He made up his mind that Townsend had been acting suspiciously and arrested him."

Sherlock Holmes leaned forward. "And then?"

"Further inquiries revealed that Townsend had visited the local hostelry and ordered drinks all round. He then raised his own glass, exclaiming - forgive me, Miss Every - 'To hell with Jackie Fisher!' Having thus damned the First Sea Lord, he lurched out of the tavern and was later observed outside Harts,watching the conflagration with every appearance of enjoyment. When the constable approached him, he was heard to boast that if he chose he could say a great deal about the *Bulwark* disaster."

Holmes's long face was very thoughtful. "It would be interesting to have a few words with friend Townsend."

Captain Hall's hands sketched a gesture of frustration. "I wish that were possible, Holmes, but sad to say, Townsend is no longer alive. The constable's superiors decided, with incredible stupidity, that Townsend was nothing more than a drunken fool with a penchant for self-dramatisation and they ordered his release after a night in the cells. Townsend returned to his lodgings and shot himself."

"Was anything found in his rooms?"

"Nothing, Holmes - no papers or letters - even the labels on his clothing had been removed."

"A real man of mystery," Holmes commented. "Presumably Townsend was not his real name either?"

"I should think it unlikely," Captain Hall agreed. "However, the incident set me thinking. Since the spate of arson attacks continued after the man's death, I think it is safe to assume he was no more than a pawn in the game and that a mind cleverer than his actually directs the campaign. Then there was the nature of the device used to cause such fires." He looked at Holmes, a glint in his black eyes. "I wanted to get our own scientific people onto it, but once again Oliver blocked me. Then came news from New York that the steam-ship *Phoebus* sailing for England with a cargo of munitions had caught fire in mid-Atlantic and had been abandoned by her crew after desperate efforts to save her had failed. The *Phoebus* did not blow up, but as described to me the fire was of the same kind as accounted for the *Bulwark* - the vast column of smoke, the flames enveloping the ship down to sea-level - and I knew intuitively that both ships fell victim to.the same infernal machinery."

"Intuition is all very well, Blinker," Sherlock Holmes began, but once again Captain Hall forestalled him.

"The German undercover operation in New York is headed by a man named Van Rintelen, of whom you may have heard?"

Sherlock Holmes nodded, smiling faintly.

Captain Hall went on: "Von Rintelen is a cunning devil and I would gladly see him behind bars, but I cannot in all conscience see him allowing such wholesale slaughter as happened aboard the *Bulwark*. The crew of the *Phoenix* had ample time to take to the boats, whereas the *Bulwark*'s men had no warning whatsoever. However, it is known to our own people in New York that Von Rintelen can call upon the services of the brilliant Dr Scheele, who has probably offered the fruits of his research to the evil man masterminding the English operation."

"Yes," Sherlock Holmes said softly and threw back his head as he quoted half to himself, "'TIGER ARRIVING VATERLAND AUGUST GIVE SCHEELE CIGARS EAGLE' Now I understand. Von Bork was ordering Rintelen to see to it that the Tiger was given Scheele's device, whatever it may be to take back to England for use here. Forgive me, Blinker," he had sufficiently emerged from his preoccupations to observe Captain Hall's bewildered expression, "I had better put you in the picture." And in a few succinct words he recounted the story of his own, unsuccessful pursuit of the Tiger in New York. Captain Hall listened to him with absorbed attention then said crisply, "'So new we have two objectives - to find out the exact nature of 'Scheele's cigars' and to bring the Tiger to book. Of the two, I think you will agree with me, Holmes, the latter is the more important." He drew a long breath. "We must catch the Tiger."'

CHAPTER XV

"I made a short list," Captain Hall explained, "and after eliminating all the improbables, I was left with three possibles." He grinned at Sherlock Holmes, whose own eyes sparkled with his appreciation of the banter. "They are, Count Negretto Sylvius, Louis la Rothière and Joseph Harrison," he ignored my gasp of outrage at the last name, saying smoothly, "all of them are known to you, of course, Holmes."

"They certainly are," Sherlock Holmes agreed and pondered for a while. "Negretto Sylvius now - would-be thief of the Mazarin Stone, sportsman, big-game hunter, master-criminal, a cool hand too, and ruthless enough but, no, I cannot in all conscience imagine Negretto in something like this. It would not be to his taste at all - and he is really too flamboyant a character even in his sixties to fit the role of saboteur." He gave a reminiscent smile. "If Sylvius had descended on a quiet little place like Sheerness in his flowing cloak and broad-brimmed hat, twirling his silver-topped cane, he would certainly have attracted some attention from the local worthies."

"La Rothière, then?" Captain Hall suggested. "No one could call him flamboyant, quite the reverse in fact."

Sherlock Holmes shook his head decisively, "Louis always preferred the quiet life - that is why he was so successful in the buying and selling of information - and why, incidentally, he found it so easy to go to ground at the beginning of the War."

"And Harrison?" Captain Hall's patience was visibly waning. "What is your objection to him?"

"That's what worries me, Blinker" Holmes took his pipe from his mouth, "I can't think of one."

"Yes, he is a cunning devil" Captain Hall nodded his snowy tonsure, "and, if he is engaged in anything he would prefer the authorities not to know about, that nursing home of his must offer the perfect cover for, whatever his past record, who is going to suspect a man who has appeared on the front pages of every newspaper in the country, shaking the hand of Lord Kitchener? To my mind the fellow should have been locked up for good when you got hold of him, Holmes."

"I agree," Sherlock Holmes puffed a cloud of smoke at the ceiling,"but I suppose it was necessary to spare Lord Holdhurst's blushes."

"Look here!" I found my voice at last. "Aren't you both taking rather too much for granted? As far as I can see, Harrison genuinely has turned over a new leaf. I can vouch for the good work he's doing at Briarbrae."

"No doubt, doctor," said Captain Hall. "Harrison never was a fool and he must have realised our security people would be keeping an eye on him when he returned to this country. For my money," his dark eyes were like bullet-holes, "the Germans could have planted him in this country as a sleeper years ago."

"A sleeper?" I repeated. "And what might that be, pray?"

"An agent who has been infiltrated into this country with instructions to lie low until his masters decide the time has come to reactivate him," Captain Hall explained with a hint of impatience. "In Harrison's case, he might have been recruited well before the theft of the Naval Treaty. I have never entirely believed that story that he just happened upon it that night. It's my belief he entered the Foreign Office to look for it after he had been tipped off by the German Embassy."

I looked at Holmes. "But you told me Harrison only turned thief after dangerous speculations on the Stock Exchange had brought him to the brink of financial ruin."

"And what I told you was true, Watson" said Sherlock Holmes, "but now I cannot help wondering if perhaps the Germans somehow arranged for Harrison to lose money so as to have him in their power and once he was in the net to blackmail him into stealing the Treaty. It would not be the first time such a thing happened."

Before I had a chance to speak Captain Hall said, "I am convinced that is what did happen, Holmes. Thanks to you, Harrison bungled the job, but when he was forced to go abroad the Germans contacted him again in Bad Ischl."

Sherlock Holmes said humorously, "You appear to know a great deal about it, Blinker."

"I make it my business to know, Holmes," Captain Hall retorted grimly. "Besides, I have access to the reports made by our surveillance agents, both European and American, on friend Harrison's movements since he was forced to leave England."

"They've been keeping a check on him, then?"

"What do you think? Obviously a watch was kept on all doubtful exiles - just in case." Captain Hall turned his head slowly and looked

Holmes in the eye. "It may interest you to know that since 1910 Harrison has made no less than seven trips to the United States. I'm rather surprised you never came across him in your guise as Altamont?"

"I never did," said Sherlock Holmes,"but that signifies nothing, of course. The Germans prefer to keep their operatives in watertight compartments, as you probably know, but I am beginning to think that maybe Harrison was in fact the `big man' poor O'Reilly referred to with his dying breath. However, all this is pure supposition: we have no proof that Harrison is the Tiger - and lacking proof you cannot arrest him."

"Quite so," said Captain Hall, adding slowly, "What we need now is for someone to get into Briarbrae to watch Harrison's movements. That is the only way we are going to get our evidence against him. Do you not think so, Miss Every?"

At the sudden question her colour rose and she mumbled that she supposed he was right. Until then I had almost forgotten her presence as I listened to the verbal fireworks between the two men, each of whom in his own way deserved the epithet `great', and I confess that Miss Every's lacklustre response rather surprised me, until I benevolently reflected that she must be worn out after the strain of the long day.

Sherlock Holmes heaved a sigh. "I suppose you are right, Blinker," he said,"though I had been hoping to do some research into the exact nature of Scheele's infernal devices. They cannot, of course, be conventional time-bombs, which would be far too bulky to be carried about without exciting comment. No, Scheele must have hit upon some-thing quite small - the 'cigars' offer a clue, if only we could interpret it. I wonder now - some kind of chemical combination might fit the bill, but how did Scheele manage to ensure that the subsequent explosion would only happen when he wished, without resorting to a clock. Well, well, I have always said, what one man can invent another can discover, but that must wait. When do you want me to set out for Briarbrae, Blinker?"

"I don't," Captain Hall said bluntly. "My dear Holmes, Joseph Harrison must remember you only too well as the author of his previous ruin and it is vital that we do nothing to alert his suspicions until we are ready to smoke out the rest of his organisation."

"Oh, come!" Sherlock Holmes's quick flush showed he had been nettled by the Captain's remarks. "Credit me with a little sense, Blinker. Do you seriously imagine I would go there in my normal persona? No doubt you could arrange for Harrison to need the services of another gardener or ward orderly or even someone to clean the boots, and," he added with a chuckle, "I'm sure I can depend on you for an impeccable set of references?"

"No, Holmes," Captain Hall's voice was very quiet, "not even a reference from Buckingham Palace could get you into Briarbrae. Harrison runs a very tight ship there and he has only three male employees; Dawlish the gardener, his son who does odd jobs about the place, both of them long-time servants of the Phelps's, and Harrison's manservant, Heaney, who also acts as his chauffeur. Apart from that, all the staff at Briarbrae are women." The corners of his mouth lifted in a smile. "Your reputation as a master of disguise is second to none, Holmes, but I have never heard that the art of female impersonation was included among your many skills."

Somewhat reluctantly, Sherlock Holmes joined in the laugh at his expense. Then he quickly became serious again. "Well, I grant you, it is a problem, but what's to be done? Briarbrae's defences must be penetrated somehow."

"We have tried," Captain Hall informed him. "The best we have been able to do is arrange for one of our men to pose as the greengrocer's assistant, who goes once a week to deliver vegetables to the back door, but has never once managed to enter the house. Not very satisfactory, as I am sure you will agree. But if only we had a shrewd young lady with the requisite nursing qualifications, I am convinced we should soon have the information we need." His eyes, deliberately opaque, studied Mabel Every's downcast face, "There is a rapid turnover in the nursing staff at Briarbrae," he said quietly, "I gather the matron, Mrs Foster, is something of a martinet. They are always needing replacements."

For once in my life I saw Sherlock Holmes taken by surprise. The significance of Captain Hall's speech was slow to sink in, but when he realised the enormity of what was being suggested, he sat bolt upright, exclaiming angrily. "No, Blinker! That is going too far, even for you! I forbid you to think of such a thing!"

"Excuse me, Mr Holmes," Mabel Every interrupted. "I'm sure you mean to be kind, but I can speak for myself, thank you." She looked at Captain Hall, saying coldly, "I'm willing to go to Briarbrae for you."

CHAPTER XVI

Having gained his objective, Captain Hall became very business-like. "I'll have some references prepared for you right away, Miss Every," he said. "There will be no difficulty about that.

It is fortunate that you come from Liverpool - much less suspicious - from Harrison's point of view, that is. Now, we shall have to work out a suitable cover story-"

"One moment, Captain," Mabel Every raised a hand. "Before we talk about that, I think you should know I am only prepared to go to Briarbrae on certain conditions and you had better hear what they are."

He stared at her, meditating. "Yes," he said at last and though his voice was even the rapidly fluttering eyelid betrayed his unease, "I should like to know that."

Mabel Every took a deep breath, like a swimmer about to launch into an icy current. "I want your personal guarantee that all the evidence previously suppressed by the Admiralty will be brought to Lord Mersey's attention during the *Lusitania* Inquiry. Also," she gripped her hands together, "I must have a signed statement from you Captain Hall detailing this arrangement between us."

Until then I had marked down Captain Hall as a cold fish, incapable of strong emotion. Now, as his weathered face darkened to crimson and he croaked, "Impossible!" in a voice thickened with fury I realised my mistake. Sherlock Holmes caught my eye, winked and looked away. Although I never heard him admit it, I believe my friend had a soft spot for women of spirit and I am sure he was immensely enjoying this David and Goliath battle played out in front of him.

Mabel Every had risen to her feet, "Very well, Captain Hall," she said calmly, "in that case I won't take up any more of your time."

The Captain let her reach the door before he barked, "Where do you think you're going?"

"Home," she answered, turning to face him, her eyes very dark in her white face. "There's no point in staying here any longer. I told you my conditions and you are obviously unwilling to meet them, so I bid you good night."

She pulled the door open, allowing the strains of the palm court orchestra to steal into the lofty room. They were playing a selection from *Floradora*, as I recall, that little number that goes, "Tell me, pretty maiden, are there any more at home like you?" I have often wondered if Captain Hall took note of the irony.

She had taken his measure all right. He was forced to sprint after her and lead her back, into the room muttering profuse apologies. "Come and sit down, my dear young lady," his voice flowed like warm oil. "Let us talk this over and see if we can arrive at a reasonable compromise."

She stiffened. "No compromises!" I have seen greater warmth in the eyes of a Pathan aiming a jezail at me. "We have had enough of that, Captain Hall. I want your absolute guarantee that you will do as I ask, otherwise I'm leaving."

It was at that moment that Captain Hall temporarily lost his head. "You set a very high value on yourself, young lady," he rasped.

"No, Captain," she slowly shook her head, "only on the truth."

"Excellent, Miss Every" Sherlock Holmes whispered behind his hand, adding, "She has him, Watson. He will be forced to give in now."

In fact it took another twenty-five minutes before Captain Hall finally yielded and promised that the transcript from the Valentia W/T station would be sent to Lord Mersey, together with any other relevant papers. "Though I have to tell you that many of them have already been destroyed," he warned. "I know for a fact that Oliver and Captain Webb worked through the night after the disaster, weeding out anything that seemed to them-"

"Compromising?" suggested Holmes when the Captain paused.

"Holmes, I have already explained the reasons for what happened," Captain Hall wearily closed his eyes.

"You have indeed," Holmes's expression showed his deep distaste, "and I can see for myself that survival must have been uppermost in the minds of the Admiralty that night - never mind who else had to suffer in the process."

"Don't let us have that argument over again," Captain Hall implored. "We are wasting time and I have to be back in London by morning." He did have the appearance of a man labouring under heavy burdens and the dark shadows under his eyes told their own story of sleepless nights.

As he moved over to the writing table, followed by Miss Every, who clearly preferred not to let him out of her sight, I caught Holmes by the arm. "One word," I said. "You know I have always regarded you as the best and wisest of men - in all conscience then how could you allow yourself to become a party to this deplorable scheme? Captain Hall's conduct does not surprise me in the least - he is obviously a man who delights in intrigue for its own sake, but for you, Holmes, you of all people, to risk the life of that poor child! Words fail me, Holmes - I simply don't know what to say - but ask yourself one question, old friend, was that the act of a gentleman?"

Sherlock Holmes appeared visibly distressed by my remarks - and to speak truth I had never spoken to him so harshly before - but before he could open his mouth to defend himself, Mabel Every called across the room in a low clear voice, "Going to Briarbrae was my own choice, Dr Watson. I won't have you blaming Mr Holmes. In any case," she left Captain Hall to his writing and came over to us, "maybe you are wrong, Mr Holmes, and Joseph Harrison is all he seems to be."

"It is entirely possible," Sherlock Holmes agreed and then his face clouded. "All the same Watson is quite right and I feel bound to warn you that you may, be exposing yourself to considerable danger, Miss Every."

"I'm not frightened of that," she declared bravely, "but there is one way you can put my mind at rest, Mr Holmes."

He nodded gravely. "I am at your service."

"Then please see to it that whatever happens, Captain Hall keeps his word to me."

He took her hand. "You have my personal assurance on that. Now, Miss Every, one word of advice - obviously Captain Hall will be expecting you to report to him. I want your promise that you will do nothing of the kind. Send your reports to me at Fulworth - and I will pass them on to Captain Hall. I am sure I need not tell an intelligent person like yourself never to put your letters with the other mail at Briarbrae. If Harrison is working for the Germans, he will certainly make a point of reading all letters to and from the house. You can circumvent him by walking to the Post Office in Woking with your reports. It is worth a little fatigue to avoid an obvious danger."

"Very well, Mr Holmes," she said earnestly, "I will do everything you say."

"Good. Now if ever you feel the situation is getting out of control, you must wire me at Fulworth and I will come to you immediately."

She nodded. "And what kind of things am I to look out for?"

"Harrison's demeanour - his relations with staff and patients - visitors who come to the house - his friends," Holmes glanced towards the busily writing figure of Captain Hall. "I would avoid contacting the man who comes to deliver vegetables at the back door. In my opinion a fellow who has failed to get into the house after all this time is hardly worth his keep as a secret agent."

"Unfair, Holmes." Captain Hall had completed his missive and was showing it ill-temperedly to Mabel Every. "I take it this is what you wanted Miss Every," his voice was ungracious. "Though what satisfaction it will be to you to ruin my career I cannot think."

There was a hint of malice in her smile. "I don't want to ruin your career, Captain Hall," she said, "only to prevent you from ruining some-one else." She put the folded sheet carefully into her bag.

"Well, well," Sherlock Holmes's calm voice bridged the awkward silence," all that remains now is for us to look forward to some interesting correspondence from Briarbrae."

CHAPTER XVII

I was not myself present at the events described below, but I have Miss Every's permission to use the letters she sent to Fulworth in the following days and I here present them, to offer my readers a coherent narrative.

Briarbrae, 8th June

Dear Mr Holmes,

Well, I have arrived safely at the house and I shall be taking up my new duties right away. Captain Hall was quite right - none of the nursing staff appears to last very long here, so, I had no difficulty in persuading Mrs Foster to employ me, even though, as I admitted at the interview, I had been out of active nursing for several years now.

"My dear," said Nurse Woods, with whom I am to share a room, "just now we're so short-staffed they would have taken you on if you had two heads and swilled down the gin like Sairy Gamp." I soon found out this was an accurate if unflattering assessment.

As you no doubt remember Briarbrae is a very large place, which is just as well, since it now has to house twenty-five patients and fifteen nursing staff, as well as Mr Harrison and his manservant, Heaney (more of him later, by the way). Space is therefore at a premium and the nurses' rooms are upstairs in the cramped quarters formerly occupied by the domestic staff when Sir Percival and Lady Phelps kept open house here. Mr Harrison occupies a bachelor flat on the top floor under the attics and Mrs Foster sleeps in the room previously occupied by Sir Percival before he was married. I understand you have good reason to remember it, Mr Holmes?

"Excellent, Watson!" Sherlock Holmes said when he had skimmed through this passage. "The lady has the intelligence to know what is important. Thanks to her, I now have a very clear picture of Briarbrae as it is now." He sighed then and when I asked him the reason he said, "It is a waste of natural talent for that girl to bury herself in the mundane routine of a private housekeeper. She would be a considerable asset in the kind of work we are doing, I've a good mind to mention her name to brother Mycroft."

"She would hardly thank you for that," was my considered, response. "Clearing Turner's name is Miss Every's only reason for

engaging in such desperate activities."

"I suppose you are right, Watson," said Holmes and turned his attention back to Miss Every's letter.

The patients are all young men, of course, she had written, and all of them, alas, badly wounded. In theory they are only here until they are fit enough to return to active service, but it is clear to me that this is merely a kindly fiction employed to keep them from despairing before they are considered ready to hear the truth, which is that, far from returning to duty,the majority of them will never be really fit again.

The other nurses tell me that Joseph Harrison is fiercely protective of his 'young men', who in turn almost worship their 'Father Joe'. Hearing them sing his praises I find myself wondering if Joseph Harrison can possibly be the cold-hearted villain who destroyed HMS *Bulwark* and her crew. But you are not interested in my speculations, Mr Holmes, so I will get down to practical things again.

During the day the patients meet together in the graceful white-panelled drawing-room. If the weather is warm enough they are allowed to sit outside on the terrace which runs the whole length of the southern side of the house. It is the favourite spot of those in spinal carriages.

I should perhaps mention that Mrs Foster's door opens directly on to the passage leading to the kitchens. Hilda Woods told me rather maliciously she is believed to have chosen that room so as to catch any of the staff trying to pilfer food.

From this you will gather that Mrs Foster is not a popular Matron, but I believe she is very good at her job.

Mr Harrison's apartment overlooks the enclosure and the stone-built pigeon-loft which houses his cherished collection of birds. Apparently Mr Harrison is an enthusiast for the more exotic breeds of pigeon - the pouter, the tumbler, the cochin-china, so staff and patients are forbidden to go anywhere near the pigeon-loft, as it has been impressed on us that these birds are very delicate and the presence of strangers might interrupt the breeding cycle, or some such matter. Otherwise, we all have the free run of the grounds.

Although I arrived at Briarbrae somewhat prejudiced against Joseph Harrison, I have to say he is kind and sympathetic towards the patients, Nothing is too much trouble for him. Perhaps he has a fellow-feeling towards them for it is obvious to me that his own health is far from, good. He is grossly overweight and his heart is not strong. Several times I have seen him turn pale and press a hand to his chest after climbing the main staircase. Once he looked so ill that I tried to help him, but he brushed me aside.

"*Anno domini*, Miss Every," he gasped. "Nothing for you to bother your pretty head about." He gave a ghastly smile. "A man does not attain to my advanced years without an ache or two, you know. And I am a lucky fellow compared to the poor lads here."

Thus he tried to make light of his condition, but the skin round his mouth had turned blue and his bald scalp shone with sweat. Before I could insist that he must at least allow me to help him to his room, Heaney came running up the stairs and rudely brushed past me. Without a word he took a small capsule from the box he carried and thrust it between his master's teeth, supporting him in his arms until the drug had taken effect, whereupon, still glumly silent, he half dragged, half carried him to their private apartments

This was my first close encounter with Heaney and, since he is such a very singular character, I feel I should describe him to you in some detail. He is a short, dark-haired individual with an almost simian cast to his features, a flattened nose and small rather bloodshot grey eyes almost hidden by fiercely bristling eyebrows. His beauty is not improved by the two teeth missing from his upper jaw and the cauliflower ears. I am told he used to box in his youth - he is now about forty - and though he was born in Brixton, he was known as the Monaghan Mauler.

He follows Joseph Harrison everywhere, like a devoted shadow, and the only time I have ever seen a remotely pleasant expression on his face is when he gazes upon his master with doglike devotion. Towards everyone else he is generally disagreeable and often comes as close as he dares to actual insolence, even when he is addressing Matron.

I had a taste of his temper myself only yesterday, when I perhaps not quite accidentally strayed into the pigeon-loft enclosure, Heaney materialised seemingly from nowhere and rushed at me screaming. I was taken aback, to say, the least, and tried to apologise, but Heaney ignored, my stammered excuses and shook his fist in my face, all the while shouting the foulest abuse. How it would have ended I can't very well say, for at that moment Mr

Harrison himself appeared in the enclosure and uttered a sharp word of reprimand. Instantly Heaney's hands fell to his sides and he shuffled away in silence.

Mr Harrison waited until he had gone before turning to me. "My dear Miss Every," he took my hand between his large fleshy palms, "you must excuse Heaney. In his anxiety to serve me he is a little inclined to be - shall we say - over-zealous." His small dark eyes lingered on my face for a moment. "He knows how much I prize my little beauties - why, I wouldn't sell even one of them for a king's ransom! And such delicate creatures, too! A stranger's presence is anathema to them. I once lost a rare nestling to the shock caused by an intruder. So, Nurse Every," his grip tightened on my hands until he hurt me, "you will be very sure to remember the rules in future, won't you?"

He was still smiling pleasantly but just before he turned to go I could swear I surprised a look of fury in his eyes. The change was so remarkable I might have been looking at a different man. And my hands still burned with the pressure of his fingers.

This incident has convinced me I ought to take a closer look at the pigeon loft, for, despite all the praise that has been heaped on him, I am quite certain Joseph Harrison is not all he seems to be.

Take, for instance, his attitude towards the patients. On the surface he is all smiles and friendliness and jollity, yet, observing him over the past two days, I have discovered that while appearing to.sympathise with their misfortunes, he is in fact reminding them of their disablement. I have heard him exclaim to a blind patient: "A magnificent sunset tonight! Such a pity you can't see it, my dear fellow." Or to a man in a wheel-chair: "Just the day for a good walk in the grounds, eh? Oh, forgive me, my dear boy I was forgetting. I do apologise." In other words, he is practising a nasty spiteful cruelty masquerading as kindness. Whether this means that he could have sabotaged the *Bulwark* I do not know, but I do not think he is a good man.

Well, Mr Holmes, I hope you will find something in all this to interest you. I must close now, as I can hear Hilda Woods coming along the passage and I am due to relieve her at nine o'clock.. We are all having to do extra duties now because another of the nurses left or was dismissed earlier today. Mrs Foster can be very exacting. I will write more fully about her in my next report.

Briarbrae, 10th June

Dear Mr Holmes,

I apologise for the delay in writing, but I found it impossible to get to the post yesterday as one of the patients collapsed and died in the early hours of yesterday mornings. It was, as they say, a merciful release. Of course, there was a great deal to do, relatives to be summoned, doctor, Rector and undertaker to be contacted and so forth. Though I had been on night-duty, I found myself pressed into service and so it was that for a .little while I found myself sitting at the bedside of the dying man.

For most of the time he was deeply unconscious, but at one point he suddenly opened his eyes and clutched my hand, addressing me in a hoarse voice as `Sally'. I naturally took this to be the name of his sister or lady-friend, but his rambling words soon made it clear that Sally was a nurse who used to work here.

`You won't go away, will you?' he constantly repeated, `Please say you won't go away!'

`Of course I won't,' I tried to reassure him. `I shall be here as long as you need me.'

`You say that now,' he moaned, gazing at me with wide fever-bright eyes, `but you all go away. None of you ever stay! Not one of you!'

Before I could ascertain what he meant, Mrs Foster rustled in, She too had been up all night, but she betrayed no sign of fatigue. Her blue uniform was as neat as ever.her cuffs immaculate, not one iron-grey hair on her elegantly coiffured head was out of place. She as very pale blue eyes and it is hard to read their expression as they are nearly always hidden behind a pair of pebble-lensed pince-nez. She reminds me of one of those severe Roman ladies you see in a museum of antiquities. She is not popular with the nurses, who refer to her behind her back as The Icicle.

I could understand their attitude when she looked me up and down and I became acutely aware that my uniform was rumpled and my cap askew.

"Thank you, Nurse Every," she said, "you can leave this to me now. Tidy yourself and have some breakfast."

I was forced to ignore the pleading look in the patient's eyes, though I think it would have meant a great deal to him if I had been allowed to stay. His words continued.to haunt me during the rest of the day and at suppertime I found the opportunity to tackle Hilda Woods about it.

"What did young Parfitt mean when he said none of the nurses stays here very long?" I asked.

Hilda drank some water. "Well, they don't," she said, putting down her glass."

"What on earth do you mean?" I demanded.

Hilda was gobbling up some meat and took her time about replying. "Just that," she said at last. "Either the nurses do something to annoy the Icicle and get the sack or else she makes life so unpleasant for them that they're more or less forced to leave." Searching with her tongue for a stray shred of beef that had lodged between her teeth, she added reflectively. "Come to think of it, I don't believe anyone's lasted here for longer than three months."

It was only logical to ask, "How long have you been here, Woods?"

"Eight weeks," she gave a lopsided grin, "so make the most of me while you've got me, Every, because the odds are ours is going to be a short-lived friendship."

"Doesn't it strike you as odd - this rapid turnover of staff?" I said.

Hilda forked up some mashed potato. (The food here is adequate but uninspiring.) "Not really," she said. "I'm not saying The Icicle isn't a perfectly competent nurse, but between ourselves, she's a bit of a sow - and these days nurses won't stand for being treated like dirt - not the younger ones, anyway. There are plenty of other places, offering higher wages than this one - and better conditions."

"But you stay," I pointed out.

"Ah, but I'm lazy," she responded with another grin, "I can't be bothered looking round, so I expect I'll stay until they kick me out."

I believe there is more to it than that, however. It is an open secret that Nurse Woods has become very attached to one of the patients, Sub-Lieutenant Harry Oldcastle, and that, rather than laziness is the reason for her determination to stay at Briarbrae as long as she can - the sad thing is, he barely notices her.

Back to business, though. As you can imagine, Mr Holmes, this conversation set me thinking, for if Harrison really is a saboteur using this nursing home as a cover for his activities, it would be only logical to keep changing the staff, since new-comers obviously would not notice any change in the normal routine.

I was still mulling this over when Mrs Foster called me unexpectedly into her office.

"I have not yet had the chance to talk to you properly, Nurse Every," she said with one of her chilling smiles. "We have been so busy over the past few days that I feel I have neglected to welcome you properly." Her English was clear and precise, the phrasing oddly old-fashioned and I was sure I could detect the faintest trace of an accent, though I could not place it.

"Tell me," Mrs Foster propped her elbows on the desk and leaned her chin on her clasped hands, "do you think you are going to like working here?"

"Very much indeed," I said.

"Good. I ask the question because I see from your references that you are very well qualified and frankly I am a little surprised that you prefer working in a home of the convalescent rather than a hospital where your talents would be more fully used."

I was glad I could answer truthfully that an old back injury had compelled me to give up nursing for a while.

"I see," Mrs Foster nodded; the sunlight slanting in through the window flashed blood red on the lenses of her glasses. "Is that not a rather strange choice, Nurse Every? There is a great deal of heavy lifting to do here, particularly the spinal cases, and for someone whose back is weak -" Suspicion deepened her voice.

"I'm much better now," I said hastily. "My back hardly troubles me at all."

The twin red suns glinted as she mused, "And yet the trouble was sufficiently severe to keep you out of nursing for seven years." She studied my references again. "It says here that you became housekeeper for a wealthy businessman - Sir Samson Crowther of Liverpool. The name is vaguely familiar, but I cannot recollect the precise nature of his interests."

The palms of my hands were damp. Sir Samson Crowther existed only in the fertile imagination of Captain Reginald Hall. If this wretched woman took it into her head to check...

If she had continued to interrogate me, as ill-prepared as I was, I cannot think what would have happened, but fortunately a diversion was created by Heaney, who strode in, announcing, "The Boss wants you upstairs. Now!"

"*Voertsek*, you fool!" Mrs Foster took off her pince-nez and stood up, her eyes were blazing. "Get out of here and don't ever come into my room like that again!"

Clearly taken aback, Heaney retreated:a little, repeating stubbornly, "But the Boss said you was to come right away."

Mrs Foster said deliberately, "Tell Mr Harrison I will come to him as soon as my duties permit; not before. Now go."

Heaney shuffled out with a hangdog expression on his face.

Mrs Foster replaced her spectacles with hands that trembled slightly. She blinked at me. "Did you want something, Nurse Every?" Apparently she had forgotten our previous exchange.

"Er-no, Matron, " I said.

She picked up her pen. "Then return to your duties."

Reprieved, I did as I was told, but the incident convinced me that my cover-story is too thin to withstand really serious investigation and I shall be lucky to last a. fortnight here - let alone three months! Mrs Foster gave herself away when she shouted that very vulgar South African word at Heaney. (Of course, you wouldn't know, but Thomas served on the old *Umbria* when she was a troop transport during the Boer War and he picked up a smattering of the Taal - the old Dutch language. Mr Holmes, I am convinced Mrs Foster is really a Boer woman. Could this be checked, please?)

In closing, I must mention one other member of staff, the gardener, Stephen Dawlish, whom the patients irreverently insist is so old he was here before the Flood, and certainly he is bent nearly double with rheumatism. He boasts such a formidable set of white whiskers that it is difficult to see his face. He is a morose, disagreeable man, avoided by staff and patients alike, and he makes life a misery for his son, a pale, shambling youth who is unfit for military duties.

Finally, Mr Holmes, may I trouble you to send the enclosed letter to Captain Turner, if anything occurs to prevent me from seeing him again. I am not trying to anticipate trouble, but I suppose it is as well to be prepared for all eventualities.

"Our little friend is becoming frightened," Sherlock Holmes remarked, turning over the sealed enclosure in his hand, "and with good reason. "The more I learn of this business, Watson, the less palatable do I find the thought of that young woman, untrained, untaught, aided only by her own considerable courage and common sense, trying to investigate matters at Briarbrae. If her next dispatch

is equally alarming, I shall be strongly tempted to go down there myself."

Briarbrae, 11th June

Dear Mr Holmes,

I believe I have made a discovery of real importance, but before I tell you what it is I had better fill in the background.

I don't know how familiar you are with nursing routines, but you may be aware it is customary for nurses to be assigned to particular patients, which involves keeping a daily check on their health, mental and physical, and reporting back to Matron. I have been assigned to look after Hilda Woods's favourite, Harry Oldcastle, who has been here longer than most of the other patients as he was wounded early in the War, losing an arm when the *Aboukir* was torpedoed last November in the Broad Fourteens. The poor boy was barely eighteen when it happened and he is considerably embittered; understandably so, as he had set his heart on a Navy career and had turned his back on the family woollen mill in Yorkshire. Now, although he is really fit enough to go home, he won't hear of it, saying his family would have no use for him now.

Rather to my surprise, he seems to have conceived a liking for me. I suppose I fulfil the function of an elderly aunt - when you are nineteen, thirty must seem as old as Methuselah. More surprising still, our friend-ship has been encouraged by Mrs Foster, who willingly agreed when I asked if the Lieutenant might accompany me for a stroll in the grounds.

"Certainly, Nurse Every, it will do that young man good to get out and about instead of moping in his room all day," Mrs Foster said, adding scornfully, "He is full of pity for himself."

"It must be very hard to be crippled for life so young!" I was stung into retorting.

Mrs Foster drummed the table with her fingers. "There are worse things than disablement you foolish woman!" she burst out, her normally pale face a surge of colour. "But what would you smug English know of hunger or disease or being herded together with a lot of strangers and kept in filth while your home is burned to ashes? Ach, you people have so very much to learn!"

I have to confess I gaped at her. She was almost unrecognisable, with her lips drawn back from her teeth in a grotesque snarl and her pale eyes blazing. She was shaking from head to foot with emotion and I would not have been at all surprised if she had struck me.

Finally she controlled herself and said with an effort, "I am sorry, Nurse, there are times when the old memories are too much for me. As you have probably guessed, I am South African Dutch, and for many years my people were at war with yours, but," she smiled painfully, "all that is over now and our two countries are friends since Louis Botha and Jan Smuts made us so. We forget what I just said - yes?"

"Of course."

"Good - then go enjoy your walk, but, please make sure you are back before seven. Mr Harrison prefers to lock up early."

As you can imagine, I was considerably shaken, but I made myself forget what had happened while I was strolling with Lieutenant Oldcastle and as the day was so pleasant I suggested we might as well go and have tea in Woking.

"No, thank you," he said distantly. "I don't want a lot of strangers gaping at me. As far as I'm concerned they can keep their damned pity!" He halted, announcing, "Sorry, I'm not fit company for anyone today!"

Before I could stop him he had plunged into the thick shrubbery bordering the drive. Alarmed by his air of desperation. I hurried after him, but he was quickly hidden from sight by the burgeoning thickets of elder and gorse.

I found him some minutes later in a clearing, staring down at a pathetic heap of blue-grey feathers. When he heard my approach he looked up and smiled, and I realised thankfully that the mood of black depression had lifted for a while.

"It looks as if Father Joe has lost one of his pets," he said. "A sparrowhawk, I suppose. I remember in Yorkshire they could be devils with-" He broke off, staring at the dead bird with a puzzled expression. "Funny," he muttered, "I could have sworn..."

"What is it?" I said.

"Well, I've never gone in for the sport myself, but pigeon-racing is a very popular sport in my neck of the woods and for my money that is a racing pigeon."

"How can you be so sure?" I said. "It looks just like an ordinary pigeon to me."

He shook his head, decisively. "Too powerfully built for a tumbler or a pouter. These fellows can outfly a hawk, you know."

"That one didn't," I remarked.

"True," he admitted, "but you can take a Yorkshireman's word for it that is not a fancy. It's one of the kind we use to carry messages on the Western Front - and the question is now what is it doing here?" He knelt down beside the bird, ignoring the cloud of flies that rose buzzing as he turned the corpse over. "There, d'you see?" With an air of triumph he pointed to the ring on the bird's leg, stamped with the initials JH.

"No message," Sub-Lieutenant Oldcastle muttered after a brief, distasteful examination of the bloodied heap of feathers, "and it was coming from Briarbrae when the hawk got it."

"How can you tell?"

"By the line of flight after it was attacked." He gestured towards the trail of blue feathers and then looked up at me, his eyes no longer those of a sick man, but alert and full of intelligence.

"Too many mysteries here, Nurse," he said, "and I've a mind to look for some answers, starting with you. Who are you and what are you doing here?"

I have no idea how I would have answered him, but once again luck was on my side, as there came the sound of someone cursing and bracken being beaten down. Making up his mind quickly Harry hauled me into the nearest thicket and forced me to crouch down beside him.

We were just in time, for the next moment Heaney appeared. He was sweating profusely and his face was red. He caught sight of the dead bird and hurried over to it with a grunt of satisfaction. While he was gathering up the pathetic remains wings clattered overhead and I looked up in time to see a sleek blue arrow flash across the clearing and fly purposefully in a westerly direction.

"Explanation time, Miss Every," Lieutenant Oldcastle said softly after Heaney had gone.

I have not yet decided whether it is safe to trust him. Of course I do not suspect his patriotism, but he has been gravely wounded and he is very young. On the other hand would welcome some help at this stage as the next logical step is a search of the pigeon loft and this may be difficult with Harrison or Heaney constantly on the look-out. If Lieutenant Oldcastle kept watch for me, though, I am certain it could be done.

But would I be justified in giving away so many secrets to a comparative stranger? It is a hard question to answer.

You may as well tell Captain Hall that his spy-cum-delivery man is wasting his time. He drives up every day with the groceries, which are then unloaded by the kitchen-staff, after which he drives away again. What can be learned from that?

I will write again after I have seen inside the pigeon-loft.

The above concludes Miss Every's third and last report to Sherlock Holmes and I well remember the shock and distress it caused him. "I told you that young woman had courage and sense, Watson," his voice was harsh with anxiety. "I was wrong. Courage, yes, but sense is sadly lacking, I fear. You had better drive us both to London right away."

CHAPTER XVIII

I wish to point out that I myself was not present at some of the events described below and my account of them is made up from the recollections of the many participants.

John H Watson, MD

Mabel Every was caught red-handed by Heaney, emerging from the pigeon-house. The man enjoyed the struggle that followed - putting the fear of God into women had long been a favourite amusement - but he was unprepared for the strength and spirit displayed by the nurse and in the end he was forced to crash his fist in her face.

Luckily, no one had seen them or heard anything, it being the middle of the afternoon with house and residents in thrall to the drowsy summertime. Not even a blind stirred at one of the many windows as Heaney lifted the unconscious woman and slung her casually across his shoulder before marching back to tell Mr Harrison.

He'd be very angry, there was no doubt about that. She'd seen everything, the prying bitch, not just the birds, but the demi-johns of acid under the floorboards, with the lengths of cut lead piping and the boxes of copper disks. Mr Harrison wouldn't think twice about doing her in. Heaney told himself it wouldn't be the first time, after all. He could still remember O'Reilly's face as he cowered away, trying to protect, his face and ribs from a spate of vicious blow, still hear his yell as he plunged down the hotel staircase to his death. Good sport, that had been, but today's would be even better if Mr Harrison let him loose on the woman.

***

"But why are we going to London, Holmes?" I shouted above the roar of the hard-pressed engine. "Surely Miss Every's safety must be our first consideration, and if what you tell me is true...?"

"Only too true, I fear," Sherlock, Holmes rubbed a hand over his unshaven chin and grimaced. "Why else would I leave Fulworth in such haste as to leave no time for my usual toilet? But I have some vital information for Captain Hall and I also need his help to extract Miss Every from Briarbrae." He sighed. "I wish she had waited for me, Watson. All day yesterday I hoped to hear from her, but the postman brought nothing and it was the same story this morning."

"You think Miss Every may have come to grief?" I pulled out into the traffic to overtake a slowly moving dray.

"Well, this continuing silence is rather ominous. In any case I had to see Hall. My researches are now complete and I am now a hundred per cent certain I know how HMS *Bulwark* was destroyed. Come, Watson, put your foot down, or whatever it is you motoring experts do. We have to be at the Admiralty before eight o'clock."

***

Joseph Harrison stared with distaste at the woman's swollen face. Wheezing slightly, he bent over and pinched the lobe of her ear quite hard. She did not stir. Harrison turned on Heaney, "You hit her too hard, you blundering fool! Now we are unable to question her, thanks to you." Overcome by exasperation, he raised his hand and flicked Heaney across the mouth.

Light though it was, the blow stung like acid and Heaney winced, but it wasn't so much the pain he minded as the thought he had displeased Joseph Harrison. In so far as he loved anyone or anything apart from his Cause, Heaney worshipped Joseph Harrison. Englishman though he was, Heaney knew he was ready to die for him, so it hurt to be at odds with him now.

"I'm sorry, Boss," he whined. "I lost me head, like. Shall I go and find Mrs Foster? She'll know what to do." He gave a pleading smile, showing the gaps in his teeth.

Like a cur-bitch that has been kicked and comes back for more, Harrison thought with mingled disgust and amusement. But he did not wish to quarrel with Heaney. The man was a fool but his huge fists and savage nature were useful weapons in maintaining the total discipline Harrison expected from his acolytes. So he said now, "Yes, go and find her for me. We have to discover how much this woman knows and - more important - who sent her here and why."

Heaney"s expression was bemused. Clearly that had not occurred to him, but it was plain as day Mabel Every could not have come to Briarbrae on her own initiative. She was obviously intelligent, but an amateur. Even so, it was disturbing that even one spy had managed to penetrate the elaborate façade he had constructed here at Briarbrae. Until now it had offered a perfect cover for the clandestine activities he was engaged upon. His German superiors had questioned the wisdom of returning to the house which had witnessed his previous downfall at the hands of Sherlock Holmes, but

Harrison had insisted that the English were a sentimental race who liked the idea of the repentant sinner and he would be welcomed back with open arms, as had indeed proved the case - with the single exception of Percy Phelps, who still seemed to believe Joseph Harrison had ruined his career.

"But the fault was his, not mine," his brother-in-law reflected, "The truth is, poor Percy would never have made the First Division, but I suppose it is handy to have someone to blame for your own failures."

Footsteps clattered along the passage and a moment later the door opened to admit Heaney and Mrs Foster. The Matron's cold eyes rested on Mabel Every's face for an instant before switching to Joseph Harrison.

"How long will it take you to bring her round?" he asked. She shrugged, "It depends, Joseph."

"On what?" he rapped, concealing his anger at the cool insolence in her voice, Never had she treated him with the respect due to The Tiger, the most feared agent of Imperial Germany. Quite the reverse, in fact; there were times when he suspected she was secretly laughing at him.

"On whether you are willing to give me a free hand," she answered, clasping her hands across her spotless white apron.

Harrison smiled, saying blandly, "You can do whatever you like, my dear, short of killing her, of course - at least," his voice hardened, "until we have the information we need."

All the same, it took much longer than they expected. Wan and exhausted, her face dirtied with tears, the woman proved amazingly stubborn, insisting over and over again that she had no associates but had come to Briarbrae of her own accord. The day wore on; downstairs the gong was ringing for luncheon and still they had no information worth speaking about.

"It is useless" Mrs Foster said at last, "She will tell us nothing, You might as well kill her and be done with it."'

"Not yet," Joseph Harrison responded, drawing his lip between his teeth while he silently pondered. At last he said, "Bring Woods up here."

"No!" Mabel Every's voice rang with shrill protest.

"Then tell me what I wish to know," and as she hesitated, "unless you wish your friend to suffer. Who sent you here?"

And in a choked whisper she breathed out the name Harrison had least expected and least wished to hear. "It was Sherlock Holmes." Then as he gazed at her, appalled her head fell sideways and she fainted.

Mabel Every's absence at luncheon was not particularly remarked upon. It was assumed she was upstairs, nursing one of the seriously ill patients, but as the hours went by and still she did not appear Nurse Woods and Sub-lieutenant Oldcastle both began to wonder.

"She said she was coming for a walk with me this afternoon," Oldcastle remarked, "I suppose she must have forgotten. Or changed her mind," he added gloomily.

Hilda Woods shook her head. "Every wouldn't do that," she said with conviction. "She's much too conscientious."

"I don't see how you can say that," Mr Oldcastle was in a mood to be argumentative, "you've only known her for a few days."

"We share a room," Hilda reminded him, "so I know her pretty well and I can tell you, Every's all right." She frowned briefly, "Except for wanting to keep the light on while I'm trying to sleep so she can write to her people. I never knew anyone write so many letters - and not ordinary letters either - more like books."

"I didn't know she had any family."

"She mentioned an old uncle living somewhere in Sussex," Hilda said, adding, "What's the matter?"

For Mr Oldcastle's youthful face had become extremely thoughtful. He was thinking about the odd incident the day before, when they had stumbled on the dead pigeon, and his own instinct to get them both out of sight when they heard Heaney crashing about. He had tried to question her afterwards, but she had put him off with light answers. Now he was beginning to realise there might be more to this affair than met the eye. The mysteries were beginning to add up: a nurse appearing, as it were, out of nowhere - Mabel Every had been extremely reticent about herself, writing letters of such length that she was keeping her room-mate awake, a man supposedly bred fancy birds, some of which turned out to be homing pigeons all this coupled to the strange incident of the previous year, when a lorry delivering what was supposed to be carbolic acid (for clearing the drains they had been told) to the house had accidentally spilled some in the drive. One of the kitchen-maids had managed to step in it and burned her foot right through the sole of her shoe. She had been given a large sum of money and turned off - and now Mabel Every had disappeared.

Putting her possible fate aside for the moment - she might simply have gone for a walk or left the job, as some of the nurses did, Mr Oldcastle thought about the spilled acid. Why would a nursing home require such enormous quantities of the stuff? Was it really carbolic acid at all? Could carbolic burn through a stout leather sole? And where was it being kept now? Not in the kitchens, surely?

***

"As you see, Blinker, the piece of lead is hollow inside," said Sherlock Holmes, showing it to him. "In the middle of the tube a copper disk has been pressed and soldered, dividing it into twochambers. One of these I intend to fill with chlorate of potassium, so." He suited the action to the words, his hands steady and precise, "Now I seal the chamber with a plug of wax and a simple lead cap.before filling the other with sulphuric acid. Have the goodness to hand me that flask, Watson, and I pray you, be careful, old friend."

Within a few minutes the tube had been rendered airtight at both ends, while Sherlock Holmes continued with his exposition. "The real stroke of genius on Scheele's part," he said, "was to hit upon the copper disk, which could be made as thick or as thin as he and his masters wished. If it is thin the two acids on either side will take but a short time to eat their way through to each other. If thick, the mingling may take days or even weeks to occur. In other words, the copper disk acts as a safe and efficient time-fuse."

"And then?" Captain Hall's dark eyes were like gimlets.

Sherlock Holmes said, "Ah, you want a practical demonstration, Blinker. I guessed you would." And he drew from his pocket a small leaden cylinder, "The copper disk is wafer thin," he warned, "and therefore combustion should take place within minutes." And he stepped back, smiling slightly when he noticed the greenish tinge in Captain Hall's normally ruddy complexion.

"You fool, Holmes, do you want to incinerate the lot of us?" he blurted and then the breath was driven out of his lungs in a choked gasp as a jet of white flame shot forth from the end of the cylinder almost blinding us with its intensity. When the flame eventually died I was awed to see the lead cylinder had utterly vanished - consumed to nothing in that searing heat.

"Well, gentlemen," Captain Hall was the first to break the silence that had gripped us all, "I take it that was the device that killed HMS *Bulwark* and her crew?"

"I would call it a strong possibility," Sherlock Holmes agreed. Captain Hall looked suddenly careworn, "The question now is what will be the next target for that infernal thing? Good God, Holmes, the possibilities are frightful! We can't hope to protect every installation at risk, we haven't got the manpower. Unless," sudden light dawned in his eyes, "you heard anything from the woman today?"

"No nothing," said Sherlock Holmes, his tone indicating that he did not care for Mabel Every to be referred to in that, somewhat casual manner, "There has been no word since she announced her intention to search the pigeon-house and I tell you quite frankly, Blinker, I am beginning to feel alarmed for her. A great deal can happen in twenty-four hours."

***

Over at Briarbrae Sub-lieutenant Oldcastle had come to the same conclusion. If only he knew the address of the old uncle person in Sussex: Father Joe and the Matron would have to come up with some answers if a relative came sniffing round. However, Nurse Woods was adamant that all of Mabel Every's belongings had gone from her room and Oldcastle was just telling himself he would have to think again, when he was struck by an idea.

"You told me she was always writing letters," he said to Nurse Woods, whom he had met by arrangement in the sunken garden after luncheon.

"Yes, she was," Hilda confirmed and the thought went through his mind that she was really quite a pretty girl, but he had more serious things to think about at the moment. "So she must have used a blotter," he said, "I wonder if it's still there?"

"There's only one way to find out, isn't there?" said Hilda Woods. "I'll go and look." And she was off running like a hare towards the house. She felt rather guilty, because although she was as worried as Harry Oldcastle about what might have happened to Mabel Every she had never in fact been happier in her life.

Joseph Harrison, relaxing in his luxuriously furnished apartment, also felt he had reason for self-satisfaction. He had finally accepted he was unlikely to get anything more out of the Every woman - she was brave but completely untrained - and after the first inevitable frisson at hearing the name of his hated enemy, he had decided that on the whole matters had worked out very well for him. Sherlock Holmes would lose his much-vaunted reputation for infallibility once it was learned that his senile dabbling had helped to bring about the destruction of one of the greatest vessels ever launched, and hard on the heels of her sister-ship's demise at that. Harrison felt he knew the British people; they were slow to anger, notoriously tolerant, notoriously forgiving of their enemies, but when once they felt their trust had been betrayed, they never forgot and never forgave. Harrison smirked: it would be an undoubted pleasure to teach his quondam countrymen a lesson in manners when Germany won her inevitable victory; tomorrow's little venture would be an apertif, enjoyable on its own account and as a harbinger of things to come.

The Kaiser had always hated the *Lusitania* and her sister *Mauretania* and had secretly rejoiced when the U-20's torpedo, sent the first to the bottom. The man who got rid of her sister as well would be made for life, one of the gilded inner circle at the Court in Berlin.

But he had no time to dream about the future now, Joseph Harrison scolded himself. He must be practical. The knowledge that Sherlock Holmes was on his trail again had persuaded him to ignore the advice of his German masters and contact his man in Avonmouth openly.

True, it might, indeed probably would, mean Straker's arrest and eventual death as a traitor, but Joseph Harrison was in a hurry: he needed Straker's motor-launch and his short-wave radio and he needed them quickly.

"Are you mad?" Straker bleated. "You ask me to contact a German submarine for you, knowing the authorities might be listening in? I'd be signing my own death warrant!"'

Harrison soothed him with a promise that provision would be made to transport him too back to Germany. Straker listened, quivering still with nerves, but finally allowed himself to be persuaded, He would make the broadcast.

Joseph Harrison smiled. "I won't forget this," he said and replaced the earpiece.

Poor Straker; but there it was, one was trained never to leave any loose ends about, and Straker had been simply that. He knew too much as well, so one had no choice but to get rid of him.

Apart from Straker, there were quite a few loose ends still. Miss Every, Briarbrae - but that was all in hand; thanks to Heaney.

By tonight, courtesy of Herr Doktor Scheele, Briarbrae would have ceased to exist, and with it Miss Every and the twenty convalescents and fifteen nurses who might, if they were allowed to live, speak a little too freely to the authorities. Most of the visitors to the home had been innocent, but a couple of them had not and Joseph Harrison knew he must never betray his fellow agents. He was sorry the pigeon house would have to go too.

Although their use in carrying messages had been severely practical, he had grown quite fond of the little beggars, homers and fancies alike, and it was sad to think of them dying like that as Scheele's cigars shot forth their lethal flames. At least the end would be quick, if Heaney had done his job properly, and there was no reason to suppose he had not done after so much experience starting with the *Bulwark*, where he had signed on as a chargehand in order to plant the devices. After that had come Harts and so many others that Joseph Harrison was unable to remember all the names. But none of them could compare with the *Mauretania* arrogantly setting out for the Dardanelles with 5,000 British troops abroad. It would be the third time she had made such a voyage, but it was destined to be her last when she slipped beneath the waves to join her ill-fated sister, another rusting hulk on the ocean floor.

And he was going to be there, Harrison promised himself, watching in safety as she went past to the mouth of the Severn Estuary, unaware that she carried within her belly the seeds of her own destruction.

Heaney must be halfway to Avonmouth by now, Harrison thought. He had sent the man ahead to, well, dispose of Straker, there was no point in being squeamish about it, and to make sure all was well with the launch before they embarked. The coast was watched, of course, but they couldn't hope to man every yard and in any case Joseph Harrison had decided to slip down-river in the *Mauretania*'s wake, naturally keeping his distance; he didn't want to be tossed about like a child's toy.

"Joseph!" Mrs Foster's sharp voice roused him from his reverie. "I am all ready for you now. Shall we be going?"

He gazed at her with poorly concealed irritation. She was wearing a grey travelling costume and a hat with a motoring veil.

Berlin's insistence that he must work hand-in-glove with this woman still rankled, but when he protested that he would be better on his own they had turned deaf ears. Of course they admired him for thinking of the scheme to turn Briarbrae into a convalescent home. Sick young men were vulnerable; they needed friends, and what better friend could anyone have than bluff, jolly Father Joe, so ready to lend a sympathetic car, so interested when they told him about their homes and families never realising, the poor nincompoops that they were giving away priceless information, which later he put to excellent use in determining where to plant the next crop of Scheele's infernal cigars.

There was no doubt Berlin admired him for what he had done, so why, Joseph Harrison asked himself, why had they saddled him with the Foster woman? True, she was good at her job - very often she succeeded in getting information when he owned himself baffled, It helped if you had no feelings and Renata Foster had become the cold automaton she now was after seeing the British set fire to the family farm in the Transvaal and had then been herded away to a concentration camp with her mother and her five sisters. She had watched them die one by one, and now there was literally nothing she would not do to get her revenge on the British.

All very well, and he admired her naturally, but she was about the last travelling companion in the world he would have chosen, left to himself. Still, Berlin wouldn't like it if Renata fell victim to the kind of little accident he longed to arrange for her.

"Yes, I'm ready," he said and stood up to put on his travelling cape.

"What about-?" she gestured towards the bound and gagged form of Mabel Every.

"Leave her," he said, "she can do us no harm, now - and in a few hours, what difference does it make?"

"But shouldn't you-?"

"My dear Renata, what a bloodthirsty creature you are!" Joseph Harrison was fast losing patience, "I have to remind you seem to have forgotten, that I am not a violent man. May we go now? I really would like to be in Avonmouth before dark."

***

"So I thought the best thing would be to send a wire to the address in Fulworth right away," Sub-lieutenant Oldcastle explained, "Of course I had no idea the great Sherlock Holmes lived there," he added. "Anyway, after I'd talked to the old woman-"

"Martha," Holmes supplied, "has been with me for many years."

"Yes, Martha, well, after I'd talked to her for a bit she agreed that you ought to be contacted and she gave me a number to ring. That's about all, really."

Sherlock Holmes patted his shoulder approvingly. "You have done very well, both of you," his smile included Nurse Woods, "Indeed it may be that you have saved - but what the devil?" he broke off, staring at a point just over Nurse Woods's shoulder, with a look of horror on his face.

The girl swung round to see what he was looking at and uttered a shattering scream. High over Briarbrae, a serpentine column of smoke climbed lazily into the sky above Tadpole Phelps's old home and hung there like a portent of evil.

CHAPTER XIX

"Come," Sherlock Holmes quickly took charge of the situation, "there is no time to be lost. That cunning devil has stolen a march on us. Miss Woods, run as fast as you can to the nearest house and alert the fire-brigade. The rest of you, come with me."

Needless to say, we streamed along the drive in his wake, pausing only briefly when the gardener, old Stephen Dawlish, hobbled from his cottage followed by his son, a vacant-faced youth.

"Do you know where the fire-fighting apparatus is kept?" Holmes demanded of him tersely.

"That I do, sir," the old man responded.

"Good," Sherlock Holmes reeled off a list of instructions, his eyes never leaving that sinister black column of smoke, which was now beginning to grow branches, like a monstrous tree. The summer breeze had a singed quality that caused my eyes to water.

Old Dawlish hustled his son away, moving with surprising agility for one so crippled. As they disappeared behind a screen of trees I heard the tinny sound of the fire alarm. By the time we arrived in front of the house, it was clear that the first priority of evacuating the patients was well under way.

Armed with the registers, one of the senior sisters was directing operations. She eyed our party with no great favour.

"Who are you?" she snapped, then, "Well, that doesn't matter now. I need your help. Our telephone instrument is out of action, so I want someone to go and alert the Fire brigade."

"That has already been done, Sister," Sherlock Holmes said calmly.

"Oh, I see," her voice lost a tithe of its certainty. "Then, if you really want to help, I need a hand with some of the patients. We got them out all right, but one or two took a bad dose of smoke."

"My friend here is a doctor," Sherlock Holmes informed her.

"Do what you can for these poor folk, Watson. Now, Sister, are you quite certain everyone has been evacuated from the house?"

She bridled. "Of course."

"What about the top floor? Mr Harrison's apartments?"

Mr Oldcastle interrupted, "Mr Harrison is away, as you know perfectly well? Why don't you go and line up with the other patients, Mr Oldcastle? People are very busy here, you know?"

The young man darted her a furious look and said to Holmes. "I'm going to search the top floor. Miss Every may be up there."

"Nonsense," snapped the Sister, "Every left us yesterday morning."

"I wouldn't be too sure of that," Sub-lieutenant Oldcastle retorted and turned to my friend, "I'm going to take a look, Mr Holmes," he said and darted into the house before anyone could try to stop him.

Sherlock Holmes glanced at me. "I hope not to be long, Watson," he said and followed.

Later he was to give me his own account of those desperate moments inside the blazing house, Heaney had done his fiendish work only too well and the main staircase was alight, the banisters crackling merrily in the terrific heat. Just in time Holmes grabbed young Oldcastle as he was about to plunge forward. "Where are the service stairs?" he demanded.

The young man's face cleared. "Of course, how stupid of me! This way - we'll have to go past the kitchens."

By now the hall was thick with smoke; both were coughing and spluttering. After a moment Holmes caught hold of Oldcastle's shoulder and pressed down indicating that it would be better if they were to crawl. The heat as they passed the kitchens was almost unbearable.

Another flight of stairs led to the former servants' quarters, which Joseph Harrison had taken over for his own use after substantial modifications. The smoke was choking and it seemed to Sherlock Holmes that the very treads of the staircase were becoming hot. He glanced behind him and saw a reddish light was already pulsing on the wall. If this staircase too caught alight they would be trapped. He was worried for young Oldcastle.

The boy had shown immense courage, but if the worst happened it might be hard for him to escape, disabled as he was. ("And not so easy either for an aged detective, Watson!" he said to me afterwards.)

Oldcastle had stopped outside a door. "Here we are," he said hoarsely.

Much to Holmes's relief the door was not locked. He flung it open, his eyes darting at once to the bound and gagged, form in the winged armchair which someone's sadistic fancy had placed so as to give the poor girl a clear view of the advancing fire.

Above the gag her eyes stared, as wild as a snared animal's. For a moment she seemed not to recognise Holmes for her body gave a convulsive shudder and her head thrashed from side to side as he cut through her bonds. When he attempted to raise her she moaned with the agony of returning circulation and hung half conscious in his arms.

Mr Oldcastle ran swiftly for the brandy decanter. "Good lad," Sherlock Holmes said approvingly, dashing a measure of the spirit into a glass, which he held to her lips. After a moment she opened her eyes again.

"Mr Holmes," she murmured, "you have come, but-" She clung to him, her body racked by a fit of uncontrollable shivering. Plying her with more brandy, Sherlock Holmes looked at Mr Oldcastle and jerked his head towards the door.

The young man immediately hurried from the room, returning grim-faced a few seconds later to report, "These stairs have caught as well - we're trapped."

Mabel Every whimpered.

Sherlock Holmes lifted her to her feet with great gentleness. "Come, Miss Every," he said, "We will get out on the roof. The Fire Brigade will have us down on the ground, in no time."

Mabel Every looked at him in amazement.

"Just a little walk on the roof." Sherlock Holmes made an effort to speak lightly. "Follow me, both of you." He opened the dormer window.

A wide stone parapet ran round the roofs of Briarbrae and, theoretically, it was entirely possible to walk the entire distance provided one had a steady head and was unafraid of heights. Oldcastle quickly proved he had both by scrambling over the leads like a mountain goat, his empty sleeve flapping beside him. He turned to smile reassuringly at Mabel Every, who was still clinging, whimpering to Sherlock Holmes, "Come on, Miss Every," he called. "If I can do it, you can!"

"I can't," she turned her head away. "I can't."

"Yes, you can," Sherlock Holmes said gently but firmly, "Try not to look down or ahead. Simply follow Mr Oldcastle and I will bring up the rear."

Balancing himself with great care, Oldcastle stretched out his hand to her. "This way, Miss Every," he said in a cheery voice, "it's a lovely warm evening for a stroll and we never did take that walk, you know. I wouldn't have thought you were the kind to let a chap down."

She gave a watery smile. "I'll try not to," she said and slowly inched her way forward.

Far below them, helping the nurses to marshall the patients to safety, I looked up and saw three ant-like creatures crawling along the ledge of the roof.

"Thank God," I murmured to myself, but my apprehensions were not stilled, for although the Fire Brigade had arrived and jets of water were being directed onto the burning façade of Briarbrae, I could see that the flames had now gained such a hold it could only be a matter of time before the roof collapsed. Every window on the two lower floors glowed with a rosy light and from time to time one of the glass panes would crack with a sound like a pistol shot as a tongue of fire belched forth to lick hungrily at the brickwork.

Their bandages and faces coloured bright orange by the reflected glare, patients and staff alike gazed in awe at the terrific spectacle and shuddered to hear the deep sullen roaring within the building as the fire greedily consumed all within, the paintings, the fine furniture that had been Percy and Annette Phelps's pride, the attics through which Tadpole and I had ranged as boys. I felt an unaccustomed pricking behind my eyes - the effect of the smoke, I told myself.

But my chief anxiety was for my friend and his two companions up there on the roof and great indeed was my heartfelt relief when the escape ladder was run up and a fireman scaled it rapidly. Within moments he returned, bearing on his shoulder the motionless form of Mabel Every. Holmes followed more slowly with Sub-lieutenant Oldcastle.

Holmes!" I cried, "My dear friend!" In the depths of my emotion I clasped his hand and wrung it heartily. "I am so very glad to see you!"

"There, there, Watson," he said, "all is well now." But I fancy I could detect an unwonted softening of that austere countenance, As always, however, he avoided any display of his feelings, saying abruptly, "Come, Watson, Miss Every has need of your services, poor girl. Look to the lady."

She was already recovering, trying to sit up, her bewildered gaze moving from the chaos on the lawns where nurses and patients were grouped together watching the dying moments of their former home, to the blaze now torching upwards from the roof. The firemen were beginning to move back, coiling up their hoses, a clear indication that they recognised there was no hope of saving the house now.

Holmes too was looking about him. "I wanted a word with young Oldcastle," he said. "Miss Every and I both owe our lives to that boy, As far as I am concerned he has no reason to fear the future."

"I believe he would agree with you, Holmes," I said drily, for I had already seen Nurse Woods run up to him and throw her arms round his neck and the young man showed no sign of disliking the experience.

"Mr Holmes!" Mabel Every's cry brought us both back to her side.

"Are you in pain, Miss Every?" I began and she shook her head impatiently. "I have something to tell you both," she said hoarsely, "about Joseph Harrison-"

"Well, well, I am sure he will be caught soon," Holmes said soothingly.

"I know where he is, " she clutched his arm and tried
to get her breath. "Mr Holmes, he has gone to Avonmouth."

"Avonmouth?" Holmes repeated and she nodded frantically.

"Yes, Mr Holmes, he means to sabotage the *Mauretania*. I heard him talking to Mrs Foster. Heaney had knocked me out and they thought I was still unconscious, so they talked quite freely in front of me. Joseph Harrison is going with Mrs Foster to a safe house - I don't know where Heaney is supposed to join them after he has-" she hesitated, "put something aboard the *Mauretania* that will finish her and everyone on board, was how Joseph Harrison put it."

Pressing a hand to her bruised swollen cheek she cried, "Please, Mr Holmes, go quickly to Avonmouth and stop them!"

CHAPTER XX

Here I have to give Captain Hall due credit for springing into action the instant he received Sherlock Holmes's urgent wire; for even as the first of a fleet of ambulances began arriving to transfer the patients to fresh accommodation, a naval car threaded its way expertly between them to whisk us back to London.

Once there we were put aboard a special train for Bristol.

"Pray God we shall be in time," Sherlock Holmes said grimly as the train steamed through the darkening landscape. I nodded, aware that he had good reason to be alarmed. Miss Every had seen enough acid under the pigeon house to set the whole of London alight. Both Holmes and I had been greatly relieved when the pigeon-house too exploded into flame, though I confess to a pang of sorrow for the unfortunate birds inside. However, uppermost in my mind was a sense of puzzle-ment that Joseph Harrison had decided to set fire to Briarbrae at all.

"Surely," I said to Holmes as the train roared through an empty station, affording me a vivid glimpse of shuttered waiting rooms and hanging sodium lamps, before it was swallowed up in the rushing darkness, "it would have made more sense for Harrison to continue the masquerade at Briarbrae which had already served him so well?"'

"No," Holmes took his unlit pipe from his mouth and looked at it sorrowfully. In our haste we had both neglected to bring any tobacco with us. "No, Watson, Joseph Harrison was far too canny not to realise he could not hope to continue his secret campaign for ever and planned accordingly. If his career must end, then let it be with a flourish and that, I believe, is the reason he hit upon the *Mauretania* as his final atrocity. He knew only too well the depth of emotion generated by the *Lusitania's* sinking, but to account for her sister-ship too would be to deal a crippling blow to British morale. No doubt Berlin agreed with him and gave their blessing to the scheme."

"But," said I, "you still have not explained why he found it necessary to burn the house with everyone inside it?"

Sherlock Holmes gave me an impatient look, "Do you really not understand, Watson? Think, man, think. He needed a body so as to make his disappearance convincing." With a macabre smile Holmes added, "Had he succeeded there would have been many bodies at Briarbrae, all of them burned beyond recognition."

I shuddered, "It is horrible, Holmes. Only a monster could have devised such a scheme - all those poor young men and their attendants, dying so as to provide Harrison with a convincing means of escape."

"Yes, they are a pretty trio," he concurred, "for I have no doubt that Heaney, and the Foster woman were also deeply implicated, which is why, Watson," he leaned forward to lay two slender fingers on my wrist. "I look to you to support me in any way necessary when we arrive in Avonmouth."

"Why, Holmes, what do you have in mind?" I asked, thinking I had never seen such a look on his face before so haggard, so old.

"It is better you do not know, Watson," he said. "However, I give you fair warning; if we capture Harrison or one of the others, they must be made to speak. Must, Watson, you understand me?"

"I'm afraid so, Holmes," I said after a long pause during which I had been forced to wrestle with my conscience, "and, yes, you will have my unqualified support for whatever you decide to do."

"Thank you, Watson," he said sincerely, adding with a sigh, "but let us hope and pray it will not come to that. Hall is having the *Mauretania* searched from stem to stern and with any luck Scheele's notorious `cigars' will come to light even before we arrive."

But when we were ushered through the steel gates to Avonmouth Dock Captain Hall met us with the news that the most exhaustive searches, carried on throughout the night, had yielded nothing,

"Then," said Sherlock Holmes, "the *Mauretania* must not sail until we have found what we seek."

Hall's eyes were weary; the stubble on his unshaven chin glinted in the grey morning light. "That is not possible, Holmes," he made an effort to keep his voice even. "Our efforts at Gallipoli are going badly and it has been decided by the War Office that fresh troops must be embarked within the next twenty-four hours. The *Mauretania* will be raising steam all day: she sails at midnight tonight."

"But that would be madness, Blinker," Sherlock Holmes insisted. "Contact your superiors at once and tell them to delay the ship's departure until there has been time to seal off the area and mount a proper search."

"Oh, is that all you want?" Captain Hall said sarcastically. "My dear Holmes, it is out of the question - you simply don't know what you are asking. I told you - the *Mauretania* is raising steam."

"Then give the orders for her fires to be damped down," Sherlock Holmes urged him. "For pity's sake, Blinker, surely it would be better to delay than risk losing the ship?"

"We are committed to sail," Captain Hall gritted his teeth. Then he said more temperately, "Listen, Holmes, I'm grateful, we all are at the Admiralty for what you have done, but now it is time for you to stand aside and leave it to us - the professionals. We are paid to do this job and we know what we are doing."

Holmes looked at him soberly and remarked, "you remind me very much of my old sparring partner, Lestrade of the Yard. He was always telling me to mind my own business too. Luckily for his reputation, I usually ignored his advice."

Captain Hall reddened but he said nothing and after a moment Holmes shrugged and walked away from him. He came to join me as I stood looking up at the cause of the dispute, the great *Mauretania* at her berth in Avonmouth Docks.

Gazing at her, I was reminded of the troopship in which I had sailed to India so many years ago. At twelve thousand tons she had seemed to my inexperienced eyes a very considerable vessel indeed, but compared with the *Mauretania*'s vast bulk she would have appeared no larger than a.tramp steamer. Even with her famous Cunard livery exchanged for drab camouflage, the *Mauretania* was an overwhelming sight, with her twelve decks, her knife-edged bows and four towering funnels; but as I stood there I was reminded of her ill-fated sister and it was as though the pale early sun had slipped behind a cloud.

"The two ships were not completely alike," Sherlock Holmes had divined what I was thinking, as he so often did. "The *Lusitania* had smaller air-vents - they made her funnels look taller."

Of course, I thought, he had sailed in both of them while on Von Bork's trail, but in those days officialdom had been glad of his help, now they preferred to ignore his advice. In his place, I think I would have walked away and left them to it and was just opening my mouth to say so, when Holmes suddenly swung round to hurry back to Captain Hall.

"What is it now, Holmes?" the Captain's voice was testy.

Holmes ignored the deliberate rudeness. "Just tell me one thing, Blinker," he rapped. "Why have your people made no attempt to investigate the crews of the lighters coaling the *Mauretania*?"

Captain Hall bridled at his tone, "Why? Because we know the firms well and-" he broke off, saying slowly, "why do you ask?"

"Because I have seen Harrison's manservant, Heaney, standing among the crew of the grey lighter down there. Don't point to it, please."

"Are you certain it is Heaney?" Captain Hall asked doubtfully. "You have never seen him in the flesh.have you? Just his photograph."

"I am quite certain," Sherlock Holmes declared. "In your place, Blinker, I would tell everyone aboard that lighter to lay down their shovels and wait for the Admiralty launch to come and take them off."

"Are you giving me orders, Holmes?" Captain Hall's bushy eyebrows rushed together like two angry caterpillars and then he answered his own question "Yes, of course you are-and you're quite right."

He turned away to issue the necessary instructions.

The men in the lighter watched the launch's approach apathetically; then suddenly there was a commotion and one of them ran to the bows and leaped overboard, his heavy body immediately vanishing from sight. Captain Hall swore volubly and was beginning to strip off his jacket, when Sherlock Holmes restrained him.

"There is no need for you to play the hero this time," he said with a smile and, indeed, one of the launch's crew was already in the water, striking out powerfully towards the spot where Heaney had vanished. Once there, he took a deep breath and duck-dived, his bare feet waving.

For a moment nothing happened and then the water boiled, as though powerful creatures from the abyss thrashed there, and the two men rose to the surface locked in a desperate struggle - and desperate it was, for they were both strongly-built men in the prime of life,and if the sailor was the better swimmer, Heaney's huge fists and what I might call ringcraft, were enough to daunt any man.

Two, three times they disappeared in a swirl of oily bubbles and bobbed to the surface again, both gasping for breath, yet still with the strength to lash out at one another - but by then the launch was along-side and more men were jumping into the water no doubt in the happy anticipation of a good fight. Their combined strength was too much even for Heaney, who was dragged unceremoniously aboard the launch, kicking and gouging and screaming curses. The sailors were not gentle with him and one of his eyes was half-closed and a great bruise darkened his cheekbone when the launch was made fast at the landing stage and the man was hustled towards Captain Hall, water streaming from his clothes, clinging to his ungainly body like liquid weights.

A commanding figure in his uniform, Captain Hall surveyed him with the superciliously lifted eyebrow of a Roman nobleman inspecting a barbarian slave.

"Bring him to my office," he said shortly.

'My office' was somewhat of a misnomer, we were to discover, for it was first necessary to eject the sitting incumbent, a Rear Admiral with a great deal of gold braid and a rapidly purpling face, who left exclaiming loudly that he was going to telephone Captain Hall's superiors in London. The Captain looked at my friend with a glimmer of laughter in his eyes. "You had better get on with it, Holmes," he said. "Oliver will likely have me court-martialled for this."

"Of course, of course," Sherlock Holmes agreed somewhat absently; he was studying Heaney, who gazed back at him with every appearance of loathing on his brutish countenance.

Finally Holmes gave a chuckle of pure delight. "Well, well," he rubbed his hands together. "If it isn't my old friend Mallen, I should have recognised you at once, but a two-day growth of beard and a black eye will change a man." He added apologetically, "I fear I am somewhat rusty, Blinker. Miss Every sent me a detailed description, even to the missing teeth, but I failed to make the connection between this man and James Mallen late of New York, an arch republican utterly dedicated to his own particular brand of Irish nationalism."

Hall shrugged. "I accept what you say, Holmes, but the name means nothing to me. How did you happen to meet up with the fellow?"

Sherlock Holmes smiled reminiscently as he drew out a chair and sat down facing Heaney. "Our acquaintance goes back quite a way now."

"That's a dirty lie!" Heaney scowled ferociously. "I never laid eyes on you afore."

"Not in my present persona, agreed," Holmes was filling his pipe from the tobacco pouch he had located within the Admiral's drawer, "But I daresay," he rammed down tobacco, "you recall Patrick Altamont?" He looked up at Heaney and laid a finger on his chin where he had once grown that horrible goatee.

Heaney started violently, his face turning to the colour of unwashed linen. "Altamont!" his voice was a croak, "No, no, it's not possible - Altamont died, he died, d'you hear? He was run down in the street - I talked to people who saw him laid out."

"They were well paid to say so." Sherlock Holmes drew on his pipe and puffed out a cloud of smoke. Captain Hall waved at the exhalation distastefully. "Yes," Holmes ignored him, "it was necessary for Altamont to die - he had outlived his usefulness, but we have no time to waste on that now. I have some questions to put to you, Heaney, or would you prefer to be called Mallen?"

Heaney's jaw set stubbornly. "You'll get nothing out of me," he growled.

"We'll see," Holmes responded imperturbably. "Meanwhile, Blinker, would you feel I was stepping out of line if I were to suggest the last load of coal put aboard the *Mauretania* might be well worth investigating?"

CHAPTER XXI

"We found twenty-five of these beauties, Holmes, effectively disguised as lumps of coal, believe it or not!" Captain Hall did not even try to hide his exultation as he held up a thin copper desk. "From what you tell me I judge the ship would have been two days at sea before the explosion occurred." He added soberly, "We owe you a great deal, Holmes."

"Not to me but to Miss Every," Sherlock Holmes corrected him quietly. "I hope you people will remember that when the time comes to draw up the balance sheet for this strange affair."

"Of course, of course," Captain Hall agreed absently, then he looked sharply at my friend. "But we are not yet out of the wood, nor shall be until Harrison and the Foster woman are safely behind bars," his shoulders were bowed and his voice wore disconsolate than I ever heard it as he said, "They could be anywhere by now, Holmes, and we lack the manpower to make a proper search."

"Then," Sherlock Holmes turned his head to look at the manacled, glowering figure of Heaney, who sat in his corner, guarded by two stalwart ratings, "we shall have to persuade our friend here to tell us where to look."

"Fat chance!" Heaney sneered.

Holmes gave him a pitying look. "I fear you do not know me as well as you think you do, Heaney," he said in a mild voice, "It is true that I am not normally a violent man, but, as my friend Watson here can testify, I have been known to suspend my principles when the occasion seemed to warrant it - as Dr Grimsby Roylott of Stoke Moran was to discover." His eyes not leaving Heaney's face, he reached into his pocket and drew from it a small lead cylinder, which he placed carefully on the table.

Sweat stood out in great drops on Heaney's forehead and trickled down his face. "You bastard, Holmes!" he gasped and writhed against his bonds like a man possessed.

Ignoring him, Sherlock Holmes looked at his watch and remarked to Captain Hall, "I estimate the acid will have eaten its way through the copper disk within an hour or even less, so you must be ready to evacuate the building very soon, Blinker."

"I certainly will!" Captain Hall declared with some vehemence. He glanced down at Heaney. "What about him?"

Sherlock Holmes shrugged. "He must take his chance," he said. "If he chooses, he can speak and live, or," his voice hardened, "he can experience in his own body the agonies suffered by those poor devils aboard the *Bulwark*."

"Poetic justice indeed!" Captain Hall gave my friend an admiring look that bordered on veneration. "Yet I must say I'm surprised to find someone like yourself willing to employ such methods, but I suppose you have now come round to my way of thinking that all's fair in love and war, eh, Holmes?"

"No, Hall!" Sherlock Holmes shot him an angry look, "All is not fair in war, as our German cousins will learn some day when their *schrechlikeit* is revealed for the barren, amoral doctrine it is, but there are five thousand men aboard the *Mauretania* and I have to weigh their lives against the existence of this miserable specimen here."

Heaney had been listening intently to this exchange and he now burst out, "You can't do this! It would be murder. I demand to be treated as a prisoner of war!"

Captain Hall looked at him incredulously and gave a short bark of laughter. "Prisoner of war! That's rich, coming from someone who helped to murder seven hundred men in cold blood."

"But that wasn't me!" Heaney's voice rose to a shriek. "Harrison planned it all. He's the man you want, not me!"

Sherlock Holmes half closed his eyes, saying with weary patience, "So you were only obeying orders, is that it, Heaney?"

"Yes. Yes!" Heaney was babbling now. "I only did as those two told me, Harrison and that bitch, Mrs Foster - they made all the decisions. I was never consulted, not once. You've got to believe me - I was a tool, nothing more."

Studying the lead cigar and once again glancing at his watch, Holmes asked quietly. "I suppose Harrison gave the order for O'Reilly to be killed?"

"He did indeed, sirs. He said O'Reilly knew too much and had, to be got out of the way, but I was to try and make it look like an accident. Sir, sir, as you're a Christian man, will you get me out of here? That thing's getting warm. I can feel the heat on my face."

"We can leave," Sherlock Holmes pressed his hands against the top of the desk, "as soon as you tell me where I can find Joseph Harrison."

Heaney gave a sob. "I can't, daren't-," he whispered, and Holmes levered himself to his feet. "Then I can do nothing for you," he observed quietly, "Come, Watson, there are not many minutes to go now, if my calculations are correct."

Taking me by the arm, he moved, towards the door.

Heaney screamed after me, "You're a doctor. You're supposed to save lives - help me, sir, please, please help me!" And he began to weep noisily.

I had been dreading this moment. Sherlock Holmes's warning on the train had not been an idle one: Heaney was striking at the very roots of my personal creed and it was hard to resist that anguished appeal, even from a man such as this. I tried to stiffen my resolve by recalling the dreadful fate of the *Bulwark*'s company and the fiery death planned for the helpless inmates of Briarbrae and after a moment I said quietly, "You have chosen your own path, Heaney, and it has led you to destruction. I cannot help you."

In the doorway, Sherlock Holmes paused to look back. "If you are going to speak, Heaney, you had better be quick. Time is running out for you."

No words can describe the terrifying malevolence in Heaney's eyes, "Damn you, Sherlock Holmes!" he cried. "May your soul burn in hell for this!"

Sherlock Holmes again consulted his watch and said nothing. With a moan Heaney sagged down in his chair like an ungainly sack of meal, the tears streaming down his face. In a hoarse, broken whisper he began to speak.

CHAPTER XXIII

"Faster, man, faster!" Captain Hall's voice fairly crackled with impatience as the great car surged along the road and screeched around corners on two wheels, the blazing headlamps erratically spearing the darkness, illuminating the high green banks on either side of us, glinting in the frightened eyes of the little wild creatures scattering in panic from the hurtling monster.

"Doing my best, sir." The naval driver was plainly a phlegmatic soul, which was just as well considering the speed we were going.

"Surely you can go quicker than that?" the Captain urged.

The driver negotiated a tricky bend. "We don't want an accident, now do we, sir?" he responded in his comfortable Devonian burr.

"No, nor do we want those devils to escape us!" Captain Hall exclaimed.

Sherlock Holmes leaned forward from the back seat to give his shoulder a reassuring pat, "Remember we have the advantage of surprise, Blinker," he said. "Harrison has no idea Heaney broke down under questioning, so he believes the *Mauretania* will set sail in complete ignorance of her deadly cargo. With any luck that will cause him to relax his guard."

"I only hope you're right," Captain Hall grunted as the car moaned round another corner. "Deuce take these country lanes!"

We were on our way to Hevening Hall,a large country house some miles along the coast from Avonmouth, where, according to Heaney, Joseph Harrison intended to remain until he could slip down-river behind the *Mauretania* in the motor-launch belonging to the owner of Hevening Hall, one Richard Straker, a reclusive man who had moved there in 1911. He had systematically discouraged all attempts by his nearest neighbours to cultivate his society and little was known about him except that he kept pigeons.

Bit by bit Holmes and Captain Hall had extracted the information they needed from the increasingly frantic Heaney. Yes, Mr Straker was a secret German sympathiser and it was through him that Joseph Harrison had learned so much about the *Mauretania* movements. No, he couldn't say who had first thought of sabotaging the vessel. All he knew was that Berlin had been enthusiastic, recognising at once the devastating blow to British morale if the *Mauretania* were to be lost so soon after the *Lusitania* tragedy. How did he know that? Well, Mr Straker had a clandestine radio transmitter. No, he didn't use it much - it was kept solely for emergencies. Normally Mr Harrison and Straker kept in touch by messenger pigeon.

"No doubt," Captain Hall said drily and immediately became very busy, firing off orders in all directions. He wanted a party of twenty ratings to go at once to Hevening Hall and surround the house. They would have to be skilled marksmen - and while they were about it, he wanted a tender to transport them there as well.

He also wanted a maxim gun positioned by the jetty where Straker's launch was kept, just in case Harrison had taken fright when Heaney failed to make contact and was already on the river. If it was true there was a German submarine coming to pick Harrison up, he intended to see to it that rendezvous was never made.

The purple-faced Admiral, much subdued after recent events, quickly agreed to every demand, and also promised to speak personally to Admiral Oliver in London, saying that the operation had his full blessing. From the relief in Captain Hall's face I realised that he had secretly been dreading the prospect of explaining himself to his formidable Chief.

Skilfully questioned by Sherlock Holmes, Heaney described the lay-out of Hevening Hall, the location of the boat house, the number of servants and so forth.

"Well, Heaney," Holmes said at last, "you have been a great help to us, albeit unwillingly, and I am grateful, I make no promises, but you may rest assured your cooperation will be known in the right quarters."

Captain Hall overheard and broke off his talk with the Admiral to say, "I wouldn't have taken you for a sentimentalist, Holmes. There is only one thing to be done with a traitor and that is to hang him."

For the first time Heaney took his eyes off the lead cigar and said fiercely to the Captain, "I'm no traitor, blast you! I did what I did for the sake of a free Ireland and," his eyes glowed with a fanatic fire "I'd do the same again!"

Sherlock Holmes gave a sigh, "Do you really believe Germany would prove a better master than England? Do you know nothing of the treatment meted out to the unfortunate Belgians?" He held up his hand before Heaney could interrupt. "I am not going to defend this country's record in Ireland, Heaney, no sane man could, but you should remember the old saying about the frying pan and the fire."

Heaney gave an unlovely grin. "We have a saying too," he said softly. "My enemy's enemy is my friend, You can put that in your pipe and smoke it, Mr Clever Holmes - and now for the love of God," his voice cracked, "will you take that cursed thing away from me? I'm a dead man anyway, but I'd just as soon not be roasted to death."

Those were my sentiments as well, but I managed to hold my tongue - just. Sherlock Holmes gave Heaney a thoughtful look and then a slow smile broke over his face.

"There was never any chance of that, Heaney," he said and. picking up the lead `cigar', he tore off the cap, ignoring the sounds of consternation that greeted his action, and spilled the contents on the Admiral's old-fashioned desk.. I have to confess my spine tingled and a pang of fear pierced me like an arrow, while Heaney lolled forward in a dead faint.

"Really, Holmes," said I, "was that necessary?" For once he appeared somewhat abashed, "I fear, Watson, I have never quite outgrown my instinct for the dramatic - my French blood. no doubt. I assure you, gentlemen, we were never in the smallest danger. The tube contained nothing but plain ordinary tap-water."

"A crude piece of theatre, Holmes." Captain Hall's normally ruddy face had turned rather pale.

Sherlock Holmes bowed his head. "*Peccavi,* Blinker," he said in a penitent voice, "*mea culpa, mea maxima culpa*. But after all," his eyes twinkled," it did persuade Heaney to speak, did it not?"

For once Captain Hall could find nothing to say.

I smiled quietly to myself inside the car. Although I did not wholly approve of Captain Hall - men of such utter ruthlessness have never held much appeal for me - I must confess I thoroughly enjoyed his occasional sparring matches with Sherlock Holmes. With the possible exception of Inspector (now Chief Superintendent) Baynes of the Surrey Constabulary, my friend had never encountered his equal, but Captain Hall was very much in a class by himself and I am certain Holmes was aware of it,

After a few more miles he asked, "At what o'clock precisely is the *Mauretania* due to pass?"

"Just after high water." Captain Hall peered at his watch. "But I wonder if Harrison will be such a fool as to hang about now? He must realise Heaney has been taken and that the area will soon be swarming with our security people. Why take such an appalling risk?"

"Vanity, Blinker - the Achilles heel of all the truly great criminals," Sherlock Holmes responded. "In my experience, vanity has sent more felons to the gallows than any other weakness."

We had reached open countryside by now and the car flashed by fields and hedgerows, all silvery in the moonlight by gleaming stretches of water and here and there the twinkling lights of an isolated farm-house or cottage, where, no doubt, the innocent inhabitants were sleepily preparing themselves for bed, without a notion that the greatest detective of all time, accompanied by the formidable Director of Naval Intelligence was hastening past to capture a notable traitor.

Captain Hall struck a match and endeavoured to study the map. "We are almost at Farley," he said and swore as the match burned his fingers. "In a few minutes we shall be outside Hevening Hall." He added with a chuckle. "The house stands on a cliff above an inlet called Dove Bay. I hope you appreciate the irony, Holmes?"

"I may, but I doubt if Harrison will," said Holmes and his eyes glinted in a way that boded no good for his quarry. I cleared my throat. "You know your own business best, of course, Captain, but would you mind telling me just how you propose to lay hands on Harrison? The man's not such a fool that he won't have posted look-outs."

"Upon my word, Watson, you are in coruscating form tonight!" Sherlock Holmes murmured in my ear.

Captain Hall was spared the necessity of trying to think of an answer by the car stopping with such a violent jerk that we were once again sent sprawling. A face materialised at the side window.

"Lieutenant Villars reporting for duty, sir!" A gold ringed arm snapped up in a smart salute. Peering beyond the young officer I glimpsed a high brick wall with a military tender parked beside it, headlights extinguished.

"Good." Captain Hall got out of the car. "Now, Villars, have any of your people approached the house?"

"No, sir," the voice was slightly aggrieved, "Our orders were to wait until you arrived."

"Excellent. Then assemble your men and let us draw our covert."

In the glare of the headlights his eyes were like shafts of

darkness above the high-bridged nose and ruthlessly smiling mouth. Although Joseph Harrison deserved and got no sympathy from me, I did not care for the savage note in the Captain's voice. Even in wartime I felt we had a duty to remember we were men and not barbarians.

After conferring briefly with the naval party, Captain Hall returned to us. "We're going in," he said briefly and already the heavily-armed men were spilling out of the tender, their boots clattering on the macadamised road. "You two had better stay her. I'm not anticipating that any of Straker's crowd will try to break out this way - they'll regret it if they do - but I'd better leave the driver with you, just in case."

"How kind." Sherlock Holmes got out of the car and stretched himself. "But I believe I can speak for Watson, too, when I say that, having come so far, we would prefer to see this business through to the end, eh, Doctor?"

"Most certainly," I said as I scrambled out to join him. My blood was already tingling with the prospect of danger and, unconsciously, my hand strayed towards my trusty old service revolver.

"Come now, Holmes," Captain Hall was trying hard not to let his irritation show, "you have done wonderfully well so far, I admit, but you simply must hand over to the professionals now. The men in that house are armed and dangerous."

"Quite so," Holmes agreed promptly, "and you are going to need every pair of hands you can get, Unless," he added pointedly, "you want Harrison to make fools of the Navy a second time."

"My God, Holmes, that was below the belt!" Captain Hall said angrily, then he shrugged. "Oh, very well, come if you must, but don't blame me if you end up with a bullet in your stomach." And he turned his back, making it clear he washed his hands of us.

"Hm," said Sherlock Holmes, watching the naval party move off down the drive towards the house. "I feel quite sure, Watson, that blaming Hall will not be my main preoccupation if such an unhappy fate were to befall me." His voice softened. "Well., old friend, we are going into action again and, not for the first time, the outcome is far from certain. No regrets, Watson?"'

"How can you ask?" I said. "I told you once before, it is my greatest joy and privilege to help you."

He gave a curt nod, then reverted to his normal half-humorous, half-cynical vein with which he normally screened his deeper emotions. "Come then, Watson! The game's afoot! Let's go and catch our Tiger!"

The drive up to Hevening Hall was bordered on either side by a dense tangle of shrubbery which I could see had been allowed to run riot over the years so that laurestinus fought with rhododendron and acuba for a modicum of light. As we moved forward cautiously I could hear the steady tramp of marching feet.

"Like a herd of elephants!" Sherlock Holmes exclaimed in disgust. "Hall should have telegraphed Straker to let him know we were coming!"

"My dear Holmes," I said, "surely you realise that to the service mind that is the main element of a surprise attack?"

He gave one of his rare laughs: then, quickly becoming serious again, he said, "All the same think it would be better if we were to pursue our own line, Watson, as we have so often in the past. Follow me now and be careful to make no noise."

He melted silently into the shrubbery and I followed, putting my feet down with the fabled delicacy of King Agag, but my precautions were hardly necessary, given the noise Hall's contingent were making, particularly when they reached the gravel sweep in front of the Victorian house with its absurd pepper-pot turrets and dismal Roman-style portico running along the façades. None of the windows showed a light and no sound reached my ears, not even when the sailors crouched down, their rifles trained on the front door.

"I don't like it, Holmes," I breathed uneasily.

"Too quiet for you, Watson?"

'Yes." My military instincts had led me to anticipate an ambush and now, despite the continuing silence, I was unconvinced that Hevening Hall was as deserted as it appeared and the hairs rose on the nape of my neck as I became aware that unseen eyes were watching me.

In the wavering half moonlight I could make out the humped forms of the young sailors, waiting for Captain Hall to give the signal to advance, but Holmes had disappeared and though I strained my ears to catch the slightest sound, I heard nothing until he suddenly appeared beside me. whispering, "Hall has posted more men round the back of the house. Let us hope it will be enough."

"Quiet!" Like a dim wraith Captain Hall passed us, a loud-hailer to his lips, "Joseph Harrison!" Weirdly magnified his voice boomed across the night, "Joseph Harrison! Richard Straker! The house is surrounded! I command you to surrender in the King's name!"

Even before that appallingly magnified voice died into silence, I heard the tinkle of broken glass and a tongue of flame stabbed the darkness, followed by a loud report. Slivers of bark flew aloft from the shrubbery not ten paces away, from me. With a cry, a sailor staggered to his feet, hands clapped to his face, blood running between his fingers.

As though the first shot had been some kind of signal, gunfire now crackled from every window in the long façade, which suddenly blossomed smoke and flame. Many of the shots went wide, but once a draught of air passing over my scalp told me that one man at least knew what he was doing. However, it was my duty to aid the poor fellow who had been injured if I possibly could and I started to crawl towards him.

Instantly, strong hands flung me face-down in the soaking grass and a pair of sinewy knees drove into my back, pinning me to the ground, "Not likely, Watson!" hissed the well-known voice. "Leave it to Hall. I can't afford to lose my Boswell just yet."

"Holmes, I really must insist-" I began and fell silent as Captain Hall's men opened fire and the battle began to rage in earnest.

For a while the defenders of Hevening Hall managed to hold their own, but eventually the weight of numbers and the accuracy of the return fire began to tell and one by one the guns inside the house fell silent, Sherlock Holmes relaxed his grip sufficiently for me to see the Captain's party storm the front door.

Captain Hall had lost his cap, his fluffy hair stood up on end; I heard him laugh in sheer exhilaration as he leapt across the threshold, his men pouring after him.

Dismissing them from my mind I got up to go and tend the casualty, who still lay on the grass, uttering piteous groans. A swift examination revealed that the bullet had done no more than crease his scalp and the wound, though deep and painful was not serious. I improvised a hasty bandage while inside Hevening Hall the Captain and his party rushed from room to room, looking for Joseph Harrison and his adherents.

They found only terrified servants and the body of a man, who the portly butler insisted, his jowls quivering with fright, was his master, Richard Straker himself.

"No sign of the woman, then?" Sherlock Holmes frowned, rubbing his chin thoughtfully.

"None," Hall gestured towards the group of prisoners emerging from the house under guard. "The servants insist Harrison left the house at noon, accompanied by Mrs Foster. Since then nothing has been heard of them. However, Straker's motor launch is missing from the boathouse, so he must be out there, Holmes, lying in wait for the *Mauretania*, of course. Unfortunately it is too dark to mount a proper search for him. There are so many inlets along this stretch of the river, it would take a day to search them and we haven't the time, or the manpower, I fear."

One of the ratings brought up his cap. Seizing it from him, Captain Hall put it on, remarking, "Much as I hate to say it, Holmes, Harrison appears to have got clean away."

"Unless," said Holmes, "you get the inshore patrols to intercept?"

"Not possible," Captain Hall said regretfully. "None of them are equipped with wireless, so we have no means of contacting them." He grimaced. "Few realise how thinly our reserves have been stretched since this War began. Luckily the Germans don't know it either."

"Quite so." That Sherlock Holmes's thoughts were concentrated elsewhere showed in his next question. "Blinker, is it possible you have a really powerful searchlight among your equipment?"

"No - only my Very pistol."

"Then that will have to do, let us go and see if by any chance we can force Harrison to reveal his whereabouts. Oh, yes," a sudden thought appeared to strike him, "and could you find out which are the strongest swimmers in your party?"

Captain Hall gave him a sharp look, but he made no comment as he gave the necessary orders.

The gardens at the back of Hevening Hall were as neglected as the drive and our party were forced to skirt overgrown box hedges and to descend flights of crumbling steps or wade across ornamental pools covered in green scum to get to the water's edge. Just below the first terrace our way led past a fantastically gabled pigeon-house where our movements caused much agitated flapping of wings.

"Evidently," said Sherlock Holmes, "the late Mr Straker was not as ruthless or not as thorough as Joseph Harrison. When we have time it would be interesting to learn what information has been conveyed here by these feathered mercuries. Meanwhile-"

Meanwhile it would take to long to detail that hazardous scramble through Mr Straker's gardens, so I will pass over the treacherous pebble sliding under the foot, the unseen flight of steps, the plunge into the unexpected lily-pond, and merely say that we arrived at the boathouse a few minutes later, panting breathlessly and, in my own case, with severely bruised shins and soaking trouser-legs.

The boathouse resembled the rest of Straker's property in futile over-elaboration. A few yards away the river flowed like black oil, eddying against the landing stage with a rhythmic suck and slap, which, together with the characteristic smell of river-mud, strongly reminded me of the hunt years ago for Jonathan Small and his dwarfish companion among the Thameside wharves.

"Well?" Captain Hall demanded. "What now, Holmes?"

"We will have to be very quiet," my friend answered in a repressive voice, "otherwise we shall lose our only chance of finding Harrison."

Watched in silence by the rest of us, he pivoted slowly on his heel, listening intently, one hand cupped to his ear. I tried to copy him but my hearing was dull compared to his and now the moon's face was temporarily hidden behind a drifting blanket of cumulus, I could see little but flowing water and the dark silhouettes of my companions. Somewhere in the distance a dog was barking.

Holmes broke his self-imposed silence to say, "A neat little problem, Watson. Tell me, what would you do now, were you in Harrison's shoes?"

"I think I should make a run for it." I answered frankly.

"Without waiting for the *Mauretania* to screen you?"

"Yes, Holmes, I feel that would be taking too much of a chance. Heaney's failure to appear must surely have convinced Harrison that his loyal servant has been caught and possibly forced to speak. I believe he will make a bolt for it."

"Excellently reasoned, Watson. Very well. Blinker, have your men place their maxim gun at the end of the jetty? Yes, good. And now have the kindness to fire your Very pistol."

The single white star soared into the darkened sky, its reflection dancing on the small wavelets that lapped against the wooden piles of the jetty and gleaming on the brass fixtures of a trimly built launch rocking quietly on the swell a few yards away from us.

There was an instant of shocked silence before the engine frantically revved and a bizarre figure in a long grey dress emerged from the wheelhouse, its arms upraised shrieking curses; I took it to be Mrs Foster. At the same moment the machine-gun commenced its angry chatter.

The launch yawed this way and that, jinking like a hare, as Harrison sought to evade the all-too-accurate gunfire. Chips of wood were gouged from her sleek sides and a section of railing cartwheeled into the air before it fell into the water with a splash. A second star from the Very pistol bloomed against the night sky. Miraculously, the small craft managed to keep going in spite of the damage inflicted by the machine-gun and every second increased the distance between her and ourselves.

"We've lost her!" Captain Hall groaned, but at that moment their engine uttered a coughing grunt and died; the launch began to drift on the current. Joseph Harrison emerged from the wheelhouse to shake his fist at us. Making a funnel of his hands, he screamed, "Too late, Mr Clever Holmes! The tide will carry me downriver and there's not a thing-"

What else he intended to say we never knew, for of a sudden his voice was overwhelmed in a great roar like the rushing of many rivers at the flood and a vast dark shape loomed suddenly against the sky. To us watching on shore, it was as though a mighty cliff had broken away and floated downstream, but to those like Sherlock Holmes who had many times watched her coming majestically to her berth, it could only be the *Mauretania,* with her beautiful, knife-edged bows and four towering funnels pouring black smoke; the *Mauretania,* racing downriver to the open sea with more than five thousand souls aboard her and the death of a beautiful sister to avenge.

At the last minute the moon broke free of the clouds and I saw the great vessel bearing down on the crippled launch lying directly in her path. The officers on her dimly-lighted bridge must have seen, must have realised that within seconds a collision would become inevitable, yet the *Mauretania* held relentlessly to her course, obeying Admiralty injunctions not to stop for any reason whatsoever; and so it was that she struck the lighter vessel full amidships, like a hand flapping at a tiresome wasp. Transfixed with horror, I saw the launch flying, keel uppermost, across the moon and then she curved down steeply to hit the water with a resounding crash that sent white fountains of spray leaping all about her as she disappeared from sight, taking with her Joseph Harrison and that strange, cold-hearted woman, Mrs Foster.

Then the *Mauretania* too had gone, the roar of her engines diminishing into silence, her trailing scarves of smoke already dispersing.

Not unexpectedly, it was Captain Hall who first broke the silence. "Well, Holmes," he said, "once again the country is in your debt."

"And in Miss Every's," Sherlock Holmes said firmly. "I hope you are going to remember your obligations to her also."

"Oh, certainly," Captain Hall responded. "How can you doubt it, Holmes? I gave her my word, did I not?"

But to me his words had a hollow ring and I wished, not for the first time, that I could see into his mind.

CHAPTER XXIII

The next day Sherlock Holmes and I joined the crowd waiting to attend the Board of Trade into the loss of the steamship *Lusitania* at Central Hall, Westminster. Among them were several in deep mourning; survivors from the wreck, I assumed, or relatives of those who had died; many of them, no doubt, in full agreement with the First Class passenger who had openly blamed the ship's Captain and officers for the many deaths.

I looked from them to the small, self-conscious group standing out-side the main doors, surmising, correctly as it turned out, that these must be the *Lusitania*'s surviving officers. In court I later identified the fellow in the straw boater and bright blue suit as Mr Jones, the First Officer, and Mr Bestic, the Junior Third - a great friend of David McCormick's, in tweed jacket and cap. Mr Lewis, the handsome Third Officer, was nervously chain smoking, lighting one cigarette from the stub of another.

To me they seemed as fine and decent a set of young men as one might find anywhere, but would they be a match for the brilliance of Sir Edward Carson, the biting wit of Sir Frederick Smith? That indeed was a question to ponder.

Big Ben had just struck ten o'clock, the last booming note dying away, merging into the never-ceasing rumble of the traffic, when the crowd stirred and there was a ripple of - how shall I describe it - Shock? Anger? as a gleaming limousine drew up beside the pavement and the burly figure of Captain Turner emerged, followed by the slighter form of Alfred Booth. My first thought was how much Turner had aged since our brief encounter in Liverpool such a short time ago: there were deep trenches below his eyes and his face was grey; my second was that here stood a man who had already given up hope; I had seen men look like that in Afghanistan.

I was about to remark to Holmes on the change when I was jostled roughly aside by a hatchet-faced woman who stepped in front of Captain Turner, impeding his path. A gasp went up from the crowd as she pressed a white feather into his hand. The Captain's shoulders slumped, but he said nothing and merely bowed gravely to her before he went inside the building. Alfred Booth followed, clearly furious.

"Upon my word, Holmes!" I exclaimed. "That was unnecessary.

Surely Turner has already had enough to bear."

"Ah, yes, Watson," said he, "to me these great public trials have always had much in common with the gladiatorial displays of Ancient Rome. But come, the doors are opening and people are going inside."

Over the next few days I came to know very well the lofty chamber where Lord Mersey, a plump man of scholarly countenance, sat on a raised dais with his Assessors. In front of him were the Press benches and the witness stand. Trestle tables accommodated counsel for the Board of Trade, Cunard and Captain Turner.

Behind them sat the legal representatives of the passengers and crew and those members of the public who had been able, like Holmes and myself, to gain entrance. As I say, the scene has been printed very clearly on my memory and if I shut my eyes I can still see that room where the final act in the tragedy of the *Lusitania* was to be played out.

I was interested to see Lord Mersey, of whom I had heard so much, and found it difficult to credit that this apparently amiable man, whose benevolent expression was enhanced by a pair of golden pince-nez, could have the reputation of one of the most feared judges to sit upon the Bench. Certainly he had been very harsh towards Captain Lord of the *Californian* during the *Titanic* Inquiry, but then, I thought to myself, he might well have had access to information which had been withheld from the general public. Of course, I did not know that it would have been impossible for Lord Mersey to approach the present Inquiry with a completely open mind, since he had been constantly bombarded with letters from the Admiralty, all of them blaming Turner, from the day his appointment was announced.

Today he was flanked on either side by his Assessors, two from the Royal Navy and two from the Merchant Marine. In a stage whisper, Holmes, who had long made it his business to know things of which others were ignorant, informed me that the imposing Admiral Sir Frederick Inglefield, the chief Assessor for the Royal Navy, had previously been in command of the Auxiliary Coastal Patrol Forces.

"You understand, of course, what that means, Watson?"

"No, Holmes, I fear I do not," I answered, frankly baffled.

"Why, man, is it not obvious?" he cried. "Inglefield will in effect be sitting in judgement on the fate of the very ship his own patrols failed to protect!"

Inglefield's appointment was a blow to our hopes of a fair hearing, of course, but for my own part I had been encouraged to learn that the second Naval Assessor, Lieutenant Commander H J Hearn, was himself a submariner and would therefore have some understanding of the odds confronting Captain Turner.

Butler Aspinall had turned to look at Holmes, spreading his hands slightly, as if to indicate that nothing had yet come from Captain Hall. He seemed to be about to speak, but before he could do so the doors at the rear of the court opened again to admit a tall man in a black frock coat, who strode purposefully down the aisle and took his seat at the table directly facing Lord Mersey.

I knew instantly who he was; those craggy features had long been familiar to those of us who had followed his spectacular career at the Bar over the years, ranging from the defence of the Marquis of Queensberry in the Oscar Wilde libel action to his long and successful campaign to vindicate the young naval cadet, Archer-Shee, of the charge of stealing a five shilling postal order; it would be true to say that Sir Edward Carson had, achieved the status of becoming a legend in his own lifetime.

With Carson's appearance the atmosphere in the crowded hall had become charged with expectancy, almost as though an invisible curtain had lifted to display the brilliantly-lighted stage. However, Sir Edward ignored the air of suppressed excitement. With a quick bow to Lord Mersey, he sat down, shot back his cuffs and began to examine some papers.

Settling his pince-nez firmly on his nose in the manner of a man who does not intend to stand any nonsense from anyone, Lord Mersey rapped his gavel for silence.

"If you are quite ready, Sir Edward?"

The Inquiry had begun.

***

I trust my readers will forgive a somewhat scrappy account of the trial, but I have to say at the outset that I was not even present for much of it, since some of the matters discussed were considered too sensitive for the general public to know about and from time to time we would all be asked to leave while Lord Mersey and his Assessors heard that part of the evidence in camera.

In between leaving the hall and returning again I observed Captain Turner very closely. He appeared to lean very much on Butler Aspinall, who was said to be a master at drawing out a shy or difficult witness, but I believed even he was going to have a hard job in showing Turner at his best, since the Captain had retreated into sullen silence, plainly thinking there was no justice to be found: for him here, and answered all questions in monosyllables. I have to admit his suspicions were not baseless, for the questioning of Robert Leith, the Senior Wireless-Officer, showed very quickly the way Carson and Smith were determined the trial should go.

The question, of course, was crucial: had the *Lusitania* or had she not been ordered to divert into Queenstown? If Butler Aspinall could prove she had, then much of the case against Turner fell to the ground. However, Sir Edward Carson knew that just as well as Aspinall and his examination of Leith was a masterpiece of subtlety. (Naturally, there was to be no mention of any signal from Admiral Coke in Queenstown, nor was the Admiral himself to be called as a witness.) Instead Sir Edward asked mildly, "On Friday morning of the 7th you received two Government messages?"

Leith hesitated, looking apologetically at Captain Turner, then he said, "Yes," in a low voice.

"Which were from a wireless coast station?" Carson pressed in his strong Irish brogue.

Leith again answered, "Yes."

"The first was about ll:30?"

"Approximately," Leith emphasised the word strongly, but he was given no chance to point out that David McCormick and not he had been on duty that morning, for Sir Edward said quickly, "And the other arrived shortly after one o'clock?"

"Yes," Leith was pale and angry now.

Sir Edward turned away from him to address Lord Mersey. "There is no dispute, if your Lordship remembers the evidence. I just want to confirm it."

'If you remember the evidence', I thought, but this is supposed to be the first time Lord Mersey has heard of it. What sort of unbiased inquiry is this?

Beside me Sherlock Holmes was biting his lip. "Come, Watson, this won't do," he said, when Lord Mersey called the next recess. "I hear Carson intends putting Turner on the stand this afternoon and after what we have just heard it is clear the poor devil has no adequate defence. I must say I am disappointed in Hall. It was not a gentlemanly act to give his word to Miss Every and then break it."

"Of course," I said thoughtfully, as we followed in the wake of the crowd straggling out of the hall, "she has his signed letter."

"And will never use it, Watson," Holmes said decidedly. "Blinker Hall is a shrewd judge of character and he knew quite well Miss Every was not the type to expose him in public, that is why he gave her his written promise. Ah, Aspinall," he greeted the Captain's learned counsel, "how is it going in your opinion?"

"Need you ask, Holmes?" Butler Aspinall's expression was harassed. "Mersey has taken a dislike to Turner, I can tell by the way he looks at the man - and small wonder after Carson's performance this morning. I tell you, gentlemen, Captain Turner will be fortunate not to lose his Master's Certificate unless I can prove he was ordered into Queenstown. If I don't Carson and F E are going to make mince-meat of him for sailing in a straight line off the Old Head of Kinsale, taking a four point bearing when he ought to have been steering a zigzag course."

"None of the other ships torpedoed in the area was doing so," Sherlock Holmes remarked. "They had no reason to as the relevant instructions had not been issued at the time."

Butler Aspinall smiled rather bitterly, "People have short memories," he said. "In the aftermath of the *Lusitania* disaster every schoolboy knows zigzagging is the proper tactic to adopt in an area infested by submarines. Dates mean nothing in such a case."

Holmes drew him aside from a couple of men trying to get past. "Then how do you propose to defend Turner?" he asked.

"He is going to say that he needed to fix his position after crossing the Atlantic on dead reckoning," Butler Aspinall replied. "It is a thin defence, but the only one possible in the absence of the signal ordering him into Queenstown. Excuse me, gentlemen, I have to get back to my client."

Sherlock Holmes watched his departing figure for a moment before turning back to me. "I think, Watson, it is time we took a hand in the matter. If Hall will not produce the signal, then we shall have to speak with the only man who can - I mean Admiral Coke himself."

So saying he steered me rapidly out of the building and signalled to a cab.

"But where are we going, Holmes?" I demanded.

He paused on the step of the vehicle. "To the Diogenes Club, Watson," he said. "Where else?"

CHAPTER XXIV

Sherlock Holmes once described the Diogenes Club as the most exclusive club in London and he certainly was not exaggerating, given that its membership consisted of the most unsociable and unclubbable men in London. The rules were strict and at first I was frankly incredulous when Holmes insisted, straight-faced, "No member is permitted to take the least notice of any other one. Save in the Stranger's Room, no talking is, under any circumstances, allowed, and three offenses, if brought to the notice of the committee, render the talker liable to expulsion." He added, smiling, "My brother was one of the founders and I have myself found it a very soothing atmosphere."

I had rarely encountered Mycroft Holmes during my association with his formidable brother, but on the occasions we had met I was conscious that this corpulent, self-confessedly slothful man possessed the same mental faculties as the younger and that Sherlock had probably not exaggerated to claim that his brother 'occasionally is the British Government'. The news that Holmes intended to recruit him to our cause ought to have cheered me, and yet...

"Do you truly believe he can help?" I asked as our cab rattled through Hyde Park Gate. "Given that the Admiralty appear to have such a strong case I would have thought it only to likely your brother would refuse to become involved."

Sherlock Holmes gazed moodily at the passing traffic. "Well, well, we shall soon find out," he said at length, "and I tell you truly, Watson, this is the last throw of the dice. If this fails, our case is lost."

The entrance to the Diogenes Club stands some distance from the Carlton in Pall Mall and I suppose I have passed through the portals a dozen times in my life. One each occasion I have been struck anew by the cathedral-like atmosphere of the place, so that one's very footsteps ringing across the marble hallway strike one as a solecism, an affront to those worthy gentleman who sat about in leather armchairs in the Members' Room, most perusing newspapers, each marooned in his chosen oasis of silence. I could not see Mycroft Holmes anywhere.

As in former years, Holmes conducted me to the Strangers' Room and left me there for a few moments while he departed in search of his brother.

When they entered the room together I hastily composed my expression so as to hide the shock I felt. Always a corpulent man, Mycroft Holmes was now a gross figure who was forced to lean upon a stick as he made his way painfully towards me, holding out a swollen hand in greeting. I did not care for the sound of his breathing, nor for the bluish tinge to his complexion which hinted at mortal sickness. Well, it was to be expected, I supposed; Mycroft Holmes was in his sixty-eighth year and I did not imagine he was the type to retire, any more than his brother.

"Well, Sherlock," he wheezed, "I was wondering how long it would be before you and Watson condescended to put in an appearance." With a grunt he lowered himself into the nearest of the armchairs, which had been positioned so as to look out over Pall Mall. "And how," he continued in an interested voice, "is the charming young lady who managed to set all the Admiralty buzzing like an overturned bee-skep. If I were younger, I believe I should very much like to make Miss Every's acquaintance, Sherlock." He gave a complacent smile.

"She is indeed an exceptional woman," Sherlock Holmes agreed, refusing to be baited by his brother. "Since you know so much about it, Mycroft, you must also realise why I have come here. I need your help."

"Of course you do," Mycroft Holmes said drily and added, "Hall came to see me yesterday, as a matter of fact, he sat in that very chair now occupied by yourself, Watson, and confided his distress that he had been compelled to go back on his word, but there it is. My masters - I imagine I need not name them to you - find it a matter of expediency to blame Turner."

"Expediency!" Sherlock Holmes repeated in disgust. He looked at Mycroft. "Can this really be you speaking, brother?"

Mycroft winced, took out his snuff box, thought better of it and returned it to his pocket. "No," he said, "you are quite right, of course, and something will have to be done, but you will have to give me time, Sherlock."

"How much time?" Holmes asked sharply.

Mycroft shrugged his enormous shoulders. "I really cannot say," he answered, "Call back here tomorrow and it may be that I will have some news for you."

***

"Mabel was here today, John," my wife informed me when I arrived home that evening. "The poor girl was in a dreadful state. I tried to calm her, but nothing I said was of any use." She hesitated before asking. "Are things really going so badly, John?"

"They're not good," I answered frankly. "Turner is a difficult witness, and at times his evidence is so muddled it is hard to make sense of it. For instance, he confessed today that he had read the Admiralty advice to zigzag in dangerous waters, yet when Aspinall re-examined him. it was quite clear he was thinking of a different set of instructions altogether, I was watching Lord Mersey at the time and I could see, he wasn't quite sure whether Turner was a traitor or simply a fool."

"Not an easy man to help then?" Violet suggested.

"Far from it!" I agreed, putting an arm round her shoulders as we went back into the drawing room. "To speak frankly, my dear, unless Mycroft Holmes can produce a miracle, our cause is lost."

Three days went by before we heard from Mycroft Holmes.

During that time, although Butler Aspinall strove manfully on behalf of his client, the Admiralty case was presented in such a way by Sir Edward Carson and Sir Frederick Smith as to seem well-nigh unanswerable. No one who looked at the bemused and isolated figure of Turner, sitting miserably behind Aspinall, or on the witness stand, his hands clenched at his sides, at bay among those he had clearly come to regard as his enemies, could have had, any doubt that, this man had been unfit to command.

To make matters worse, Lord Mersey was no longer troubling to hide his contempt and suspicion, at one point remarking while Captain Turner was giving evidence, "You see what these answers are worth when you test them. They are not worth much, anyway."

Only once did Turner hit back at Mersey and that was when he rapped out that he did not navigate a ship on guesswork; but for the most part it was a dismal experience to watch him faltering against the most brilliant advocates of the day and I was profoundly relieved when Holmes and I were summoned back to the Diogenes Club.

This time he was not alone when we entered the Strangers' Room. A fresh-faced man in a tweed suit more fitted for the country than the town sat in the chair by the window, directing an inquiring look at us with a pair of very bright blue eyes.

Mycroft Holmes waved a flipper-like hand in his direction. "Allow me to present Vice Admiral Sir Henry Coke, lately in command of the Auxiliary Patrol in Queenstown."

Open mouthed, I looked from Sir Henry to Sherlock Holmes who, for once, appeared equally taken aback.

"Mycroft?" he said in a questioning voice.

The elder brother shrugged. "You asked for my help, Sherlock, but for a while I could not see my way to it. Then I remembered Henry here was a former habitué of the Diogenes Club, so I arranged this meeting. For reasons of his own, Henry was happy to comply - is that not so?"

"Yes," the Admiral said shortly. "As Mycroft knows, my career has been wrecked by the *Lusitania* disaster. Immediately after it occurred I was ordered to haul down my flag and transferred to the reserve." He gave a wintry smile, "It is safe to assume this was a mark of their Lord-ships' displeasure. Well, there is nothing to be done about that, but," his voice grew more emphatic and he leaned forward, his face darkened by a heavy frown, "I will not stand idly by and watch a fellow seaman thrown to the wolves for a crime that was none of his doing. No, by God!"

His voice had risen almost to a shout and Mycroft Holmes looked nervously about him as if he feared the noise might reach the ears of other members of the club.

"Perhaps," Holmes suggested helpfully, "the Admiral might care to tell us what happened in his own words?"

Thus encouraged, Sir Henry Coke did just that, recounting in detail the steps he had taken to try and protect the *Lusitania* on 7th May. "I knew I would have to stick my neck out," he said gloomily, "but I had to do something, gentlemen. God knows what they thought they were up to in London - I just couldn't get any sense out of them, When I pointed out the ship was approaching very real danger, they insisted I should simply keep on sending the generalised warnings of submarine activity which had already been passed to Turner the night before. Admiral Oliver strictly forbade me to give him more detailed or up-to-date information."

"Why was that?" Sherlock Holmes's voice was sharp.

"The Admiralty were anxious the Germans should not find out we were monitoring their wireless signals in case it forced them to change their codes."

"Yes," Holmes said thoughtfully, "I can understand that very well, but it still does not explain why they so signally failed to protect the *Lusitania*."

"No, it does not," Admiral Coke agreed and took a deep breath. "That is why I decided, on my own initiative to bring her into Queenstown until I was absolutely certain the danger was passed."

He looked Holmes squarely in the face - tired, troubled man who had lived ever since with this nightmare. "As we now know my signal brought the *Lusitania* directly into the path of the torpedo which destroyed her. But for that," he added slowly, "she might still be afloat."

And that, I thought, was the key to the whole sad business: Admiral Coke's well-intentioned bid to protect the *Lusitania*.

"You have been remarkably frank with us, Admiral," said Sherlock Holmes, "but you still have not explained the persistent Admiralty denials that any such signal was ever sent to Captain Turner. Over and over again their Lordships have insisted that the *Lusitania* was not called into Queenstown. How do you account for that?"

"Service loyalty, Mr Holmes," the Admiral said curtly. "Among themselves they are ready enough to condemn me as a fool, but in public they will close ranks to protect a fellow seaman, if need be until the Last Judgement."

"But Captain Turner is a seaman too," I pointed out rather indignantly.

"Different club, Dr Watson," Admiral Coke's voice was apologetic, "Decent fellow and all that, but not one of the Grey Funnel Line, d'you see?"

"And yet you came here today," Sherlock Holmes reminded him. "Why was that?"

Coke avoided my friend's penetrating eyes, saying, "Because of what Mycroft told me about the *Bulwark* - and because, when it comes to the point, I find it sticks in my craw to make Turner a public scapegoat. I'm no saint, Mr Holmes, but neither, thank God, am I that kind of blackguard."

Nodding gravely, Sherlock Holmes looked at his brother, "Can anything be done at this late stage?" he asked. "Or will Mersey refuse to consider fresh evidence?"

"No, he won't do that," Mycroft Holmes assured him. "I have dined with him from time to time and I can tell you that, for all his finicky way he is a stickler for truth and a lover of justice. But first he would require to be convinced of any irregularity in the way in which the Admiralty case has been presented."

Sherlock Holmes remained lost in thought for a moment. Then he said, "Hall mentioned a copy of the signals sent to the *Lusitania* on the 7th, which had been forwarded from the wireless station in Valentia. Is that still in existence and if so where is it now?"

"Inglefield has it," Admiral Coke told him, adding with a faint smile, "I know what you're going to say, Mr Holmes, you want me to tell Mersey. Well, why not? Having come so far I can hardly balk at the last hurdle, eh?"

I never learned with what words Mycroft Holmes and Admiral Sir Henry Coke persuaded Lord Mersey of the extent to which the Admiralty had tried to mislead him, All I know is that, when he returned after the recess, the next day, his brows were knitted and his expression so grim that his Assessors stared at him in surprise.

However, he said nothing and listened, seemingly unmoved, while Sir Edward, Carson quizzed Captain Turner on his navigation - the way he emphasised the word was an urbane flicker of contempt - of the *Lusitania*.

Turner mumbled something and Carson promptly reverted to the question of zigzagging. Why had the *Lusitania* been sailing in a straight line when she was attacked? Turner looked at him and made no reply.

"He doesn't go out of his way to help himself, our worthy Captain," murmured Sherlock Holmes.

It was at this point that Lord Mersey suddenly leaned across to snatch Admiral Inglefield's bundle of papers. White-faced the Admiral tried to grab them back but desisted when he saw Mersey's expression. The Court became very still as Lord Mersey leafed rapidly through the pile of Admiralty documents, containing all the often-contradictory advices and suggestions which had been showered on Turner and other merchant captains since the beginning of the war. Finally he picked up the flimsy sheet which I presumed must be the celebrated copy of the signals sent from the Valentia wireless station and read through it, his face perceptibly darkening. At last he looked up. "Sir Ellis, will you approach the Bench, please?" his voice was cold.

Sir Ellis Cunliffe, solicitor to the Board of Trade, came forward, looking anxious. Lord Mersey selected two papers and held them out to him.

"I have here," he said, "two copies, supposedly full and complete of the wireless signals sent to the *Lusitania* on the morning of 7th May. As you can see, Sir Ellis, they differ in one important respect - this copy," he held up the one he had taken from Inglefield includes a signal in naval code which was sent to the *Lusitania* at two minutes past eleven, whereas this one does not. Now," he gave the unhappy lawyer a sweetly sarcastic smile, "perhaps you will be kind enough to tell me which of these two documents is correct. Silence!" he added sharply to the buzz of speculation that ran through the court-room. "Well, Sir Ellis?" Cunliffe hesitated, glancing nervously at Inglefield, whose face was now dark with fury. The other Assessors looked bewildered, the young submariner staring at Inglefield, the two merchant captains whispering among themselves. Reporters scribbled industriously.

"Well?" Lord Mersey repeated.

Sir Ellis said quietly, "Sir Frederick's copy is the correct one."

Instantly journalists sprang for their feet and made for the doors to contact their editors. But Lord Mersey had other ideas and sharply ordered the Court to be cleared. What pressure was exerted on the newspapers I cannot say, but it is certain not one of them reported the exchange between Lord Mersey and Sir Ellis Cunliffe.

Mycroft Holmes, a friend of Mersey's, afterwards told me that the Assessors were then asked to submit to His Lordship in writing their opinions as to whether or not the *Lusitania*'s Master could be held to blame in any way for the loss of the ship. Of the four only Admiral Inglefield, stubborn to the end, insisted on Turner's guilt. Lord Mersey's personal opinion can be divined from his resignation from the Bench immediately after the Inquiry as well as from a remark he made to Mycroft Holmes, "The *Lusitania* case," he said heavily, "was a damned dirty business."

After we had all been called back into the court-room Lord Mersey smilingly thanked his Assessors before giving his verdict and I confess I felt my heart beating faster as I listened to the measured tones.

"The conclusion at which I have arrived is that blame ought not to be imputed to the Captain. He exercised his judgement for the best. It was the judgement of a skilled and experienced man and he ought not in my opinion to be blamed." Mersey took off his pince-nez, adding rather savagely, "The whole blame for the cruel destruction of life in this catastrophe must rest solely with those who plotted and those who committed the crime."

"There you are!" the man in front of me commented. "A whitewash from beginning to end! Look at Booth grinning all over his face! He knows he's got away with it."

"Turner doesn't look too happy, though," his friend remarked.

"The poor chap seems to be in a bit of a daze. Must be quite a shock to find you can still walk away without a stain on your character after being put through the mill by Edward Carson."

He added with obvious relish. "Our noble Attorney-General does not look at all pleased."

Following the direction of his gaze, I watched Sir Edward tidying away his papers with quick, impatient fingers, But his annoyance was as nothing compared to the fury of Admiral Inglefield, who barely waited for Lord Mersey to leave the Court before striding out, looking neither to the right nor the left. The other Assessors followed more slowly, the two merchant captains nodding affably to Turner before they left.

The Captain was on his feet now, shaking hands with Butler Aspinall, who had done so much for him, and with Alfred Booth, for whom Mersey's verdict must have come as a tremendous relief, for had Turner been condemned, the mud would have stuck to Cunard as well, so I imagine relief must have accounted for some of the warmth of Alfred Booth's smile as he heartily shook the Captain's hand, while reporters surged round them, the questions coming thick and fast.

"Captain Turner, you must be a very happy man at this moment - would you mind telling us your immediate plans?"

"Captain, what are your feelings towards the submarine commander who sank your ship?"

"Captain Turner, while you were in the water did you think you were likely to be rescued?"

"Mr Booth, do your plans include a rôle for Captain Turner?"

A brief but telling pause followed the last question. Turner looked down at his feet. Alfred Booth said evasively, "My immediate plans, gentlemen, are to have a quiet dinner somewhere and recover from this eventful day."

Before he could be asked any more questions he opened the door of the limousine which had drawn up beside the pavement and stepped inside. Turner was about to follow him when Sherlock Holmes called his name.

He turned. "Who-?" he began.

Holmes interrupted him smoothly. "Explanations can wait until later on, Captain. I suggest we repair to the house of my friend here," he grinned at me, "and I will undertake to satisfy your very natural curiosity and that of Mr Booth as best I can."

Turner studied his face closely and I noticed that some of the life had returned to his expression. "Did you ever sail with me?"

"I did indeed, Captain, but I confess I am surprised you remember a mere steward from the Second Class," said Sherlock Holmes and Alfred Booth exclaimed, "My God, Tom, don't you recognise him? It's S-"

"Later, Mr Booth," Holmes climbed nimbly into the car and made room for me to sit beside him. "Well, Watson, what are you waiting for? Tell the chauffeur we want to go to Ealing."

I had asked Violet to prepare for six guests before leaving the house that morning, though I had not then felt able to say whether we would be having a celebration or a wake. Too nervous to come to Westminster in case the verdict went against Captain Turner, Mabel Every stayed behind to help her. The bruising had faded somewhat from her face now, but it was still very noticeable and when I asked her how she had accounted for her injuries to the Captain, she replied that she had claimed to have fallen in the street.

"You should have told him the truth," I said.

"No," she responded instantly, "I wouldn't want Thomas to feel he is under any kind of obligation to me."

"But my dear girl-"

"Please, Doctor, try to understand." She looked away from me. "Thomas is not free and I have had to learn to hold my tongue, other-wise I would have to give up being his housekeeper."

"Can you be satisfied with so little?" I said, marvelling.

"It is not little to me!" she flashed. "I have his friendship and that is a great deal." Her face clouded. "Or I did have it until I came to London. Now he must think I deserted him in his hour of need."

She had been naturally overjoyed when I hurried into the house to give her the good news, but the eager smile quickly died from her lips when Turner entered and stood looking at her in silence.

"Thomas," Mabel Every said softly.

Unsmiling, he nodded to her. "Hallo, Mabel." His manner was as cool as if he had been greeting a total stranger. Without speaking again, be followed Alfred Booth and Butler Aspinall into the drawing room. White with distress, Mabel Every took a step after him. I caught her by the arm.

"Give him time, Miss Every," I said, "This has been a terrible ordeal for him."

"It isn't that, Dr Watson," she blinked back tears. "I was afraid of this. He blames me for leaving him in the lurch."

"Then," Sherlock Holmes said briskly, divesting his brother of his hat and stick, "we shall have to tell the Captain the real reason for your departure from Liverpool, shall we not?"

Given the exigencies of wartime, I felt Violet had done very well to produce a passable cold collation and some fairly tolerable wine at such short notice. (The latter was in fact a gift from my colleague, Dr Armstrong, and was accompanied by a short note asking me how much longer he would be expected to look after my patients as well as his own. Needless to say, I intended to take the hint).

However, Violet might as well have spared her pains, for none of our guests displayed much appetite and soon plates were pushed aside while the company settled down to talk about the *Lusitania*, with Butler Aspinall saying to Holmes, "I don't know how you managed to do it, but it was a masterstroke to show Mersey how cleverly the Admiralty had tried to mislead him. But for that I am sure we would have heard a very different verdict today."

Mycroft Holmes smiled with brotherly pride, "it is not without reason that Sherlock has long been known as the last court of appeal."

Holmes said with uncharacteristic modesty, "In this particular case, Mycroft, it was your own intervention which turned the scale. However, I have to say," he looked at the silent Turner, "that our contribution was negligible beside that made by Miss Every here. Of course you could not know it, Captain, but this young lady would not rest until she had tracked me down, insisting that a great wrong was about to be done to a man whom she believed to be innocent."

He smiled. "As Watson has recorded, I am not an admirer of the fair sex, with certain notable exceptions - Irene Adler, it goes without saying, and a Miss Violet Hunter." He stared directly at my wife, who blushed. "Well, now I can add the name of Mabel Every to their number. For I tell you, Captain, that but for her this country would still be threatened, by a great and evil man and Aspinall would have lost his case today."

Before Turner could ask him what he meant, Holmes launched himself into a hasty narration of recent events, beginning with Miss Every's search for evidence among the *Lusitania*'s crew and her visit to my surgery armed with the same, which prompted me to send a wire to my friend, Holmes proceeding then to Captain Hall's intervention and the young woman's courageous mission to Briarbrae, the unmasking of Joseph Harrison, the part played by the *Mauretania* in his violent death.

Turner's eyes gleamed strangely at this and he murmured half to himself, "Yes, she would do that - she knew."

Everyone sitting round the table understood he was referring to the strange, almost mystical bond existing between a sailor and his ship, the stuff of legend through the ages. As a mere landlubber, I have an open mind about these things, but it is true that Turner had frequently captained the *Mauretania* and in that sense it seemed very fitting that she should have played her part in the demise of Joseph Harrison.

Turner was now looking at Mabel Every. "And you went through all that - for me?" he said in a wondering voice.

"I had to," she assumed a practical tone. "After all, no one at Cunard had ever met Mr Holmes, whereas we were - well, not exactly friends, but-" she hesitated, trying to think of the appropriate word.

"Acquaintances," Sherlock Holmes supplied with a sly sideways smile at me.

"Exactly!" said Miss Every. "So I was the obvious person to bring McCormick's journal to London, I'm sorry I had to burgle your study, Thomas," she added.

Turner dismissed that. "You might have been killed," he said. "Eh, lass, if I'd known-"

"That was why I couldn't tell. you, " she said, at which Turner got up rather abruptly and went out of the room. Mabel Every looked after him in dismay. "Let him be, Miss Every," Sherlock Holmes said gently. "All this must be somewhat overwhelming. He will come back when he is able."

Sure enough, Turner returned a few minutes later, a little paler than usual but perfectly composed. "I'll say one thing," he remarked to Sherlock Holmes, "I don't think a lot of your friend Captain Hall - putting Mabel here in danger and then breaking his word to her. That's not how a man should behave."

"I think," Holmes said reflectively, "that he probably had no choice in the latter instance. From what Admiral Coke told us, he was anxious to honour his promise to Miss Every, but he was up against a very powerful machine directed by Oliver, whose own part in this sorry business was far from glorious - do you not agree, Mycroft?"

"Maybe," Mycroft Holmes said, ever the civil servant, "I have to admit he did not do as much as he ought to protect the *Lusitania*."

"Certainly he did not, considering he had days to make up his mind and took absolutely no action at all," Sherlock Holmes's voice was scathing. "To my mind he ought to be removed from his post forthwith before more damage is done. I shudder to think what might happen if our ships were to become involved in a major action against the German fleet if Admiral Oliver is still in charge of the War Room."

Sherlock Holmes's foreboding was well justified. The following year, during the night of 31st May/1st June Captain Hall's department intercepted and deciphered no less than seven German signals indicating the whereabouts of the German Hochseeflotte. For reasons which have never been properly explained, the Admiralty failed to pass on any of them to Sir John Jellicoe, commanding the British Grand Fleet at Jutland, with the effect that the, German enemy was allowed to slip away under cover of darkness and a great opportunity was lost, which might well have shortened the War, As the man in charge of the War Room and thus directly responsible for supplying Jellicoe with the intelligence he needed, Admiral Oliver must take his share of the blame for what happened.

John Watson.

"Let us hope you are wrong, Sherlock," Mycroft Holmes was plainly uncomfortable with the direction the discussion was taking and his uneasiness was augmented when Butler Aspinall said, "Fine masters you serve, sir!" making no effort to hide the scorn he felt.

Mycroft Holmes shrugged his shoulders. "We did not make this War, Aspinall," he reminded the lawyer quietly, "but since it has been forced upon us we have to fight with whatever weapons come to hand, some of them not very pretty." He gave a rueful smile.

"I have been a government servant for many years, the corridors of Whitehall are more familiar to me than my own home, but I have to confess that at times even I feel at sea in this brave new world of ours." He sighed, "I daresay I am too old to adjust to current imperatives."

"And what are those imperatives?" Violet demanded softly.

With a faint edge in his voice Mycroft Holmes said, "Do I have to explain them to an intelligent woman like yourself, Mrs Watson? Very well, within the confines of these four walls I am prepared to admit that two men were guilty of failing to protect the *Lusitania* - Admiral Oliver and Captain Webb - but you will never get me to admit it in public."

"And that, of course," said his brother, "is the real *Lusitania* conspiracy - not the one hinted at by Tadpole Phelps, for I am satisfied in my own mind that there never was any British intention to sink the ship - what happened was a combination of sheer ill luck and stupidity as so many catastrophes are - but there certainly was a concerted effort by everyone at the Admiralty from Winston Churchill and Lord, Fisher down to conceal their own failures and heap all the blame upon one man, Captain Turner."

Mabel Every said excitedly, "If Thomas were to offer his story to the newspapers, you and your colleagues would look very silly, Mr Holmes."

Mycroft Holmes gazed in alarm at the fierce, troubled girl. "I very much hope you will do nothing of the kind, Miss Every!" he exclaimed. "The effect on American public opinion were such a story to get out could well be disastrous. Besides," although his lips smiled his eyes did not. "I would not care to see such a charming young lady as yourself confined at Donnington Hall!" Although he spoke as in jest, I could tell he meant every word.

"Mycroft..." Sherlock Holmes began and his brother turned on him. "I shall require your guarantee as well, Sherlock," he announced. "Nothing of this affair must be spoken of outside these four walls."

"I see," his brother leaned back in his chair.his chin pointing at the ceiling, "and just how do you propose to enforce all this, Mycroft?"

"I do not make idle threats," Mycroft Holmes said quietly, "and in your own case, Sherlock, you have much to answer for breaking into confidential Admiralty files, inveigling old colleagues into disclosing matters that were meant to be kept secret, trading on your reputation so as to ride roughshod over established procedures." He shook his head in mock sorrow, "Really, Sherlock, it is difficult to think of a crime in the civil service manual that you have not committed!"

So he had merely been having a joke at our expense! I wanted very much to tell him stiffly that I did not appreciate his sense of humour when Violet intervened, "I really cannot see how you hope to keep all this quiet, Mr Holmes," she said crisply.

"Even if we all agree to keep silent, people are bound to ask questions. For instance, how are you going to explain Joseph Harrison's disappearance?"

Mycroft Holmes reached for a cigar and clipped off the end, looking about him for a match. Mabel Every silently supplied him. With a nod of thanks, he struck the match and held it to the tip of his cigar until satisfied it was properly alight. He drew on it with a sigh of satisfaction. "I see little problem there, Mrs Watson," he said through clouds of pungent smoke. "We all know Harrison died bravely trying to save the young men in the nursing home - as did the Matron, Mrs Foster."

Mabel Every could no longer contain herself, "Sub-lieutenant Oldcastle and Hilda Woods could tell a very different story!" she declared. "Agreed," Mycroft Holmes studied the ash on his cigar, "but they will not, for the simple reason that it has been explained to them that Lady Phelps is surely entitled to mourn her brother with pride as well as sorrow - also the fact that it would not look good for British security if it became known a nest of traitors had remained unscathed for months while committing dastardly acts of sabotage up and down the country."

"And I suppose that is all you care about?" she challenged him. "You don't want your precious Admiralty to look silly in front of other people!"

"I admit that is a major concern at present," Mycroft Holmes nodded. "And he's right there, Mabel," Captain Turner spoke unexpectedly. "That's why we have to agree to say nothing, lass."

"But why?" she looked at him uncomprehendingly. "These - people made you suffer. They should pay for it! Oh, Thomas," she blinked back furious tears, "don't you care?"

"Of course I care, Mabel," he responded calmly reasonable, "I'd much rather none of it had happened at all, but there it is - so I'll not make a public exhibition of myself, nor see this country's name dragged in the mud just to clear my name."

"Some would," her voice was almost unrecognisable.

"Aye, they would, no question, but I'm not that sort, Mabel, and never will be." Observing her distress.his eyes softened. "Don't think I'm not grateful for all you did, Mabel - though I'm glad I didn't know about it at the time. I'd never have had a moment's peace, worrying over you - but it's finished now, lass, I've been cleared as much as I ever will be - now all I want is to get back to sea again."

"And so you shall," Alfred Booth said firmly. "I was going to delay the announcement until we were back in Liverpool, but you might as well hear it now." He paused for effect, "Ladies and gentlemen, allow me to present the new Master of the SS *Ultonia*, sailing for Nova Scotia a week on Friday." He added apologetically, "Tom, I'm sorry she's such a small ship after you've been used to commanding the big ones, but with so many of our vessels in Admiralty hands-" He sent a distinctly unfriendly look across the table at the imperturbable Mycroft Holmes.

Turner cleared his throat, "Ten thousand tons-" he said huskily. "Not to be sneezed at by any means. Handy little ship, too, I have no regrets, Mr Booth. I'd go to sea in a barge if need be." He said no more and I have the distinct impression he could no longer trust his voice.

A little while afterwards our guests left us to go their separate ways; Captain Turner and Mabel Every to catch the express back to Liverpool and Alfred Booth to spend an evening at the Reform Club with Butler Aspinall. Just as she was going out of the door Mabel Every stopped suddenly and turned to my friend.

"Mr Holmes," she said, "I don't believe I ever thanked you properly for all you did. I shall never forget it and nor will the Captain."

"No, indeed," Turner said heartily.

Holmes smiled, a little embarrassed by the display of gratitude. To cover it he held out his hand to Miss Every, but she disregarded it and leaned up to kiss his cheek instead.

"Goodnight, Mr Holmes!" she cried and followed Turner down the front path. Sherlock Holmes watched her go in bemused silence. "A remarkable young woman, that," he said finally. "But perhaps it is just as well she is going back home."

"Quite so," I agreed, just managing to keep a straight face. Not many individuals, particularly if they were women, had managed to disconcert my friend Holmes as thoroughly as Miss Mabel Every and I had rather relished the spectacle.

Mycroft Holmes, too, was making ready to depart; I presumed to join the other misanthropes at the Diogenes Club. But when he took the coat I handed to him he turned to his brother, saying, "I hope you will find the time to come and see me in a day or two, Sherlock - you too, Watson. I believe HMG is going to be in need of your services very soon."

Holmes stared. "What on earth are you talking about, Mycroft? Harrison is dead."

"Maybe, but are you quite certain the rest of his people have been picked up? I shudder to think what may transpire if there are any more of those infernal lead cigars lying about. But my main headache is this fellow Von Rintelen. According to all the reports he's the best our enemies have had since Von Bork - and I want him, brother, I want him over here and safely under lock and key."

Sherlock Holmes laughed. "First catch your hare, Mycroft!" he said. "Von Rintelen is likely to be a slippery customer."

"Quite so," Mycroft agreed, smiling all over his face like a fat Chinese buddha, "that is why I have made arrangements for a caretaker to look after your property in Sussex, Sherlock, and also for a locum to take over the duties of your practice as from tomorrow, Watson." He consulted his watch. "Shall we say ten o'clock tomorrow morning at the Diogenes Club? Goodnight to you both, oh, one other thing, pray thank Mrs Watson for her splendid hospitality." Raising his hat, be stalked down the path, leaving his brother, normally the master of any situation, for once entirely at a loss for words.

Just before we parted prior to going to bed, I remembered to ask the question that had been nagging me for some considerable time since our visit to Liverpool, in fact. "Holmes," I said, "when we went to Turner's house you seemed to take particular notice of one of the photographs on his desk."

"Did I?" he said vaguely, but his expression belied the careless response and I said warmly," You know very well you did - and I feel I must ask you the reason if I am to complete my records of this case."

Holmes said seriously, "I doubt if it will ever be possible to make a complete record of the *Lusitania* Case, Watson. Too many documents have been lost at sea or else wantonly destroyed by human intervention."

"Yes, but the photograph?" I pressed him.

"I take it you mean the one showing Turner with His Majesty the King, who had just made him a Commander in the Royal Naval Reserve?"

"The very one!" I said, "Why did it seem to you so very significant?"

"Because it explained Turner's conduct to me - the obstinate silences, the refusal to defend himself in Court by attacking the Admiralty, his reluctance to have anything to do with us, Watson, despite Alfred Booth's sanction."

"I know all about that, Holmes. I was there, remember," I said with some degree of acerbity, "but you still have not explained how the photograph helped you to resolve the puzzle."

Holmes drew on his pipe. "Simply that it reminded me, Watson, as I should not have needed reminding, that a Commander in the RNR is as much under Admiralty orders as Blinker Hall or Admiral Oliver or Sir Henry, and Turner, remember, received his commission directly from the hands of the King himself, which would mean much to a man like him. And now, my dear Watson, I suggest you charge our glasses and light one of those excellent cigars I see over there and let us enjoy a few moments of calm, old friend, before we lay our plans for the trapping of Franz Von Rintelen."